Twingenuity Book ~~

$\mathcal{A}$ $\mathcal{K}$INGDOM OF $\mathcal{S}$UN $\mathcal{A}$ND $\mathcal{S}$HADOW

DANIELLE HILL

A Kingdom of Sun and Shadow

Copyright © 2022 Danielle Hill

www.daniellehillwrites.ca

Possible trigger warning: Abuse, alcohol, anxiety, profanity, sexuality, violence.

Cover Design: Celingraphics

Logo Design: rebecacovers

ISBN 978-1-7779909-0-9

To my own Princess Amara

ESTRELLA

CATLIA

NIX

Kingdom of Solvna

SAFEHOUSE

Shadow Lands

Kingdom of Coldoria

CAELESTIA

PROLOGUE

A hooded figure stood alone, blending into the darkness as fog and mist filled the room around them. An ominous voice spoke, causing the figures' head to tilt up slightly as a thick cloud of smoke swirled around them, making visibility even more impossible.

Sisters born of sun and moon incarnate,

Powers of the Goddesses they shall inherit.

A selfless sacrifice shall mark a new world of light and life,

When this power becomes too much, a new evil will rise and history rewrite.

There will come a day when the sun is again reborn.

The sun and moon shall realign.

It shall be on the day that sisters reunite,

Their forces together they shine their light.

Three moons hence their chance will come,

Prophetic lore may come undone.

"And so it begins." The figure spoke before the smoke consumed them completely.

CHAPTER ONE

Avery

With sweat streaming down my brow, I awoke with a start. In my frantic dream my sheets had tangled around my legs. *That was such a weird dream. Why did it feel so real?* The thought of that shrouded figure in the dark chamber made me shiver.

I staggered over to my bathroom and splashed water on my face. My golden blonde hair, damp and stuck to my head. My deep green eyes appeared as sunken and tired as I felt and my skin much paler than usual. *Who knew a dream could take so much out of you?* I bitterly laughed to myself. I looked like I had spent the night fighting demons as opposed to sleeping for ten hours after bingeing Netflix.

Checking my bathroom clock, it read forty-five minutes past seven. *Crap!* I had to hurry if I wanted to make it to work on time. Even though I was only working as a temp for the summer before going back to college to figure out what I wanted to do with my life, I still wanted to make a good impression.

Taking the quickest shower of my life and practically applying my makeup during red lights on my drive, I zoomed in and sat at my desk with mere seconds to spare. Breathing a sigh of relief, I began sorting through the mountain of forms on my desk.

"Yoo-hoo!" Sang a sweet voice from behind my chair. I froze. I loved Lola, but I knew all too well the sound of her call for social interaction.

Spinning around in my chair, I came face to face with my closest work friend.

"Thank God it's Friday! A bunch of us are going to check out this new club, Sirens. You in after work?" Lola flipped her platinum hair, looking effortlessly glamorous at this early hour.

Glancing down at my nails, I realized how badly they needed to be painted. "Umm, I was planning to watch this new Netflix original I had my eye on tonight."

Lola rolled her eyes. "It's our last day here, and who knows when we'll get the chance to work together again!"

I laughed nervously. "But they already sent out a memo saying that there will be cake at lunch. That seems like a decent party to me."

Lola sniffed, clearly unimpressed by my inability to gauge fun. "Avery, you never come out with us! When do you think we will get this chance again? Seriously, I don't think you've seen any of us in the same room once outside of this office."

Trying, and failing, to make my groan sound more like fun laughter, I replied, "I don't know, you know clubs aren't really my thing."

Lola peered down her perfect, straight nose at me. "You are coming tonight."

"That didn't sound like a question." I felt my night being taken away from me as I realized my excuses were dwindling.

"It wasn't. I refuse to leave your desk until you agree to come out tonight. Besides, your movie will still be up on Netflix tomorrow."

I sighed and rubbed my face in my hands, probably further smudging my rushed makeup job.

"Fine, but I can't show up if I'm still here trying to get this work done. If you distract me for too much longer, I'll be forced to stay late."

Lola squealed and hugged my neck, the hug felt more like a temporary stranglehold.

"Oh my gosh you won't regret it! Work hard and make sure you don't turn into a pumpkin."

Lola bounced off and I was left sitting behind my desk. I loved Lola; I really did. She was such a nice girl but sometimes she could be a little much. We've worked at a few places together through the temp agency. We were just two completely different personalities. She was fun and confident, in herself and her life. She was working these temp jobs to get by until she made it big as an actress, while I was doing it to try and figure out what I wanted to do with the rest of my life.

The lights in the club set the room in a kaleidoscope of vibrant colours. The flurry of faces felt more like scenes from a dream than actual people I could interact with because of the bright strobe lights. I groaned internally as an excited shriek sounded from the bar behind me.

"O-M-G, you actually made it!"

I turned, painting on a sweet smile as my eyes met Lola's. "I said I would, didn't I?"

"Well, yeah. But you *actually* came. Usually, I beg you until you agree to come, and you cancel or find an excuse to leave almost immediately."

"Well, don't get too excited. I'm still trying to come up with my excuse for tonight." I tried to play it off as a joke but the frown she gave me made me glad that I wasn't the one trying to pursue a career in acting.

But Lola was right, I don't get out much. She's the type of person that goes out every weekend and I'm, well, I'm not. I'm not saying that there's anything wrong with that. It's just not really my thing, I get pretty anxious around crowds. She's so outgoing and I've always admired and respected that about her.

Feeling out of my comfort zone already I noticed Lola in her short, tight white dress. It seemed to glow against her fake tan, flawless as usual. Then I remembered I was wearing the only dress I owned, other than my old high school prom dress. The top half was black and the shirt had a nice green geometric pattern on it. I couldn't help pulling it down in fear I was showing off too much leg, even though my dress was undoubtedly longer than Lola's. She looked amazing and was definitely a lot more confident in herself than I was.

"So, what are you drinking?" Lola demanded, shocking me out of my own little world. "It's on me as we are celebrating such a momentous occasion."

"Uh, a root beer is fine."

Lola huffed a laugh. "A rookie beer? I don't think so. Seriously, what are you drinking?"

Helplessly looking to the bartender for direction, but he was too busy chatting up a busty brunette to be of any use. "I guess I'll just have whatever you're having."

Lola smiled at my apparent good taste and turned to walk up towards the bartender. She flipped her hair as she stood next to the brunette and leaned over the bar counter getting closer to the bartender. His eyes went right from the brunette to Lola. He smiled at Lola as she proceeded to order.

"Here." Lola shoved a short fat glass with dark liquid into my hands. I quickly downed it and shuttered as it burned my throat long after it went down. Watching Lola, I wished I had the same kind of confidence, even just to be able to get the bartender's attention long enough to get that root beer.

Turning back to the bar, it became evident that the bartender was making progress with the brunette, so I gave up hope of getting another drink. With a sigh, I pulled my attention away from the bartender and back to Lola, only to find that she was gone. Already in deep conversation with a harem of attractive men at a booth. Leaving me to fend for myself. "Great." I mumbled.

Clearly abandoned by my awesome friend, I allowed myself to leave the stuffy place to get some fresh air. The club was on the bigger and busier side of town. The only part that actually had anything open past eight p.m., really.

I decided to walk back to my apartment by taking the shortcut through the park. Lola probably wouldn't even notice my absence until the next morning anyway.

It was such a nice autumn night that I actually enjoyed the walk—it was peaceful. The bright, silver waxing moon as well as the shimmering stars framed the beautiful night sky as though it was an expensive work of art. It shone in the night sky and warmed my heart like a friend I could always rely on.

My hand reached up to caress the necklace I wore around my neck, a sparkling silver crescent moon that twinkled along with the stars above. It was the only memento I had of my birth parents.

A rustle in the bushes made me whirl around in shock and almost trip over my own feet. I scanned the area expecting a lion, or tiger, or bear to jump out in front of me. I couldn't move, I froze waiting to see what would happen next. Nothing. After a few moments of silence, I took a deep breath and convinced myself I was alone. I turned back and continued on my way home, walking much faster than I was earlier.

I made my way through the empty park and was now walking down the long quiet street that my apartment was on. As I walked past each storefront, I couldn't help but glance at the windows to ensure there was no reflection of someone following me. *Maybe Lola's right, I do watch too much T.V.*

A low whistling noise sounded from behind me. Hoping it was only the wind I slowly turned around to see a dark figure peeking around the corner of the alley way I had just passed. They blended in with the shadows, almost as if they were translucent, except for their large glowing red eyes.

I rubbed my eyes in shock. *This can't be real.* Just as I removed my hands from my eyes the figure was gone. I blinked in disbelief before I continued. Only a few blocks away I decided to run the rest of the way home. *I could probably use the workout anyway, right?*

I sprinted to my building door and dug around my purse for my key card to get in. *Ugh, why do I always have to bring so much crap with me in my purse?* I finally pulled out my card and tapped the lock. The light turned green, and I breathed a sigh of relief as I opened the door.

The building was empty and almost too quiet. I looked around the lobby as I made my way to the elevator. As I passed the front desk, I glanced behind it to see if Mr. Anderson was behind it taking a nap, he tends to do that sometimes, but even he was gone. I shrugged it off and waited for the elevator to get to the lobby floor. *I'm losing it. I definitely need to watch some cartoons to get to sleep tonight.*

Once inside the elevator I figured I should probably send Lola a quick text to let her know I left and that I was home safe and sound. I hit send on my phone as the elevator doors opened to floor four. I walked out and turned right to see that my apartment door was opened slightly. I slowly made my way to the door in a panic with my phone in one hand ready to call 9-1-1. Examining the door, it didn't seem like a break in, and as I was pulling my phone up to call for help, I heard a familiar voice.

"Avery? Is that you honey?" I exhaled in relief and ran into my tiny apartment. "Mom!" You nearly scared the life out of me, what are you doing here?" As I ran in I could see her sitting in my living area with a mysterious middle-aged man. He was dressed in a professional black suit with a navy-blue tie, and he wore black, thin-framed glasses.

I watched him nervously. "Hello, Miss Avery, my name is Lawrence. I have been sent here to bring you back home."

"Uh, I am home," I said as I gestured around my bachelor apartment. My eyes shifted from him to my mom hoping she'd tell me that this was a prank, she did have a very weird sense of humour. Scanning my mom's face to see if she was serious. Her usual dark brown eyes were now pink and puffy.

"Mom, what's wrong? Have you been crying?" I couldn't help but to narrow my eyes at this mystery man. I hated seeing my mom like this, she was the most kind-hearted, loving person I knew. "I swear if you hurt her, I will hurt you one hundred—"

My mother cut me off, "No, Avery, it's nothing like that. Lawrence called me earlier and told me that something had been following you all night."

"You mean after the club? Like on my way home?" *I knew I wasn't seeing things. And did she say* something *was following me?* Suddenly I felt my mom's arms around me as her dark brown hair was practically suffocating me. I was so lost in my own thoughts I never even noticed her get up from the couch, but for a moment I felt like I needed this.

I pulled away. "I still don't know what's going on." I stared at my mom trying to get a read on her. She was even paler than usual. I watched as Lawrence stood up and walked over to us. "I was sent by my employer to watch over you and protect you but now I feel as though you are no longer safe here."

"Employer? Watch over me? Are you the person who was following me back at the alley?" I was not scared anymore, now I was pissed. Who was this guy and why the hell was he watching me?

Lawrence's eyes shifted from my mother then back to me before a soft smile formed on his lips, not really reaching his eyes. "Miss Bate, I had the absolute pleasure of working for your parents for most of my career. However, it is with great sadness to inform you that they passed away a few years ago."

Is this guy for real? I thought as I pointed a thumb at my mom.

"No, Miss Bate, your birth parents."

I felt like someone shot me in the heart. I loved my adoptive mother, so I never gave much thought to my birth parents, but it still hurt to find out that I would never get the chance to meet them.

As a tear slid down my cheek, I tried to recompose myself. "Well, they didn't want me, so I guess it doesn't matter."

"That's not the case at all. They loved you very much and had excellent reasons for sending you away. They always wanted to reunite with you, but sadly never got the chance."

And now they never will. Confusion took over my senses.

"Please Miss Bate, I need you to trust me. We need to leave immediately; I promise I will explain everything in due time."

"Leave? I can't leave!"

My mom placed her hand on my shoulder. "You need to trust him, Avery. He has always been looking out for you." I had to wipe my eyes before another tear had the chance to slide down my cheek. "You know him?" She just nodded in response. "And you trust him?"

She hugged me again and then handed me a small suitcase she must have already packed for me. "Go with him, Avery."

CHAPTER TWO

Avery

I followed Lawrence to his car, curious as to who his current employer was, and who was following me in that alley earlier. What did they want with me?

Lawrence opened the back passenger side door to a black 1967 Chevy Impala. I took my seat admiring the black leather interior. It was giving me serious *Supernatural* vibes. *I always hoped if I were ever to be in this car I'd be in the back seat with Jensen Ackles.* The thought made a small chuckle escape my lips as Lawrence walked around the car and joined me in the backseat. I wondered who was driving since Lawrence was sitting in the back with me. I tried to peek out of the tinted windows, but all I could see was my own face reflected back at me.

Exhaustion suddenly overcame my senses and I felt myself drifting off to sleep. Lawrence took out a pillow and blanket as though he had planned for this all along. "Sleep now, Miss Avery. I know you have many questions and all shall be revealed in due time."

My eyes became heavy and I struggled to keep them open. *What the hell is going on?*

I awoke to find myself still inside of the car. *Ahh crap.* I lifted my head slowly and was pleasantly surprised that I wasn't dead. I took in my surroundings and noticed that Lawrence was still sitting in the back with me. *My mom told me to trust him, but can I?*

As I rose, Lawrence straightened and smiled softly. "Miss Avery, we have arrived. Please put on this cloak, keep your head down and do not say a word. No one should be on our path, but for your safety it is best if you were not recognized should we interact with anyone."

I nodded, too preoccupied with the unbelievably luxurious material of my black velvet cloak and fear of who the heck I was about to meet to bring myself to speak. As the car came to a stop, Lawrence got out and opened the door for me. I looked back at the car and had to do a double take. Instead of the Impala, there was now a horse drawn carriage in its place. *Was I transferred into this thing while sleeping?*

I slowly spun around and took in the stone castle covered in ivy. It felt like I stepped into a magical world straight out of a fairy tale. The castle was so large I couldn't see where it ended, just that the walls seemed to go on forever. The driveway we had pulled up in was large and circular with an enormous fountain in the middle. The fountain had several tiers with streams of water making arches in the air before landing seamlessly into the tier below.

Turning back towards the carriage, I realized that it was gone. Standing before me now was a tower attached to an enormous castle that shot up into the night sky. Lawrence gestured forward and I noticed that, hidden behind the ivy, was a stone door that blended into the wall. Lawrence opened the door to show me a giant spiral wooden staircase, which I guessed I would have to climb. *Hopefully we don't have to go up too high.*

Thankfully, the tower had no windows, so I didn't focus on how high we were climbing, leaving my full brain capacity to scream about my calf muscles. We stood before grand wooden doors engraved with symbols and pictures that made my imagination take flight.

Lawrence whispered, "Miss Avery, are you ready?"

I thought briefly about how the last twenty hours had been crazier than the entire twenty years I'd been alive. *I guess if he is planning to murder me, I may as well see what lies behind these doors.*

Slowly the wooden doors opened, soundless in their movements. A woman with a regal blonde golden updo, and freckles that framed her emerald eyes stood before me.

Frozen in place, I took in the face of the woman in front of me, my mouth falling open in utter shock. A distant wail filled my ears and resounded throughout the cavernous entrance, growing in volume until the sound was so loud that I instinctively moved to cover my ears. It was only then — as my chest rumbled despite the muffled sound — that I realized that the deafening shriek was coming from me.

Amara

She's screaming at me. I watched this familiar but strange woman with a mix of awe and doubt. Taking a step forward, hoping to calm her down before the guards descended upon my chambers.

"What the hell is going on? Who are you? Why do you look like a better dressed version of me?"

"I know you must be confused, Avery."

"Well, isn't that the understatement of the century." Her arms flew up as she shook her head.

You have no idea.

I gestured for Avery to sit on my bed, which she hesitantly did, and I began pacing as I attempted to explain. "I was confused when I first found out as well. What I am about to say is extremely important, and unfortunately we do not have much time."

Avery's eyes narrowed. "Well, how about we start with this—who the hell are you?"

A laugh escaped my lips before I could compose myself again. "As you have probably already guessed, I'm your twin sister. I am Amara Marie Asteria, Princess of Soluna."

Avery snorted at me. "*You're* a princess? Really? What, princesses kidnap people for fun nowadays?"

I stifled a sigh and tried to explain as best I could. "Unfortunately, due to time constraints, drastic action had to be taken."

Avery's eyes flicked with horror. "Wait, if you're a princess, does that make *me* a princess?"

"Technically yes, but it is a lot more complicated than that." I placed my head in my hands, willing my training in etiquette and patience to kick in. I glanced at the clock and realized I only had ten minutes to get to the stables before he would come for me.

Lawrence seemed deeply uncomfortable as he adjusted his tie and tugged at the collar of his shirt, which was saying a lot for him considering he was not one to show much emotion. He bowed. "I will take my leave now, Your Highness. If you need anything, please do not hesitate to call. I will only be outside the door." The look on Lawrence's face indicated that he hoped I would not require him to come back in.

I smiled at my trusted friend. "Thank you, Lawrence."

I turned back to Avery, who was now standing in front of one of my many full-length mirrors, with utter uncertainty etched on her face.

"Our parents were the King and Queen of Soluna. They passed away a few years ago, may they rest in peace." I paused and took a deep breath before continuing. "Lawrence has been regent ever since. He has been training me so that I can ascend the throne after my twenty-first birthday. It is said that the true heir of Soluna is not one but two specific people. These two people would bring Soluna into its most glorious age of prosperity. Until recently I thought that it meant that I had to be married. Then I found out about you, and now it all makes sense."

Avery was quiet for a moment, nodding slowly while biting at her bottom lip though she was trying to put her thoughts into words. "How does any of this make sense, and how did you find out about me anyway?"

"It happened several months ago. There are some people out there who believe, even married, I am unfit to rule."

Avery's eyes widened slightly and I thought back to the day.

"I was in our parent's private study, desperately trying to find something, anything, that would reaffirm that I am the rightful heir. I was reading through the books in one of the many bookcases, when a secret door opened behind the bookshelf. That's where I found it."

Avery's eyes were now sparkling, completely entranced by my tale. "There was a small room behind the bookcase, about the size of a broom closet, filled with old pictures and books.

The pictures on the walls caught my eye, because they were of myself and my parents."

Letting out a harsh breath I waited a moment before I continued, "I noticed after a moment that, in most of the pictures, my parents had two, identical, blonde babies, swaddled in pink. I took one of the pictures off of the wall and written on the back in our mother's handwriting was, 'Amara and Avery, two months old.' And then it all made sense."

Avery nodded quietly again, her gaze down as she fidgeted with her fingers. "No offence, Amara, you seem nice and all, but this is a lot to take in. I'm happy with the way my life is. Why don't we just go and tell these people they were wrong? Then I can go back home, and you can rule alone."

"No!"

Avery flinched at my sudden outburst and her eyes shot back up towards me.

"There is no reasoning with them. They are mostly noblemen and members of the Solunian court. This situation needs to be handled delicately. We need real proof."

"Aren't I proof enough?" She gestured to herself as though I had forgotten we were identical.

"Unfortunately, no. As I mentioned, there is talk of an ancient prophecy that speaks further about the Kingdom of Soluna and the need for two people to rule. People have searched for this prophecy for centuries but nothing has ever been found. I need to find it and bring it back."

Avery raised a brow. "How can you find it if people have searched for centuries?"

I whispered softly. "It is my only hope."

"The sooner we sort this mess out, the sooner I can go back to my own life. So, when do we leave?"

Laughing in uncertainty, I said, "I do need your help if we are to succeed, but not in the way you think. I need to travel to the outskirts of my kingdom in order to find this prophecy, and this trip may take a while. I cannot leave my kingdom for that long without raising suspicion, so you will be staying here pretending to be me while I am gone."

Avery wore a disoriented expression on her face, eyes squinted and mouth opened. "Excuse me? You want me to be you? Seriously? I don't know anything about you. You're a freaking princess. How the hell am I supposed to convince people that I'm you? Wouldn't it be better if I went for the prophecy and you stayed here?"

I was already shaking my head before she finished her sentence. "No. I know my kingdom well and am aware of the dangers I may face. You will have Lawrence here to assist you. He is the only one that can know, and the only one you can trust."

Avery seemed highly skeptical, so I tried to further reassure her. "You can trust Lawrence. No matter how badly you mess up, he would not allow anyone to harm you. You can trust him with your life."

"I don't know if I can do this, Amara. I'm not even slightly qualified."

I glanced at the clock, already late. "Avery, you have to, there is no one else who can do this." My eyes met Avery's once again. "The Kingdom of Soluna needs you. I need you."

"So what? I am supposed to just forget about my own life and stay here for how long?"

"However long it takes for me to find it." I met and held her gaze.

"What about me? What about my life? I don't know how to be a princess and I don't want to." She raked her fingers through her hair, almost as if she were about to pull it out.

"Please," I breathed.

Avery finally conceded. "Okay fine, I'll do it."

I thanked her and ran into my dressing chambers to quickly change. Luckily, my outfit was already laid out. I changed into my long lace up black pants and attached my scabbard to my belt then threw on a loose white shirt. Grabbing my black velvet cloak while checking the time once more. *Now I am really late.* I ran back into the main bed chambers and made my way to the hidden doorway that Avery had just entered through.

My eyes flicked back to Avery before opening the hidden passageway, "Thank you." I said smiling one last time before pulling on my hood and making my way down the spiral staircase and through the short secret path to the stables.

"Took you long enough, Princess. I was about to send out a search party."

I rolled my eyes at my oldest and most trusted friend. "A queen is never late."

Wesley chuckled, saddling up my horse for me. He leaned in closer to me and whispered into my ear, "You aren't queen yet."

I glared at him while I jumped up and straddled my horse. "Whatever. Are you ready?"

The smile on Wesley's face turned into a concerned frown. "Are you sure you want to do this?"

"I do not have a choice."

He draped the saddlebags over both of our horses. "So did you tell her the full truth or just your version?"

"You know I couldn't. It's for her own good. Now let's go, as you said, we're late."

Just like that his smile was back as he mounted his horse. "As you wish."

Avery

The second I agreed to help, Amara hightailed it out of her—now my—room so quickly I wondered if she even wanted to bother meeting me. Before I had the chance to take in the giant space, Lawrence walked back in.

"Miss Avery, thank you for your service to our kingdom." He bowed, and I had to stop myself from bowing back.

"I hear you are the man I can trust," I tried to joke, but I was truly terrified.

Lawrence smiled warmly at me. "You can trust me with your life, Princess. You can come to me with any questions or concerns you may have, and I will stay by your side whenever possible. The only caution I will give is discretion. Do not talk to anyone if you do not have to. Do not say more than you believe necessary, and trust no one. I am the current regent so I can be busy at times however, this may help as I can teach you about Solunian culture and many people will suspect I am preparing you to take the throne."

I tried to look regal nodding in response but gave up quickly. "Thank you, Lawrence. I will need all the help I can get."

"Is there anything else I can aid you with?"

I shook my head, unable to think let alone form words.

"You should get some rest, you will have a big day ahead of you tomorrow." Lawrence said as he turned to leave the room.

I called to him as he walked out the door, "Good night."

He turned back slightly, bowing his head in acknowledgement before lifting his gaze back to mine.

"Welcome to Soluna, Miss Avery."

CHAPTER THREE

Avery

The bright morning sun shined through the giant wall of windows to the right of where I laid on the four-post bed. Yawning, I opened my heavy eyelids, taking in the ginormous room around me and allowing my memories of last night to come flooding back. *Oh right, I'm a princess now. Great. All right Avery, you can do this.*

Surprised by how modern everything was, I realized I never got the chance to really take in this room or castle last night; everything happened so fast. Though the castle walls were made of stone and the exterior reminded me of something from one of my high fantasy movies, the inside was not what I had expected. The room had electricity and I hoped to God that meant running water and plumbing.

First day pretending to be the twin sister you met yesterday and know absolutely nothing about. Who is also a princess. I pulled the gigantic overly plush covers over my head and groaned. *What is wrong with me? I didn't ask for this, sure who hasn't dreamed of something like this after watching a movie or reading a book. But reading it and living it are two completely different things.*

After a few moments I slowly sat up. *I might as well get this day over with.* I clawed my way out of Amara's many overly plush pillows and disentangled myself from the multiple layers of thin, expensive, silk sheets.

Standing up, I was almost surprised by how cushy the rug felt beneath my toes. Sighing internally, I tried to muster the willpower to be prim, proper, and positive for the rest of the day.

Sighing, yet again, I walked over to Amara's ginormous walk-in closet that was three times the size of my apartment back home.

Let's find out what is considered fashion here.

Surveying the first section of the closet before me I noticed the style of clothing reminded me of the perfect blend between modern and medieval. I came across a lovely dress and decided to put it on. The top half was a white corset style with long sleeves while the skirt had a beautiful blue pattern.

I think I'm going to explore the castle a little while I try to find Lawrence.

I took a deep breath and opened Amara's main doors from her room, not the hidden ones I came through last night. The first thing I noticed once I made it into the hallway was the guards stationed on either side of the doorframe.

Trying not to bring too much attention to myself, I nodded in greeting as each of them placed a hand over their hearts and bowed in sync. Taking in another deep breath and trying to recall all the movies and books I'd seen and read; attempting to channel my inner princess.

All the corridors were exactly the same. Stone floors, walls, and ceilings. They were cold and dimly lit. The only light came from torches hung every few feet and the windows were just holes in the walls. It was such a contrast to how modern the rooms, at least the one I had been in, had seemed. There was no electricity, no heaters, no anything that even resembled the buildings back home.

I wondered if the parts of the castle that were like this had been part of an original build while the rooms were built more recently. It was the only thing that had made sense to me. This castle had secret stairwells and passageways which matched the old style of the corridors.

After wandering around aimlessly for several hours, I had finally found a door that led outside. As I opened the door, I felt the sunlight warm my face. *Thank goodness, fresh air.*

I figured, based on the impressive plants and bright flowers, that I was in a well-maintained castle garden. There were colours everywhere. I breathed deeply, enjoying the floral scents as it coursed up my nose.

As I continued along the marble path throughout the garden I stumbled upon a beautiful white gazebo. It had lights hung above the top of it with blue and yellow rose bushes around the exterior. Just behind it there was yet another garden with a tiny waterfall like fountain in the center. I could hear the water trickle as it fell to the small pond below. *This is incredible! I'd love to come back here at night when this is all lit up.*

A rustling behind me made me jump and spin around. Lawrence emerged and smiled at me. "There you are, Your Highness. I was wondering where you ran off to."

I smiled, relieved that this was not some secret monster-filled garden. "I was lost for a while, but I finally found an exit." I gestured around me. "I love this garden, it seems so peaceful."

Lawrence seemed to agree. "I am glad you like it, Princess; I have always admired the royal gardens myself."

In the distance the fields were so full of flowers that the grass appeared to be made from different colours. Weaving together into the space before me, like a beautifully interlaced rainbow.

I was too busy admiring the tranquility to notice that there was a couple inside the gazebo sitting at the white iron bistro set. They got up and made their way towards us.

The women's chestnut brown hair was pulled into a regal updo. A royal blue dress hugged her tiny figure. Along the bodice was elegant gold embroidery, disappearing along the top of the skirt like stars on the night horizon. The man had dark blonde, slicked back hair. It shined from all the gel holding it in place. He wore a simple suit and a scowl on his face. They both looked to be in their mid-thirties.

Lawrence silently moved to stand closer to me and whispered, "That is your cousin, Chaz, and his wife, Vivian, the Duke and Duchess of Caelie. I had no idea they were visiting the castle. This complicates things."

Chaz and Vivian had walked up to us, and I turned to face them. Chaz placed his right hand on his chin while he looked me up and down as if he was studying me.

"Hello, cousin," he said as he crossed his arms, still waiting for answers I didn't know.

I went in for a hug but instead of opening his arms to welcome me, he took a step back and held his arms up in front of him as if he was trying to push me away.

Chaz sneered, "What are you doing?"

"Saying hello to my favourite cousin," I said more as a question than a statement.

"You're acting weird. Come on, Vivian." He stalked off then added, *"I'm watching you."*

Well, that went great.

31

When they were out of earshot Lawrence let out a low whistle. I faced Lawrence again in complete shock. "I don't understand, you said he was family?"

Lawrence pulled at his collar while he adjusted his tie, but his monotone voice didn't falter. "Yes, but he believes he is the rightful heir to the throne."

"Why would he think that?" I wasn't sure if I really wanted to hear the answer.

Lawrence let out a heavy sigh as he pinched the bridge of his nose. "He believes the next king should be of Solunian royal blood. Since your parents never bore a son, he is the only real male left in the royal bloodline. So, he believes he should ascend the throne."

"That's terrible. When Amara said that there were some people who didn't want her to be queen, I didn't think it would be family." Even though I didn't have much family, or know I did until recently, the thought of someone you called family doing something like that left a weird feeling in the pit of my stomach.

"Well, if it were not family, they would not really have much of a claim to the throne. Though there are a few that share in his beliefs, it was your fathers dream for the two of you to rule and I'll be damned if that moron, Chaz, becomes king." Lawrence slammed his fist into the tiny table between us. I hadn't known him long at all, but this was the first time I saw much emotion in anything he had said. His chest rose as he took a deep breath when he spoke again, his monotone voice was back. "I have worked with your family for many years, your father and I were very close. I was your parents most trusted advisor before they passed, and I became regent soon after."

We sat for a while in silence. I didn't know how to answer—how to feel. I just got here; I didn't even know this place existed twenty-four hours ago. Now I was being told that it was my fathers dream for me to co-rule? *Wait a second... Does that mean Lawrence knew about me before Amara found that picture? My mom* did *say he had always been looking out for me and to trust him.*

My breaths quickened and I started biting at the cuticles of my nails, trying to muster up the courage to ask Lawrence exactly what he meant by that. He knew about me, that I knew and understood but for exactly how long? Why did they get rid of me in the first place if they were just going to watch me from afar? And why the hell would they want me to rule a kingdom I knew nothing about. That didn't sound like the actions of someone who wanted this. *I* didn't want this. I wanted to go back to my normal life, sure it was boring but I liked it that way.

Just when I was finally going to ask him for answers, he broke the silence.

"I have some matters to attend to. Do try to be more careful, Miss Avery. If you run into anyone else, please just nod and continue walking. Do not strike up any unnecessary conversations." He looked at me with uncertainty in his eyes.

"Wouldn't that just be kinda, I don't know, rude?" I asked. "And I have a lot of questions I need answered. I was just completely uprooted from my life. How long do you expect me to just stay here playing princess?"

"Believe me, it will not raise any questions. But as to your questions, I promise I will answer in due time. It is just not the right moment."

The right moment? I rolled my eyes dramatically. "And when will this perfect moment present itself?"

"If I am being completely honest, Miss Avery, when I have the time to answer them all." He replied flatly.

Lawrence walked me back inside the castle. It was a short walk, but it seemed like forever since we just walked in silence.

He mentioned that it was my father's dream for us both to rule together. My mom said he had always been looking out for me and to trust him. But did I? I am supposed to just put my life on hold and wait around for answers. I blew out a harsh breath and decided to focus on the beauty of the garden as we walked back along the marble path.

We stepped back into the castle corridor and Lawrence groaned beside me, *"You have got to be kidding me. Is everyone visiting the castle today?"*

I followed Lawrence's gaze to a man who was standing at the top of a set of grand, extravagant stairs. *Damn, he's so freaking hot!*

I couldn't take my eyes off of him. "Who is that?"

"That, Miss Avery, is the crowned prince of Coldoria, Prince Alexander the third, and Princess Amara's fiancé."

"Seriously? He's a prince?" I replied, still unable to take my eyes off of him.

Finally turning back to Lawrence, his face wrinkled slightly as he pulled at the collar of his shirt, "As I mentioned, try not to say much and just leave. I really must go, but I'll find you later."

Before I could question him again, he was gone. Just as Lawrence left, Prince Alexander descended the stairs and started heading my way. He seemed about as friendly as Chaz.

Nervous, and unsure of what to do in this situation I did the first thing that popped into my head, *He's a prince.* "Prince Alexander." I curtseyed with a huge smile on my face.

As I slowly began to stand up fully again, I admired his appearance. He was even more gorgeous up close. My gaze made its way up from his chest and back to his face. My eyes immediately fell to his, I stared into them as they began to shift from blue to green and back. I could have gotten lost in them for hours trying to figure out which colour they were closest to. They were so bright and stood out so prominently against his golden-brown complexion.

I finally managed to pull my gaze from them and noticed his deep brown curls, they were like the perfect balance between elegant and eccentric. My eyes wandered down to his perfect jawline next just as it clenched, quickly snapping me back to reality and I wondered just how long I'd been staring at him.

"That's Prince Xander to you."

Who does this guy think he is? I crossed my arms. "What's your problem?"

"She's acting weird." He watched me with a frown and furrowed brows.

"No, I'm not!"

Prince Xander shook his head in disbelief. "What?"

"You said I'm acting weird, I think I'm acting perfectly fine thank you very much."

He let out a bitter laugh. "Whatever, you're acting like a lunatic."

"I am not!" My arms flew out beside me in protest. *Is he for real?*

"I see you bothered to show up. I'm surprised you haven't bailed yet." His arrogance showed through his smirk.

What is he talking about?

"Just look pretty tonight and try not to embarrass me. Have you seen Erik?"

"Who?" I somehow forgot to play my role.

"I don't have to deal with this. Soon, I will have two kingdoms to run."

It didn't sound like a threat, but as though Prince Xander was exhausted by the thought of managing so many people on his own. Huffing again, he walked off.

"Where are you going?" I called out to him.

"Away from you."

What a jerk! I don't know what she sees in this guy.

Amara

The sun was high as we travelled south. Wesley and I both knew the kingdom well enough that it was far too easy to make it this far unnoticed. It was unlikely that any of the villagers would have recognized me, but we still would not risk it. They were quiet at night, especially the further south we got.

Now that we had made it past the cities and villages and had entered the overgrown forests earlier this morning. I believed it to be safe enough to remove my cloak as the remainder of the journey should be this way and it would be unlikely to come across anyone within the forest.

Most of Soluna was this way, unused, dark woods. I never would have thought to come out here if it had not been for my mother's journals. They spoke of a safehouse that I believed to be the key to finding the prophecy, at least I hoped.

Wesley and I used to come out this way when we were younger but had never gone too far. We studied maps and loved the idea of running away where we could be who we wanted to be. But that was a child's dream. We were the biggest kingdom in Caelestia and yet we used less than half of our land. It was not like it was a frozen wasteland like most of Coldoria, so why was it not used? It was like a piece to the puzzle was missing and I needed to find it almost as much as I needed the prophecy.

Lost in my thoughts, I grumbled as a branch smacked me in the face. I should have been paying attention.

"We've been at it all night and we still have a while to go, Princess. Maybe we should take a break and let our horses rest?"

Suddenly, Wesley stopped and jumped off his horse. He reached up, grabbing my arm gently to signal for me to stop. I instantly drew my sword from its scabbard in preparation for whatever Wesley had sensed.

The bushes in front of us began to rustle just as I prepared to jump off of my horse, a squirrel leapt out of the bushes and twitched its tail at us before scampering away.

My gaze shifted from the bushes back to Wesley as he stood with his blade in one hand. Fits of giggles exploded from my stomach, nearly knocking me off my horse as I laughed at my dumbfounded warrior.

Wesley frowned, until a snort escaped from me. I froze from embarrassment as we stood there for a moment just staring at one another in silence. He soon began to laugh even harder than I originally had, I joined in as well, no longer fearing the rampage of the killer squirrel.

When we finally stopped laughing, I realized how close Wesley and I were. Gulping, I tried to clear my head.

"Don't worry, I will never let any harm come to you."

"I can protect myself." Heat crept into my cheeks and I quickly turned away, squaring my shoulders. Out of the corner of my eyes I noticed Wesley still watching me intently.

"We should keep moving until we find the safe house. According to her journal, it's located along the western border of Soluna and about a full day's travel by horse, so it shouldn't be too much longer now."

Wesley smiled as he jumped back onto his horse. "After you, Princess."

CHAPTER FOUR

Avery

I was back in my new bedroom. *I didn't expect it to be this difficult. Maybe I should take a nap, this is exhausting.* Sighing, I retreated back to Amara's bed but as soon as I reached it, there was a knock at the door. *It's probably the guards from earlier telling me that they are back in their positions, I didn't see them on the way back.* I made my way back over to the door and opened it.

A *High School Musical* Zac Efron wannabe strolled into the room like he owned the place. He leaned forward and kissed me.

What the hell?

"You ready?" He smirked as he double checked that the door was locked. "We don't have much time." He turned back towards me and eyed me up and down before he began to strip.

Oh my God! I shut my eyes and abruptly turned away, smacking my head off one of Amara's bed posts. I groaned as I rubbed my forehead.

Not Zac's hand brushed my shoulder, "Are you all right? That must have hurt. Let me see." He came around to face me once again and I made the mistake of glancing down to a, now fully stripped, man showing far more than I had wanted to see.

"What do you think you're doing?" I shook my head as I took a few steps back. Pushing his hand away from my face when he tried examining the new mark I could already feel forming.

"Oh, I think you know." I heard him take another step closer. *"Gods, you are sexy right now."*

"Get. Out. Now!" I yelled as I stared up at the ceiling and prayed he'd gather up his clothes and leave.

"Is it your head? Do you need me to get you something?"

"No, I need you to leave, now!"

"Jeez, if you weren't in the mood you could have just said so."

I waited a few minutes and heard his belt buckle rattle, relieved he was putting his clothes back on and finally turned back to make sure he actually left. He was almost out the door when he turned back towards me.

"Try not to look too hot tonight, or I won't be able to keep my hands off you." He winked and then finally left, closing the door behind him.

I quickly made my way to the door myself, opened it slightly and wondered where these guards from earlier had been. I closed the door again and made sure to lock it this time. *What is happening? I don't know anything about Amara or this place and it is already becoming too crazy for me.*

Amara

40

Wesley followed me for miles without question. I was warmed by his faith in me. The sky opened and rain began to pour down out of nowhere. The sun was also beginning to set, creating a dangerous environment for us to travel in. "The safehouse is just up ahead." *Thank Gods.*

"Of course, after you milady." Wesley smiled as though he was happy to be spending time with me, not at all bothered by the sudden rain.

"I'm going to survey the area and ensure there is no present danger."

"All right, I will meet you inside." I replied and waited for him to be out of earshot. I was glad he was not with me for what I had to do next and prayed it would actually work.

I turned to the ruins before me and held up my arms to the sky and closed my eyes. I recited the words I had memorized from my mother's journal that seemed to be of another language. When I finished, I opened my eyes and there it was, a secret magical safehouse.

I opened the door and breathed a sigh of relief as the lights immediately flicked on. I walked into the kitchen where a pot was steaming over the stove and fresh bread lay on the table next to me. I could not help but smile and the delicious smell filled the room. I investigated the cupboards for dishes and utensils for myself and Wesley. I scooped some stew into two separate bowls and cut us both some slices of bread and laid them on the table.

I heard Wesley's footsteps descending the creaky stairs, I had not even heard him come in the front door.

I went back into the common area to meet him at the bottom of the stairs. He was now dressed in a new pair of dry pants. I studied him; my gaze moved from his messy, dirty blonde hair that fell perfectly over his light brown eyes. Then, my eyes moved down to his bare chest and arms.

"I made us something to eat," I finally said, meeting his eyes once more.

"You should take those off," he said as he gestured to my clothes.

"Pardon?"

"Your clothes are soaked from the rain, you should change into something dry before we eat or you'll get sick."

"Right, of course. You go ahead and start eating. I'll be back down shortly. After we eat we can start our search for more of my mother's research."

He took a few steps closer. "That can wait until morning, it's been a long day. I'll run you a warm bath after I finish eating and you can relax and then get some rest. I'll keep guard tonight."

"Come on, Wes, you really don't need to. You must be just as tired as I am right now."

"You know I won't be able to sleep tonight anyway," he protested. "I'll be too worried." He paused again and his face stiffened. "When I agreed to accompany you on this quest, I promised I would protect you, Princess."

"Protect me from what exactly, may I ask?" I was more annoyed than anything at this point.

His tone softened again. "I don't know, but I won't let anything happen to you."

"I'm not some damsel in distress needing your protection or saving Wesley."

"I know, you are far from it in fact. However, that doesn't change the way I feel about you."

"The-the way you feel about me?"

"You are the princess of Soluna, future queen, and my best friend. I will always want to protect you, whether you need it or not."

I finally gave in and sighed, "Fine, stay up if you must. But, at least try and get some sleep tonight, even just for a few hours." I retreated upstairs before he had another chance to argue.

Avery

After walking around this maze of a castle searching for Lawrence for what seemed like hours, but in reality, was only about thirty minutes, I finally found him in a large ballroom. *Finally!*

The room was dressed in navy and gold décor. I was in awe, a huge golden chandelier with diamond shaped crystals dangling. The crystals twinkled like stars as the lights from the chandelier shone down on them, making the entire ballroom sparkle. Navy and gold patterned tapestries danced upon the ceilings inviting any guests below to join in.

I walked over to where I saw Lawrence standing with a woman. She was dressed in a navy dress with a white button collared shirt underneath and a gold tied bow around the collar of her shirt.

She's dressed like the rest of the female staff here.

Lawrence looked up and smiled at me, "Princess."

The woman turned to face me and curtseyed, "Your Highness."

Oh great.

"You are excused, Stella." Lawrence said and the woman turned back to face him, curtseyed one more time before finally leaving us.

I whispered to Lawrence so none of the staff would overhear, "I don't understand what's going on. People here are crazy. I know I'm not used to living in a castle but should there really be this many people here?"

Bags had formed under Lawrence's eyes. He rubbed at his temples as he mumbled. "No, there shouldn't be." He took a deep breath in composing himself, "I completely forgot that there is supposed to be a ball held here tonight."

"Seriously? A ball!" I admit I was a little surprised. "I thought those just happened in fairy tales and cheesy hallmark movies!"

Lawrence seemed confused. *I guess they don't have hallmark movies here.* They're my guilty pleasure, especially the holiday ones.

"Unfortunately, not. Prince Alexander's entire family's here. You will be expected to dance with him."

Lawrence sighed. "This ball has been planned for months, I apologize for not alerting you sooner but, this is supposed to be your engagement ball. Miss Avery, this is not just a ball to celebrate the joining of the two royals, it is also the merging of two kingdoms. It is, foremost, a diplomatic event."

"Yeah, about that, he's such a jerk! Why is she even with him?" I didn't mean for it to come out as rude as it did but I couldn't help it. *Prince Xander's the worst.*

Lawrence nodded, "Princess Amara is not with him by choice. As she mentioned some people think she should be married to take the throne. That is where he comes in. His father,

King Alexander the second, sees this as the perfect opportunity to combine the two kingdoms."

He sighed again, "Please just try to keep the peace tonight. Believe me, I know how much of a, as you call him 'jerk,' Prince Alexander can be. However, we need this unity between the kingdoms. His entire family will be there, including diplomats from both kingdoms and dignitaries from neighbouring kingdoms with whom we are forging alliances."

"Uh-huh. Why did Amara agree to this? I know it was an arranged marriage, but God, was he the only guy available?"

Lawrence coughed in a way that I suspected stifled a laugh, "This *guy* rules over the second largest kingdom in Caelestia, after Soluna. Not to mention, our greatest enemy until twenty years ago when you and your sister were born. A tentative peace agreement was forged with the promise of this union."

"If we made peace so many years ago, why does he still have to act like such a prick?"

Lawrence adjusted his tie, "Essentially, you and Amara are very different people, so she has a higher tolerance for, as you so eloquently worded it, 'pricks.'"

Before I could protest, Lawrence called the maid back in.

"Your Highness, Stella has your options for tonight. As this is a diplomatic event, you have the option to wear our traditional blue and gold, or Coldoria's burgundy and black."

I smiled, grateful for the subtle context.

"Stella, can you please escort the princess back to her chambers and assist her in getting ready for tonight's ball?" Lawrence worded it as a question but that is not how it came out.

"Of course, Lord Regent," Stella said as she, again, curtseyed at him.

I walked a few steps behind Stella as we walked back up to my room. Lost in my own thoughts. *I wonder how many people will actually be there tonight, I hate crowds. Ugh, this must be what Prince Xander and Not Zac were referring to earlier.*

Before we knew it, we were standing in front of my door. Stella opened and held the door for me. I nodded my head to her as I walked through. "Thank you, Stella."

She followed me in and somehow the options were already hung on a rack in the middle of the room. *I don't know if I should be creeped out or impressed.*

I surveyed my options. One was a gorgeous burgundy dress with lace overlaying a long, silk skirt. With a classy slit at the side and a high neckline, the dress was easily one of the most gorgeous pieces of clothing I had ever seen.

Stella smiled. "Prince Alexander picked that one out for you himself."

I snorted. *I love it, but after he was such an ass, I won't give him the satisfaction of wearing it.*

The second option, an equally gorgeous floor length navy gown with a gold belt and a thick golden metal neckline like some kind of built-in necklace. It reminded me of something a Greek goddess would wear.

"I'll wear this one!"

Stella smiled and then helped me into the dress. *"You look beautiful."*

"Thank you so much, Stella," I said, my back still towards her. She reached up to take off my necklace, but I stopped her. "It's fine." I quickly tucked it under the neckline of the dress.

Stella gestured for me to sit at the vanity, and I obeyed. She styled my hair the same way I had it, just fixing up some parts that may have come undone. She braided a few pieces to meet

46

at the back of my head, leaving the rest of my curls to flow well below my shoulders. I smiled at her reflection in the mirror just before she headed towards the door.

"Thank you, again." I called out and she stopped mid-step.

"Of course, Your Highness." She said while turning towards me and curtseyed, as she always did, then left.

I walked into Amara's closet. *A girl could get used to this.* She had amazing taste. To the left of me were shelves that were built into the wall that ran from the floor all the way up to the ceiling, filled with shoes. *This is more shoes than in the shoe stores back home.*

I walked over to the shoe wall. Slowly walking from one side of it to the other, running my hand along the one shelf. I found a pair of sparkly gold heels that laced up my calves. *These are perfect and totally go with this Greek goddess theme!*

I quickly put them on and admired myself in the closet mirror. *You got this!* I said as I stood in a superhero stance with both fists on my hips, still watching myself in the mirror. I took a deep breath and left.

Lawrence was waiting for me outside of the ballroom. "You look lovely, Princess, your guests await."

"I wish your parents could see you now, they'd be so proud."

Avoiding his gaze and trying not to let my eyes water I whispered. "Me too."

"Excuse me, Miss Avery?"

"Um…nothing, let's get this over with."

I painted on a smile and tried to channel confidence. Taking in another deep breath as I walked towards the doors. There were two men standing on each side of the double doors. They opened the doors for me and apparently, every other guest for the evening.

I did a slow lap of the ballroom, trying to smile at everyone, but I was so mesmerized by the décor. *I thought they were practically finished decorating earlier, boy was I wrong.*

There were tables set around the walls of the room with extravagant white sparkling ostrich feather centerpieces. There was a large rectangular table along the northern wall with gifts piled high. I couldn't help but roll my eyes.

If this is just the engagement party what is the actual wedding going to look like? The thought of Amara actually marrying Prince Xander sent shivers up my spine.

In the center of it all, under the giant chandelier, was the dance floor. There were already couples dancing and gazing lovingly into each others' eyes.

Behind me, the main doors to the ballroom opened and my jaw dropped. Prince Xander and Not Zac walked in together. I walked over to interrogate them, thinking Prince Xander had something to do with Not Zac's stunt earlier.

"Thanks for helping me find Erik." Prince Xander's voice dripped with sarcasm.

"That's Erik?" I squealed.

Prince Xander scowled at my outburst, "Yes, my best friend and attendant Erik. You have met many times, and your stunts for attention are getting old."

"That's your best friend?" The man apparently named Erik gave no indication that the prince, his best friend, knew where and what he had been doing earlier.

I gulped, wondering what kind of person Prince Xander was if the man he was closest to was a total scumbag. "I-I have to go."

"*Is she alright?*"

Instead of responding to Xander, I heard Erik's voice ring out, "*Why would she come up to me in front of Xander?*"

I spun around to question him, but they both looked just as confused as I felt.

"W-what?" I stuttered.

"*Why is she acting so weird?*"

My eyes narrowed at Not Zac. "I'm not weird!" I demanded.

Prince Xander grinned smugly at me. "Could have fooled me." He and Erik both broke out in laughter.

I turned to Erik. "What are you even doing here?" I asked, crossing my arms and deepening my glare.

Xander's brows furrowed. "And what are you doing here, Amara?"

"Uh, because I have to be? Because we can't celebrate *our* engagement party if one of us is not here." I raised a hand as I shook my head in disbelief.

He maintained his grimace of disgust as his one eyebrow raised slightly and his nose wrinkled. "No, I mean why are you here talking to me? Don't you have someone else to go bother?"

I could feel my jaw clench. "Believe me, this is not my idea of fun. Do you always have to be so damned sarcastic?"

Prince Xander smirked. "Yes."

Anger rose in my chest. "You're infuriating!"

"Only for you, my queen." His smirk widened as he slightly bowed, mocking me.

Erik's eyes shifted. "I'll give you guys some alone time." As he walked past me he whispered in my ear, "What did I tell you about looking so good?"

Before I could even turn around to glare at him, Prince Xander grabbed my hand and began to drag me to the dance floor. "We are required to dance. May as well get this over with."

I rolled my eyes internally at his grand gesture. "Such a romantic. I'm amazed I'm not fighting off other women for the chance to be your betrothed."

He's the most annoying man I've ever met. It only makes it worse that he's so ungodly attractive.

Prince Xander placed my hand that he was still holding onto his shoulder, grabbed my other hand in his, and his free hand fell around my waist. He held me much closer than I thought was necessary to convincingly dance.

Even though I couldn't stand the man, I had to admit that dancing with him felt different. Butterflies fluttered in my stomach and I was suddenly very, very warm in the face and chest. I didn't want him to see how red I assumed my face was, so I rested my head against his chest and watched our feet as we danced.

He jerked in surprise but then pulled me in even closer than before. *I don't know why he makes me feel like this.* Maybe it was the way he held me as he placed his chin on the top of my head as we danced, or maybe it was just because I finally got him to shut up.

"Amara...Amara?"

I was too wrapped up in the feeling to remember my role. *Oh right, that's me.* "Y-yes, Prince Xander?"

"Could you *not* step on my feet?"

I know it was foolish to enjoy spending time with him, but did he have to ruin it by running his mouth?

"S-sorry," I couldn't help but stutter as I removed my head from his chest.

Xander's eyes widened for a moment then mumbled. "It-it's all right."

What, no sassy comebacks or sarcastic remarks? What's wrong with him? Did I step on his foot so hard he's delirious from the pain? Based on the odd expression he wore, I didn't want to rule that out.

"And Amara," he whispered so quietly I almost didn't hear him.

"Yes, Prince Xander?" My gaze shifted once again to the floor.

"You can just call me Xander."

I stopped dancing and just stood there for a moment, slowly looking back up at him, surprised by how differently he was acting compared to just minutes ago. I smiled at him and placed my head back on his chest as we continued to dance.

Just as I laid my head back down, the rhythm of the music changed, more upbeat and faster paced. Everyone around us started spinning in sync. They lifted one another in time to the music. Panic set in as I didn't know what to do. Both of Xander's hands were now on my waist as he lifted me up just as everyone else in the room had done the same.

Once my feet hit the floor again, he took one of my hands in his and spun me around. I couldn't help but laugh as I tipped my head back and let him guide me around the dance floor. We twirled, and laughed, and I didn't step on his feet too many more times. The song ended and was replaced by yet another slower one.

"She seems so different today."

I continued dancing while trying to decide if I should take that as a compliment or not.

"And she looks so beautiful tonight. I mean that dress."

Okay, what the heck is this guy thinking? Saying all of these weird things. It's like he has no filter.

My eyes met Xander's bright blue-green eyes for a moment, showing nothing in my expression but a genuine smile that I got to dance with a handsome prince at a ball.

"And that smile."

His lips didn't move. Am I hearing his thoughts? Have I been hearing people's thoughts all day? This isn't possible! I felt my chest tighten as panic squeezed at my lungs. *Oh my God, what is wrong with me?*

At the same moment, I heard Xander's voice but again, his lips didn't move, *"Is she all right?"*

I couldn't answer, my throat felt like it was full of lead and my head felt devoid of air.

Xander actually managed to show some genuine compassion and pulled me closer, "Hey, are you okay? Your face is pale."

My eyes went wide and Xander's arm around my waist tightened as if to better support me. "Amara, are you all right?"

I let out a scream as I covered my ears with both hands and bent over into a standing fetal-like position.

Everyone was staring at me.

"What's wrong with her?"

"Is she all right?"

"What a weirdo!"

"Does she need help?"

"That girl has problems."

"What a drama queen!"

"Someone should help her."

What is wrong with me? Am I imagining this? I must be! This is impossible! Isn't it?

Xander placed his hand on my elbow. "Are you okay?"

"I-I have to go!" I pushed his hand off where he was still holding me and just ran.

"Yeah, she's lost it."

I didn't know if it was the stress, or realizing that I had some weird power, but I was suddenly bombarded with thoughts. I felt like my brain was being both compressed and expanded, and both sensations made me feel like I was going to explode. I could hear everyone in the room's thoughts. And what was the topic on everyone's mind? Me.

I fell forward grabbing my head, experiencing the worst migraine of my life. The sounds were so loud and jumbled I could no longer make out any words. It was like a wall of angry white noise. The room spun while everything and everyone became a blur. I thought I was going to collapse. I screamed once again, not knowing if it was words or just sounds as there were too many others' thoughts in my head to focus on my own.

I took a deep, gulping breath, and fled towards the closest door I could locate with minimal brain function. I stumbled to the door like I had been shot. Apparently, whatever I had screamed was loud, because the room had been overcrowded before, but I didn't have to push a single person aside to get to the exit.

I forced my legs to push on, no room in my brain to create a single thought of my own or process what was happening. I ran out the balcony doors so fast I nearly flung myself off of the edge of the terrace.

Gripping the rail, staring down six stories, I tried to focus on my breathing. Thanks to my outburst, people were giving me distance in hopes they didn't catch whatever special brand of crazy I was supplying.

The distance and fresh air helped. The banging, pounding noise in my head had lessened to an ever-present buzzing, like a broken T.V. I took a few steps back to further myself from the railing in fear of falling since I still was unsure of my balance and sanity. I wrapped my arms around myself as I watched the bright glowing moon above me and tried to focus on that. The nausea subsided enough for me to notice Xander standing by my side, looking genuinely concerned.

"What the hell was all that?" As our eyes met he must have seen the pain I was trying to control as his stare and tone softened, "Come here." Xander scooped me up and held me close to his chest, walking me back towards the ballroom.

"I need to get out of here." I managed to whisper.

"Don't worry, you'll be okay." With Xander's kind and confident words, I allowed him to walk me back through the ballroom and to my bedroom. The last thing I remembered was Xander placing me on my bed.

Amara

It was late at night. I have no clue how late, but the moon shone strong and true in the night sky through the open window. I could hear Wesley pacing downstairs. *I wish he would just get some rest.*

I quietly opened my bedroom door and made my way to the stairs a few steps away, tip toeing so he would not hear me. I took a step and the floor creaked. I froze hoping he did not hear me.

"Hello?" He called, not too loud to wake me if I was sleeping but loud enough for me to hear otherwise.

He sighed and continued pacing back and forth. I let out a deep but quiet breath myself, relieved that he did not catch me.

I peeked around the corner, down the stairs, and watched him. I sat down at the top of the stairs and watched him. *Why won't he just listen to me and get some sleep.*

He stopped his pacing and for a moment I thought he was about to look up at me, but instead he pulled out his sword from his side and practiced his form and stances and I thought back to all those years ago and our training.

"You need to work on your counters," Wesley said as he threw me a wooden sword from the side of the stables.

"When can we switch to real swords?" I complained.

"When you can beat me with a wooden one." He countered with a devilish grin and then grabbed a second wooden sword for himself. "One!" he called out as he aimed for an overhead attack, and I defended myself in the position I knew as one. "Two!" He called out again as he threw another attack my way. I quickly extended my arm outwards and parried the attack.

He continued to shout out numbers as we practiced. He did not land a single blow and eventually stopped calling out numbers and let my intuition take over as we continued our sparing. Wesley went in for another overhead attack when, again, I defended myself in what I knew as position one. It absorbed the full force of the blow. I pushed back with the wooden sword, and he retreated. As he stepped back, I kicked him in the chest with all the energy I had left in me, knocking him to the ground.

I stood over him smirking and I panted trying to catch my own breath, "So, am I ready for a real sword now? I pointed my sword downward at his chest.

He winked at me before he swept my legs out from under me, knocking me right down next to him. He laughed and then said, "I guess we can start with them tomorrow."

I yawned and tip-toed back to my room to attempt to get some more sleep myself.

CHAPTER FIVE

Avery

Deep within the darkness, a shadowed creature moved with cat-like grace. The darkness was so thick I couldn't make out much more than some arms and legs. The creature seemed to bow to the same cloaked figure from my last dream.

"Shadow Lord, how are things progressing?" The shadowy figure tipped its face towards its cloaked master.

The cloaked figure spoke in a voice that sounded both feminine and masculine at the same time. "The grimoire is now mine, soon all of Soluna will be too."

I woke up with a start. *What the hell is a Shadow Lord?*

My head was pounding, and my heart racing. *What the heck is with these weird, vivid dreams?*

Rolling over in my bed I realized I was still wearing my dress from the night before. *What happened last night?* I tried to sit up, and as the sun hit me, my headache worsened. *That dream was messed up. It actually mentioned Soluna, whatever it was. I* shivered at the thought of that cloaked figure again. *Maybe I should mention this to Lawrence.*

Rubbing my head again, the events of last night came flooding back to me. Oh no, last night. What happened? The last thing I remember is Xander bringing me to bed. Crap! Did I really hear people's thoughts last night? Or was that just a weird dream too? That is completely insane. It just doesn't make sense. People can't read other people's thoughts, can they? I definitely didn't have this problem before coming here.

The alarm clock on the nightstand read 11 a.m. *Wow, I must have really slept in.*

A constant throbbing in my forehead and around my eyes had increased and I worked up the willpower to leave my bed to find some aspirin. Crawling my way out of the many layers of blankets I made it to the edge of the bed and decided the first place to check was the nightstand drawers. *Talk about the world's worst hangover.*

I began to lose hope after the sixth drawer that contained only jewelry, a diary, and a frightening amount of makeup. I headed to her ensuite to continue my search. *Do they even have pain meds here? Because if they do, I can't find them!*

After checking the medicine cabinet and failing to find anything that could be of use, I gave up. Turning the handle, I let the cold water from the vanity run for a few moments as I watched myself in the mirror. My eyes were red and sunken, face almost a sickly pale. I blinked in disbelief. *Is this all because of this weird new power or was it something more? The dreams I've been having have become more frequent, but they still weren't as terrifying as the ability to read other people's thoughts. Then again, I could try to use this to my advantage here, I don't know anything about these people or this world.* Finally removed from the trance of my reflection, I splashed the water on my face, as if it would help.

The water did not do much for my pounding head, but it certainly helped my morning vision. I hadn't realized until then how much my eyes had been squinting. The room around me seemed to open just as my eyes did. The bathroom was enormous. Not only did it have the working vanity and toilet, it had a giant jacuzzi tub and a lovely glass shower.

Stepping closer towards the shower I noticed the marble tiles along the floors and walls of it, very different from the stone I was used to for most of the castle. There was a waterfall shower head above which took up the entire ceiling of the shower. Six different jets lined the tiled walls.

Oh, this is so much better than aspirin!

I leaned over to turn on the shower faucet when there was a knock at the bedroom door.

Seriously? Does someone time this or what?

"Just a minute!" I yelled while hopping around, trying to change out of my dress and into something a little more practical and sort of tame my hair before walking over to the door.

The small bloom of hope in my chest was crushed the minute I saw Not Zac's smug grin on the other side of my open door.

"Oh, it's you. Great."

Missing my sarcasm, Not Zac strolled into my room and, again, began to strip.

"Seriously, what is your problem?"

He paused with his shirt half-off. "What's the issue babe? You already rejected me once. If you're not careful, I'm going to start thinking you don't like me anymore."

"I didn't give you that impression last time?"

Not Zac gave up trying to unbutton his pants and sauntered over towards me with a large grin pulling at the corners of his mouth. "I don't know what kind of game you were playing last night, coming up to me while I was with Xander, but I liked how risky it was."

He tried to close the space between us as I slowly backed away from him until my back met the wall. I looked over my shoulder half expecting and fully hoping that it wasn't really a wall when I noticed we were next to the fireplace. I silently grabbed the iron poker that was hung next to me and hid it behind my back just as his fingers grazed my cheek, ticking a strand of hair behind my ear.

"There's just something about you recently, I don't know if it's this new game you're doing or what, but I like it." He smirked. "We both know you love the way I make you feel, let me remind you of that."

I smiled at Not Zac again and attempted a seductive voice as I replied, "You know, there is something I would like, and only you can help me."

Not Zac leaned forward and whispered in my ear, "Tell me."

I pushed him back with one hand and pulled out the iron poker from behind my back with the other as I pointed it towards him like a sword.

"I would love to shove this poker so far up your ass that you—"

"Okay, okay!" Not Zac winced and took several steps back before I could even finish my sentence. "Jeez," he mumbled as he put his shirt back on. "But I'm loving this hard-to-get thing. I'll see you later."

He opened my door and as he did, I could see Lawrence on the other side of it. Erik avoided eye contact as he bowed his head to Lawrence and walked through the doorway. Lawrence walked in with confusion written all over his face as he stared at me still wielding the poker.

His confusion quickly turned into worry. "Princess, what is going on? Are you all right?"

I grumbled and surrendered my weapon to Lawrence. "Erik may have had a hard time understanding what I was saying."

Lawrence laid the poker back up against the fireplace before he spoke. "He is an even bigger pain than Prince Alexander, if you ask me." I laughed, half at what he said and the other half at his monotone voice saying it. "Get ready, Miss Avery, there are some other matters we must discuss. Meet me outside of your room when you are ready." He exited almost as quickly as he had entered the room.

I took this time to have a quick shower. All the while replaying the events of last night. *I must have imagined it, right? This is insane.* I lifted my head as I let the water run down my face. *I can't seriously be reading people's thoughts. Then again, I never would have believed I was a princess a few days ago, but this is next level.*

I took longer than probably necessary in the shower before finally getting out. I put on more appropriate princess-like clothes from Amara's closet and ran a real brush through my hair, brushed my teeth, and put on shoes before making my way out of the room to meet Lawrence.

We headed down to the main corridor of the castle, the entire time he droned on about political engagements that I was too tired to focus on as my head pounded.

When we turned the corner, Xander was standing in the hallway with some woman. "Why is he still here?"

Lawrence's lips twitched slightly; I had wondered if I had imagined it. "Why is *who* here, Miss Avery?"

"Prince Xander." I gestured with my head in their direction.

Lawrence nodded knowingly. "Prince Xander will be staying here for a while during the wedding planning. His father thought it would be a good way for you to get to know each other. I think it sounds like a disaster, but what would I know?"

Smiling a little at his loyalty, I asked. "And who is that with him?"

"That is Lady Victoria. She's a little bit different, to say the least. She is very close to Sir Erik and Prince Alexander."

"Yeah, they seem pretty close." I said, glaring back at Xander.

Xander turned and looked directly at me, so Lawrence urged me forward towards them, whispering, "Just remember to be nice and keep it short."

When I reached Xander I plastered a smile on my face. "So happy you're still here."

Xander gave me an equally fake smile. "So happy to be here."

God he's such an arrogant ass.

"She's the worst."

So definitely not a dream.

Before I could even think of a response or way to use this to my advantage, Victoria curtsied. "So happy to meet you, Princess."

Xander placed a hand on Lady Victoria's shoulder. "You don't have to be nice to her, Vic. She's not worth it." Turning, he said, "Let's get out of here."

Be nice, Avery.

Before he could flee, I said, "Can I talk to you for a second, Prince Xander?"

"Whatever. Wait for me in my room, Vic." He leaned down and kissed her cheek. "I'm so glad you're here."

Brown, flowy hair slipped just over her shoulders as she turned her head to gaze up at Xander. Her bright blue eyes sparkled as they watched him attentively, and cheeks flushed as she ran a hand up his arm.

She smiled. "I'll be waiting for you, Xand." She rolled her eyes as she walked past me.

Seriously? I'm standing right here. And Xand? Wow, how original.

Xander cut off my inner babbling, "So? What do you want?"

"I just wanted to try to apologize," I bit out, chewing on the bottom of my lip.

Xander gasped and then laughed. "You almost had me for a second there."

I yelled, throwing my arms up in frustration. "I'm serious, okay! Why does everything have to be such a challenge with you?"

"And what exactly are you apologizing for?" he asked, arms crossed, and brow arched.

"For running out on you the way I did last night." *What else would I have to apologize for?*

"So, the only thing you want to apologize for is freaking out in the ballroom? You have nothing else to say to me?" He loomed closer.

"What else would I have to apologize for?" I inclined my head, my eyes met his.

"Oh, I don't know. Why don't you tell me?" His anger seemed to grow. A more condescending tone crept in as he took another step closer.

"Try sleeping with my best friend."

What?

"I-I don't know what you mean," I denied, taking a step back, my eyes shifted from him to the doorway and back.

"Right, well if that's all, I have someone waiting in my room for me, as you know." He winked.

"Lady Victoria, right. How could I forget?" I rolled my eyes and tried not to gag.

"My, my, Miss Amara, are you jealous?" Xander's smirk was back, he slowly took another step closer.

"What? Me? Jealous? No! But in case you've forgotten, we're engaged."

Xander's eyes narrowed like I said something I shouldn't have. *I hope there isn't some engagement ring that Amara had forgotten to give me to wear.*

Xander's whole face wrinkled. "How could I forget? But you know, our agreement still stands."

Agreement?

I tried to look disinterested, raising one arm up and admiring my still unpainted nails. "Remind me again what that agreement was."

Xander scoffed. "This marriage is strictly political. You can be with whoever you want, and so can I. As long as we're discreet."

My mouth dropped open. "We agreed to an open marriage?"

A smirk pulled at the corner of his lips. "What, princess? Did you have a change of heart?"

"N-no, of course not. You just—" I paused for a moment before meeting his gaze once more. "Don't seem like that kind of man."

Xander gave me a flirty smile. Leaning in closer, he said, "Don't tell me you're falling for me now?"

"I'm going to mess with her a little."

My eyes narrowed. *Like hell you are. Two can play at this game.*

"There's just something about you." I tossed my hair dramatically and closed the little distance left between us, our noses practically touched.

Xander froze. *"What the hell is she doing?"*

I was having too much fun messing with him. I leaned in even closer, this time my lips gently brushed his ear as I whispered, "I just don't know how much longer I can control myself."

I slowly pulled my head back trying to meet his eyes with mine but as I did, I noticed his gaze was focused on my lips.

"What is happening right now?"

He must have somehow felt my gaze as he slowly lifted his eyes to meet mine once more, "I tend to have this effect on women." He caressed my cheek in a way that made me feel he was mocking me.

I took a step back from him and glared. "I really hate you."

"There's a fine line between love and hate." He threw me a quick wink and left before I could even think of something to say back to him.

I can't believe this guy. Why did I even do that? Ugh, this man drives me insane!

Amara

Sweat dripped down my face as I awoke, frantically gasping for air. *What the hell is a Shadow Lord?* Taking deep breaths, trying to steady my breathing and heart rate, I closed my eyes. *It was only a dream.* But much like my other ones, it felt too real.

I sat up in the bed allowing the sun shining in through the window to warm my face and calm me. *It was just a dream. It was just another, weird, creepy, dream. That mentioned Soluna. Maybe I should look for anything mentioning a Shadow Lord in the library while I'm here, just in case.*

Taking another deep breath and holding it for several seconds before letting out a long exhale I told myself, *you can do this. There must be something here that can help you. Some sort of clue, anything.*

Deciding it was time to get up, I made my way over to where I hung my clothes last night to dry. There was a water stain on the ground underneath where they hung, and I was glad that they were now dry. I pulled on my shirt, followed by my pants. My sword was on the nightside table in its scabbard where I had left it last night, not wanting it to be far away from where I had slept.

I scanned the tiny room to make sure I had not forgotten anything. The room was much smaller than my bed chambers back home. My closet was larger than this. Everything was made of wood and seemed to be falling apart. The bed was nothing more than a mattress on the floor, but that had not mattered to me. I was here for a reason, and I was not going to let anything get in my way.

Passing a full-length mirror, one of the only pieces of furniture or décor in the room, I noticed how messy my updo and makeup had become. I removed the pins that were now failing to hold up anything and ran my fingers through my long, messy hair as I shook my head attempting to make it presentable now that it was down.

I decided to head to the bathing chambers to quickly wash up. There was no running water, the plumbing here was nothing like back at the castle. Two buckets of water sat next to the tiny tub. Steam was coming out of them, and I figured it had to be the safehouse that had done this, much like the dinner that was made last night. I washed my face, and any makeup I still had on, off before heading downstairs.

I was hoping to see Wesley passed out down there, but no such luck. *I guess he did not get any sleep after all.*

When I made it to the kitchen, Wesley was sitting at the small wooden table eating something out of his bowl, eyes fixed on whatever it was he was eating. I cleared my throat and His eyes immediately flicked to me.

"Wow, your hair!" Wesley gaped at me.

"What is wrong with it?" I groaned as I ran my hands through my hair, picking at the ends I could see expecting to find something in it.

"Nothing! It's just been a while since I've seen you like this. You don't often let your hair down." His smile was soft.

"What is that supposed to mean?" I raised my chin.

"It's just. Well, you've been acting queen for so long now you haven't been able to look or act the way you used to. Like the Amara I know you truly are." He lifted a shoulder in a half shrug.

"Are you saying I have changed?" I slumped into one of the chairs at the table.

"Maybe a little. It's not necessarily a bad thing. I just don't want you to have to change who you are just so you can become queen. You used to be so careless and free. And now you—you just aren't.""

"That's the point!" I snapped instantly shooting back up from the chair, knocking it over in the process. "I'm supposed to care! Care about this kingdom, it's people, this world. No one wants a careless queen."

"Maybe I do." He took a step closer, and my eyes shifted. "Just be the queen I always believed you could be. You're amazing and you shouldn't have to change." His genuine smile changed into a mischievous grin. "Besides, I don't want you getting rusty."

"What do you mean rusty?" I arched a questioning brow at him.

"Well, when was the last time you got to get any training in really?" He teased, eyeing me up and down as if he were examining me.

"Are you trying to say you could take me in a fight now?" I huffed a laugh.

"Hey, I never said that. You are definitely someone I would not want to mess with." He lifted his hands in mock surrender as a grin pulled at his lips.

I snorted a laugh this time but quickly decided to change the subject. "We should get started on the hunt for something that can help us here. There is a huge library I was thinking we could investigate to see if we can find any more of my mother's journals or something mentioning anything about the prophecy." *And anything about a Shadow Lord.*

"That's a great idea! Lead the way, my queen."

He wiggled his eyebrows while he mockingly bowed to me and I pushed him over, knocking him right on his butt.

I raced up the steps and down the hall, laughter escaping me as I threw open the library doors. I was immediately struck with awe, my jaw dropping at the unbelievable sight before me.

CHAPTER SIX

Avery

I stormed off down the hall and nearly walked into someone. "Oh my gosh! I'm so sorry!"

A girl I'd never met before stood in front of me, her long black curls bounced as she steadied herself.

Where's Lawrence when you need him, I have no idea who this girl is.

"Don't worry about it, happens to the best of us." Her light brown eyes shined as she smiled.

She seems nice enough.

"You're Princess Amara, right?"

"Uh, yeah. I'm sorry your name is slipping my mind. I feel like such a jerk." I felt so dumb and awkward even though I knew I shouldn't.

She laughed it off. "Don't worry we've never technically met before anyway." I let out a sigh of relief as she continued, "It's nice to finally put a face to the name. I was here for the ball last night. I should probably get going soon but to be honest, I'm just too exhausted."

Finally! Someone I can sort of be myself around. She's never met Amara so I don't have to try as hard since she has nothing to compare me to.

I smiled at her jokingly. "Well, I hope you had fun last night."

"Oh, I did. I met a lovely stranger, but of course my father would never approve."

"Why not?" I asked. *Wasn't everyone here last night some type of nobility or something?*

"My father never approves of any of the people I actually approve of. But I suppose that is the life of a princess, right?" She sighed.

So, she's also a princess.

"Why did I just tell her that? She just seems so nice and nothing like I pictured from the stories I've heard."

Oh crap, what stories has she heard about me? I mean Amara, and who is telling her these stories anyway?

"My name's Hazel, by the way." She extended a hand and I shook it.

"Princess Hazel, nice to officially meet you."

"Please, just call me Hazel." She seemed to be deep in thought for a moment, but nothing came through when I tried to use whatever weird new power I now possessed. "I have an idea! Come with me." She pulled my hand that was still clasped in hers.

I don't know, I have a lot of stuff I have to do today. As you said, the life of a princess, right?" I jerked my thumb towards the exit, hoping she was buying the lame excuse I managed to come up with.

"Trust me you and I both need this. You looked a little overwhelmed last night." She rubbed her arm and she gave me a tight lipped smile.

Great she saw that. I tried to see if I could use my newfound powers to figure out what she had planned. *Cool, I have absolutely no control over what I hear and when I hear it. As if this couldn't get any worse.*

I watched her carefully, trying to read her body language since I had no idea what she was thinking. She seemed genuine and kind. To be honest I could use a friend around here aside from Lawrence, if you could even consider him one.

I hope I don't regret this. "Okay, I'll come with you!" I replied reluctantly.

"Perfect! But first we need to stop at your room so, lead the way." She cheerfully clapped her hands together once as she bobbed on the balls of her feet. I wasn't sure if I'd even seen a grin as wide as the one, she was throwing my way and I walked past her slowly, trying to read anything from here.

"This is going to be so much fun!"

I walked back up the stairs and down the corridor to my room as Hazel followed closely. I opened the door slowly, half expecting something or some*one* to jump out at me. I walked in still a little wary of what might jump out, but luckily it was empty.

"All right to the closet!" She cheered and I pointed her in the direction of Amara's walk-in.

What the hell is she doing?

After a few moments she came out in an oversized burgundy button up top that she had tucked into some black leggings, a pair of black boots, and a hooded black velvet cloak.

I raised a questioning brow at her. "What are you wearing?"

She placed both hands on her hips as if it were obvious. "A disguise, duh. I put one out for you too, go put it on!"

"But why?" I tried to get another read from her, but again couldn't.

This would be a lot more helpful and less creepy if I could actually control it.

"We're going to sneak out and have some fun. We can escape this princess life for a few hours and just be normal."

It's like she's the one that could read my mind. How did she know I just wanted to be normal again?

"But won't someone notice our absence?"

"Not until it's too late if we're lucky." She grinned. "Besides, you look like you could use a stress-free day after last night."

I conceded, "All right, I guess I'll go change." I retreated into the closet to find an outfit laid out on the cushioned seat in the middle of the closet.

Might as well just go with it, what do I have to lose? Ha, famous last words.

I couldn't help but laugh when I put on the outfit and saw my reflection in the mirror. She had picked out an almost identical outfit to hers. *This must be the fashion of the people outside of the castle.* I guessed. I had on a pair of black leggings with a long, loose fitted dusty pink top, with equally long and loose sleeves and a pair of brown boots. I walked back into the other room to meet her and she held up another black velvet cloak with a wide smile on her face.

I put it on and pulled the hood up over my head and Hazel beamed with excitement, "You look amazing! Very civilian-y." She laughed as she pulled up her own hood and headed towards the door but I stopped her.

"Seriously?" I raised an eyebrow at her.

"Trust me, this plan is genius!" She started towards the exit once more and headed out the door. "You coming?" she called from the hallway.

"Here goes nothing I guess."

I followed closely behind Hazel as we swiftly made our way out through the servants quarters. We did not pass a single soul on the way out. They were probably still too busy with the clean up from last night's lovely event.

The afternoon sun warmed my face as we crept through a part of the castle grounds I had yet to see. A large wooden building stood to the left of me, I turned to see horses just outside of the building and inside a wooden fence. The smell of fresh and slightly sweet hay filled me as I watched the horses eat.

"Come on," Hazel whispered as she pulled me forward.

We made our way to a line of trees and just beyond the tree line was a large stone wall that must have wrapped all the way along the castle grounds. Hazel looked back at me and grinned. She pointed to a small hole in the wall that was just big enough for a smaller person to fit through. She squeezed her way through, and I followed suit.

On the other side of the wall was a small forest path that led directly into the village just outside the castle.

We walked down a street in the little village. All the buildings were made of stone. The shops looked so small but unique. The village itself reminded me of an older era, the streets were covered with old gaslight streetlamps, people were walking around or travelling by horse. The roads were all dirt roads, no pavement in site. Yet, when I looked inside the shops and buildings, they had electricity just like the castle.

This is beautiful.

Hazel broke the silence, "That was almost too easy."

"That's what worries me." I couldn't help but feel uneasy. I had no idea who this lady was or where we were going. Sure, she seemed nice enough, but was I really just going to continue to follow strangers wherever they wanted to take me? It seemed like a theme lately and I'd watched enough movies to know I shouldn't be doing it and yet, here I was.

"You need to stop worrying so much, we're fine. I do this all the time back home."

"That doesn't make me feel better about this, and where are we going anyway?" I tried to change the subject hoping that getting some answers would ease my mind.

"Well, I was going to take us to a coffee shop. But I have a better idea." The largest grin grew on her face and my stomach filled with knots.

"Follow me!" she yelled as she ran ahead.

This woman is crazy. But, I like the idea that I can actually be myself around her and not some sister I don't even know.

I did as she said and caught up to follow her again. She walked into a building and I couldn't quite make out what the sign said as it needed to be replaced badly.

Once we stepped inside, she spun around with her arms up in the air. "Ta-da!"

I frowned as I crossed my arms. "You took us to a bar?"

She was far too excited. "A what? No, I brought you to a *karaoke* bar!"

"During the day?"

Her excitement turned to a slightly concerned look. "I thought you could use a good time. You seem stressed about something. I know we just met so I didn't want to pry. I thought this could help. Plus, there won't be as many people here during the day."

She speaks her mind, and I would know. I really admire that in a person.

"Okay, but what are we supposed to do?"

"Drink and sing!" she cheered.

"And how is embarrassing myself with my horrible singing supposed to make me feel better about embarrassing myself from last night?" I threw my hands up and gestured to the room around us.

"Just trust me. Plus, we're the only ones here right now, so technically you'll just be embarrassing yourself in front of me." She tossed me a devilish grin and I just rolled my eyes as I caved.

"Fine, I'll do it. But I still don't get how this is supposed to be a stress reliever."

She giggled. "Yay! So most importantly, what are you going to sing?"

I was pleased to see that she was right, the place was pretty much empty. I don't know what came over me, but I was actually going to do it.

Who knows what kind of music they even have here?

"I'll go get us some drinks from the bar while you decide." She ran over to the bar and shot back just as quickly. Luckily, I already knew if I was going to be doing this, there was only one song I'd be singing. *Can't fight the moonlight.*

She placed the mixed drink that was intended for me on the table and slid it towards me. I picked it up and downed it before putting it back down on the table between us and grabbing her drink from her hands and downing that one too. Pleasantly surprised when I found a mischievous smile on her face instead of the angry pout I was half expecting.

"I'm going to need both of those if I'm really about to go up there," I teased.

"Oh, I like you." She laughed as she pushed me towards the stage.

Halfway through my song the bar doors opened. Three people walked in and headed straight for the bar. I tried not to look their way but found my gaze kept finding its way back to them. Two of them were dancing while the other just stood there, eyeing me suspiciously. Then it clicked, it was Xander, Erik, and Lady Victoria. *Great.*

Xander made his way towards the stage and me.

What the heck is he doing? Can he see through this disguise? I mean it's not really that good of a disguise anyway.

I adjusted the hood of the cloak and tilted my head down in hopes that he wouldn't recognize me. He just continued to stand there, hands in his pockets and eyes fixed on me. I tried concentrating on the words to the song, the last thing I needed was this extra pressure not to mess up.

"Usually her voice is really annoying."

Guess the disguise didn't work. Can he just leave already? This is super awkward.

After a few more moments he finally walked away. I waited for him to get all the way back to where Not Zac and Lady

Victoria were over by the bar before I got off the stage after I finished the song.

"Jeez, that was so embarrassing." I covered my face with my hands as I reached Hazel back at our table.

Her mouth hung open like a gaping fish. "Are you kidding? That was incredible! Did you even realize how good you sounded? Wait until you hear all these other amateurs later when the bar fills up." She waved her hand dismissively.

I laughed awkwardly. "Yeah, right. Can we take off these cloaks now?"

She dramatically rubbed at her chin like she was thinking it over before replying, "I guess so, we just have to be careful. I mean I guess it is probably drawing more attention to us by wearing them inside anyway."

I took it off and laid it on the table between us. "Much better!" Hazel just laughed and I couldn't help but join in. "So, what are you going to sing?" I asked her.

"Nothing, I would never embarrass myself like that!" She laughed.

"Are you kidding me?" I threw my hands up in surprise.

"I have another idea!" She raised her hand and pointed her finger upwards. *"Shots!"*

I spoke through my hand as I bit my nails nervously. "I don't think that's such a good idea. I mean it's the middle of the day, should we really be doing shots right now?"

She tilted her head and raised an eyebrow at me. "How'd you know I was going to suggest shots?"

I tried to think of anything that wouldn't make me sound like a crazy person admitting, 'Oh, you know, I just read your mind. No big deal.' I faked a smile and blurted out the first logical sounding thing I could think of, "I just feel like we are already great friends and I know you so well."

Hazel shrugged. "Fair enough." She chuckled. "We always have to be so proper and respectful. I think it's time we live a little."

"All right fine, but you're buying!"

"You're on!"

We walked over to the bar and there they were. Xander, Erik and Lady Victoria dancing away in front of the bar counter.

Hazel let out a gasp and I turned to her. "No way!" She ran up to them and greeted them, "Hey, guys!"

I was in disbelief and didn't know what to do. I figured it was better to go up to them with Hazel rather than hang out alone until she returned so I followed her. I awkwardly stood beside her trying to avoid eye contact with any of them, especially Xander.

Xander turned around and seemed even more surprised as he cocked his head to the side and wrinkled his face. "Hazel! What are you doing here?"

My curiosity got the better of me. "You guys know each other?"

Hazel took a step back, now facing both me as well as Xander and let out a snicker, "Unfortunately."

Watching Xander, I tried to read his expression or mind. *Was she another one of his 'friends'?*

He just rolled his eyes. "Yes, unfortunately, she's my sister."

CHAPTER SEVEN

Avery

"She's your what?"

"My younger sister. Are you deaf or just stupid?" His tone was as arrogant as ever.

I couldn't help but snap, "Are you always such an asshole?"

Hazel answered before he had a chance to. "Yes!" She burst out into laughter.

Xander took a step closer as he barked, "You are just—"

"Enough!" Hazel interrupted again and put her hands up in our directions as if she was trying to hold us both back from a bar brawl. "I took us out for a good time, and that's exactly what we're going to do. All of us! Understood?"

"Understood," Xander and I both mumbled more to ourselves than to each other or Hazel.

Hazel was quickly back to her cheerful self as if nothing had just happened. "Good, now let's go do some shots and really get this party started!"

"Now you're speaking my language!" Victoria cheered as she did one last provocative dance move before she and Erik followed Hazel to the bar leaving me and Xander alone together.

Xander surprised me by taking a few steps towards me, closing the distance between us. His smug face tilted down as he towered over me.

"Can we just try to get along? At least for today." I tried to sound as nice as possible.

He paused briefly, placing one hand on his chin as he continued to survey me like he was really putting some thought into what I had just suggested.

"I guess I can put up with you for a day." He didn't wait for a response before turning away and heading over to where everyone else stood at the bar.

God, he's so infuriating.

We'd been at the same bar for hours; the lights had dimmed and the place slowly started to fill as the day turned into night. I was seated at the bar trying to order a drink but it seemed no matter where I was I still lacked the confidence to get a bartender's attention. People sang, danced and crowded the bar around me.

As I scanned the rest of the room, Xander caught my attention. He and Erik had been on the opposite side of the room in a booth. His gaze fixed on me. I tried to pull away but as he noticed my eyes met his, his stare seemed to intensify. Erik hit his shoulder playfully which seemed to snap his gaze away from me and back to Erik. They seemed to be in deep conversation. I tried not to watch them but found myself nearly staring at them from the corner of my eye just as Victoria seemed to join them.

She sat down next to Xander, so close she was practically on top of him. This time it wasn't hard to avoid looking their way. I turned back to the bar in another sad attempt to get the bartender's attention.

"Whiskey, and whatever she's having." I didn't have to turn around to see who it was, I recognized his voice. Erik propped his elbows up, leaning onto the bar counter next to me. I shot him a sideways glance and one corner of his mouth slanted up.

"I wanted you to know that I'm sorry. I've probably been coming on a little too strong lately. I shouldn't have just assumed things would be like they were before. But did you really have to pull a weapon on me?" He snorted a laugh but before I could answer, Xander and Victoria had joined us at the bar.

"We've been here for long enough. I've got another place we should check out with real music." Victoria said as she narrowed her eyes in the direction of the man singing on stage.

Hazel approached from out of the crowd and must have somehow heard as she was the first to answer Victoria. "I don't know." She turned to me. "What do you think Amara?"

It had been such a long day. Though, I'd be lying if I said I hadn't enjoyed myself. As much as I'd hate to admit it, they were all kind of fun to be around. "Why not? Let's do it!"

"I can't wait, they have the best rooftop!" Erik cheered then downed his drink the second the bartender handed it to him.

I could feel my heart start to pound in my chest, "Rooftop? You never said it was a rooftop club."

Xander turned and faced me. "It's my favourite place, but if you want, we can go somewhere else or just stay here."

I was taken back by his surprisingly nice offer and quickly glanced at Victoria who seemed equally surprised and extremely unimpressed.

"I don't want to ruin everyone's night if you all really want to go. I'm just kind of, sort of, terrified of heights." I hated to admit that, I didn't want them to think I was weak or something. "You guys go ahead. I'll just head back to the castle."

I started to turn around but stopped when I heard Victoria. "They have a great dance floor downstairs, too, don't worry." I couldn't tell if she was genuinely being nice or just putting on a show.

Erik was all too excited. "Yes! Let's go!"

The floor of the downstairs dance floor lit up and changed colours to the beat of the modern music that blasted from the speakers. An actual disco ball twirled above us and shined as many different lights hit it reflecting them back down towards us. It reminded me of something straight out of Saturday Night Fever. The only difference, aside from the music, was the clothing and the dance moves.

Much like many of the clothing I had seen from Amara's closet, their clothing was pretty modern. Basic tops and pants for the men, some even dressed in buttoned up dress shirts and pants, but not many. The women wore dresses similar to what I would see back home but a lot less form-fitted to what they wore in clubs in my world. Of course, many wore dresses with corset tops, but the rest of the dresses weren't that different.

Hazel was dancing with a gorgeous man and an equally beautiful woman. She smiled and winked at me as she caught my eye, then brought her attention right back to her dance partners as she threw her head back laughing at something one of them had said. I couldn't tell which of the two she was into more and wondered if she was trying to decide the same thing for herself.

I meant to turn around to face the group again when I stumbled and backed right into Xander. His hands found my waist to catch me but didn't remove his hands after I steadied myself. I glanced back over my shoulder at him, and he just shrugged and smirked. I quickly jerked my head forward as my cheeks flushed and we started to dance together.

"This is kind of nice." *Crap, did I just say that out loud?*

"What is?" I lifted my chin slightly, peeking over my shoulder at him again and he actually smiled which amazed me.

"I don't know? This. Not being at each other's throats," I mumbled as I scanned the crowd once more, unable to meet his eyes. Then, he just stopped dancing.

Great.

He leaned in closer, his lips grazed my ear as he spoke. "Come with me."

I hesitated at first. I mean he was a total jerk even if we were being civil for tonight. He must have noticed my doubt as he chuckled and grabbed my hand, leading me in the direction he wanted to go.

He led me to the back of the dance floor and up a set of stairs. The lights were much dimmer than on the actual dance floor considering there were no disco balls or strobe lights. I rubbed my eyes with my one free hand trying to adjust to the sudden change in lighting. I squinted and was glad that he was still holding onto my hand as he led the way because I couldn't see a thing.

We got to the top of the stairs and stars lit up the sky. Light rain drops brushed against my face. That's when I realized we were outside. He took me to the rooftop. I immediately froze and ripped my hand from his.

"And just when I thought you were actually being nice." He genuinely seemed surprised by what I said.

"What'd I do this time? I can't control the weather, you know."

I snapped, "Not that! I actually don't mind the rain but you took me up here to scare me! Maybe even push me off the roof?"

Xander just laughed which just made my blood boil. "Now you're just being ridiculous." He rolled his eyes. "I thought maybe I could help you get over your fears. You're going to be queen soon enough and I thought it'd be a nice thing to get over so you could show no fear. That's what I get for trying to be nice." He turned to head back down the stairs but I caught his arm to stop him.

Now who's being the jerk?

"Xander, wait. I'm sorry. I shouldn't have said that. So, I guess what I'm trying to say is thank you."

"Don't mention it. Literally, don't tell anyone." That smirk of his began pulling at the corner of his lips and I couldn't help but breathe out a small laugh but for some reason I couldn't look at him, so instead I watched the stars. Heat crept in along my face and chest. "So, what is it that scares you about heights anyway? I just think you're missing out on so much. It's beautiful up here."

I already felt extremely uncomfortable just by being up there, even though we were nowhere near the edge.

"I don't know, to be honest. It just makes me feel so dizzy and light headed. Like I don't have any control. That I could fall at any moment. I know it sounds dumb but it's how I feel and whenever I look down it gets worse and all I can picture is falling." The heat I was already feeling in my cheeks had moved to the rest of my face and chest.

Xander didn't say anything for some time, I finally glanced up at his face. His eyes were scanning my face like he was examining me for something.

"Well, have you ever actually fallen?"

"Well, no."

"See you have nothing to be worried about." He laughed, actually laughed at me.

"Are you seriously *laughing* at me right now?"

"N-no." He stifled another laugh as he covered his mouth with his hand, the corners of his lips visibly curving upwards.

"What? Just because I haven't actually fallen doesn't mean I won't and it certainly does not mean I am just magically over my fear now." I wrapped my arms around myself for comfort.

"I know, but the only way to get over your fear is to face it. What are you going to do when you're queen and you have to address your subjects from the balcony?"

Hopefully I won't still be pretending to be Amara and won't have to ever do that.

I took a deep breath. "I don't know. I never thought about that."

Xander sounded so calm even though I was losing my cool. "Like I said, the only way to get over your fear is to face it."

"Okay, Mr. Big Shot, what's your biggest fear?"

"What? Why?" He hesitated. "This is about you, not me."

"I told you mine, so you have to tell me yours. It's only fair." I gave him my best mock-smile.

"Becoming king," He mumbled as he rubbed the back of his neck.

"What? You've got to be kidding me!" My arms flew in the air in disbelief.

"I'm just scared I won't be ready and I'll let everyone down as a ruler. Or worst of all, become my father."

I didn't know how to respond to that. I didn't know anything about his father or ruling a kingdom. We both just stood there gazing up at the sky and took in the stillness of the night as the rain continued to fall silently around us.

Xander eventually broke the silence. "Like I said, this is about overcoming your fears, not mine. Just look around at how beautiful it is. I'm up here with you and I promise I won't let you fall, okay?"

"Okay," I breathed.

I slowly turned around to try to take in the so-called beautiful rooftop he kept going on about, and it wasn't hard. A pergola stood before us, and I made my way beneath it. It did little to escape from the rain that continued to fall but I didn't mind. The stars shone bright in the sky through the holes in the top of the pergola. Warm yellow lights intertwined with vines that wrapped around the columns.

I carefully followed a path that led to the rest of the rooftop. The slight rain must have scared anyone else off of the roof as we were the only ones up there. I actually loved the rain, to me it seemed to make the moon and stars shine even brighter.

"You're right, it's beautiful," I whispered, unsure whether or not he actually heard. "As long as we don't get too close to the edge." His footsteps echoed nearer and he was soon standing next to me again.

"I told you, this is my favourite spot in Estrella."

"Estrella?" I wondered.

"Yeah, you know, your capital here in Soluna." He shot me a questioning glance and I smiled at him.

"Right, of course."

His gaze didn't falter for a few moments before he smiled softly back at me then back to the sky above us as he continued, "Everyone thinks I go out partying every night. But the truth is, I love sneaking off just so I can come up here and be alone. It's just so peaceful, there's something so calming about it."

He's really opening up to me.

"I know exactly what you mean, not with the heights part, but I love just being alone and taking in the beauty of the night. Sometimes all I need is a good book underneath the moonlight."

Xander turned and faced me. I finally felt comfortable enough to meet his gaze once more. But this time I couldn't pull away and neither did he. We just stood there together under the moonlight and the stars staring at each other as the light rain trickled down our faces. I felt my face heating up again but this time it wasn't because of my fear of heights as he smiled at me.

God, how could I forget how hot he is? I couldn't help but smile back with what I could only imagine was the most ridiculous grin.

"Amara! Xander! There you are!" Hazel called as she ran over to us, leaving the woman she was dancing with earlier behind as she waited by the stairs.

"Yup, here we are," Xander answered.

Hazel waved over the woman and she reluctantly made her way over to us with her hands over her head as if she was trying to protect her hair from getting wet, unfortunately it did not help much.

"Amara, this is Charlie." She turned and pointed to the woman before turning back and gesturing to me. "Charlie, meet

Amara. AKA my new bestie. Oh yeah, and this is my stupid brother." She teased and Xander just rolled his eyes in annoyance.

"Princess." Charlie did a quick curtsey.

"Oh, please just call me Av-mara!" *Oh shit!* I faked a cough hoping they wouldn't notice that I just about blew my cover. "Amara, you can just call me Amara." I smiled.

They all stared at me with questioning looks, then at each other. *That was way too close. Maybe I've had a little too much to drink tonight. I need to be more careful.*

"Come on, let's get out of the rain and get back to dancing!" Hazel said in her usual cheery tone before starting to dance where she stood.

"Honestly, I think I'm just going to head home. I'm exhausted." I wasn't lying. I really was exhausted, keeping up this act is hard and not to mention tiring.

I could see the disappointment in Hazel's eyes. "I can walk you back if you want?"

I put on a brave face. "No, it's fine. You stay here and have a good time. I'll be okay." I left before I gave any of them a chance to object.

I was standing on a street corner under a lamp post trying to make out the names on the street signs, as if I actually knew where I was. The rain was coming down a lot harder than it was earlier on the rooftop.

Now, which way was it back to the palace again? Great. This is just perfect. I stood there lost and wallowing in my own self pity. Just as I was feeling sorry for myself, a familiar egotistical voice made me jump.

"Someone must be lost."

I turned around to see Xander with the biggest smirk on his face. "That obvious huh?"

"Come on, I'll walk you back."

"You really don't have to do that."

"And be held responsible if something were to happen to the precious princess? Hard pass."

His laugh was almost as beautiful as his eyes. He had the kind of laugh that made you join in. He was really making me feel better tonight. *Maybe we just got off on the wrong foot?*

"Lead the way," I said as I did a stupid bow pointing towards the way I believed to be the direction back to the castle. I instantly regretted doing so. *That was so lame, what am I thinking?*

"Uh, it's actually this way," he said and started walking ahead of me while I trailed behind and face palmed. *Stupid.*

He slowed down and waited for me to catch up. We walked side by side in silence. The village we walked through was dead, not a soul to be seen. If not for the rain it would have been eerie but the sound of the rain made it feel more peaceful and serene.

"I surprisingly had a great time today. So, thank you." I decided to break the silence with a bit of honesty.

"If I'm being completely honest, so did I." His signature smirk was back.

"Shall we call a truce? I feel like we don't have to completely hate each other. Right?" I was trying to play it off as a joke but the second it took for him to answer felt like forever to me.

"Well—" He paused. "Not completely." He winked and let out a genuine and amazing laugh while I let out a breath I had unintentionally been holding in before a small girlish giggle escaped my lips.

"Today wasn't too hard. I think we can keep it up."

"You may have a point there," he said in an even lighter tone than before.

Is he flirting with me?

I tried my best to not let it show how much he was getting to me. "I mean, at first I thought you were just some conceited, arrogant jerk. But now I think you're a fun, conceited, arrogant jerk."

"Oh, wow, you really have a way with words, Amara." His tone dripped with sarcasm.

"Hey, I said fun! Plus, you're actually pretty easy to talk to." I bumped my shoulder into his playfully as we continued walking.

"Well, if we're trying this whole honesty thing. I always thought that you were just some arrogant, completely insane, careless princess that I'd have to marry."

Well, he's got the insane part down pat.

"And now?" I breathed.

"And now—" He paused and shot me a mischievous look. "I think you're just some princess I have to one day marry."

My eyes narrowed. *Was that supposed to be a compliment?*

"Not to mention stunning."

Well, if he wasn't complimenting me before he definitely is now. Contain yourself, Avery, you're not supposed to know what he's thinking. Normal *people don't know what other people are thinking. But when have I ever been normal?*

"Just some princess, huh? Thanks." I dramatically rolled my eyes.

He smirked again. "You know what I meant."

Before I knew it, we were back at the hole in the wall that led back into the castle. We stepped through it one at a time and made our way back inside the castle in silence. We stood in front of the bedroom door. I turned to face him before heading inside, unsure if I should say anything.

I froze and all I could come up with was, "Thanks," before quickly fleeing inside and shutting the door behind me.

Amara

The library was practically the size of the entire rest of the safehouse. The walls were covered from ceiling to floor in books. A skylight in the center of the roof let in the perfect amount of light from the sun that I wanted to bathe in.

Wesley and I had been looking through dusty books four gods knew how long now trying to find anything helpful.

The loudest, most obnoxious sounding yawn came from behind me where Wesley was standing about ten feet away, arms stretched out, not even covering his mouth. As he opened his eyes from the stretch-yawn, we locked eyes and his mouth instantly changed into a grin as he chuckled.

"Sorry."

"That's what you get for staying up on 'guard' all night. Why don't you go get some rest and I'll keep searching?" He closed the distance between us, now standing directly in front of me.

His voice quickly changed into a lower, deeper tone as he leaned in even closer than before. "Have you been spying on me?"

"What do you mean? Have I been spying on you?"

"Well, you said you knew I was up all night." He pulled back again to where he stood a moment ago and raised an accusing brow at me.

"I mean I just assumed; you *did* say you wouldn't sleep. Oh wow, this book looks interesting!" I turned my face back towards the wall of books and grabbed the first book I saw as I tried to bury my face in it.

"I was only joking, Amara, don't worry. Plus, you're right, I haven't gotten any sleep. I think I'll go and try to lay down. Just call for me if you find anything."

I waved a hand at him with my face still buried in the random book I pulled off the shelf but watched him out of the corner of my eye as he made his way towards the door. He glanced back at me briefly before exiting and my eyes quickly shot back into the direction of the book. I did not even dare take my eyes off the inside of the book until his footsteps sounded from down the stairs. Feeling relieved, I placed the book down and continued my search.

There's got to be thousands of books in here. This is ridiculous. I made my way to the table and chairs that were set up in the middle of the room. Slumping into one of the chairs, I crossed my arms on the table and smashed my head down into my arms. *I didn't expect this to be easy, but I just wish I had some kind of a clue or an idea of what to do. If I can't even do this maybe everyone is right, maybe I'm not meant to be queen.*

Drumming my hands in irritation along the table, I hoped something would just fall into my lap. I threw my head back against the chair and let out a loud groan. Realizing this would not help me, I reluctantly pulled away from the table. My hands on the edge of the table ready to push the chair back to get up. I felt something small and smooth brushed against my one fingertip. *What the? Is this a button?*

I pressed it and waited for something to happen, but nothing. *Forget it! How many secret rooms and passages could one royal kingdom really have?* I started to walk towards the door to take a real break just as the room began to shake. The floor started moving, sliding into each other as a large opening formed.

I slowly made my way towards the opening in the floor and looked down. There was a dark, extremely narrow set of stone stairs. *Apparently, it can have many.* I was just about to take the first step down the stairs when Wesley came running in.

"Amara! Are you all right? What was that? An earthquake?" His eyes darted around the room as if searching for answers.

"An earthquake? Really? It was not that bad. Not even a single book fell off the shelves, calm down." I waved a hand dismissively.

"Well then, what the bloody hell was it?" he asked just before peering down the staircase. "What is that?"

"I do not know, but I am dying to find out. Come on!"

"As always, after you, milady." He grinned.

Just as I went to take my first step down, I lost my footing, falling forward with a yelp as I tried and failed to get a hold on anything except air.

"Amara!" Wesley shouted, his voice the last thing I made out before everything went black.

CHAPTER EIGHT

Avery

I woke up to the sunlight beaming down on my face. I sat up squinting at Amara's purple velvet drapes as I waited for my eyes to adjust. *I need to remember to shut those tonight before bed.* I yawned as I stretched my arms out before falling back into the overly plush bedding. *I could get used to this bed. I had such an amazing sleep last night and best of all, no nightmares.*

I took a deep breath, breathing in the calming scent of lavender. I smiled slightly to myself and rolled onto my side, curling up with the comforter. Happily sighing to myself. *Yup. This is the life.*

As if planned, there was a knock at the door. "Come in," I said as more of an instinct than actually being ready for someone to walk into my room as I laid in bed. I shot back up as the door slowly opened, frantically trying to straighten out my bedhead. Stella walked into the room and curtsied.

"Your Highness, The Lord Regent would like a word with you in the throne room." She paused, giving me a quick once over then continued, "When you are ready, of course. Do you need assistance getting ready?"

"Ugh, that won't be necessary, Stella. Thank you."

She curtsied again before leaving. I flopped back onto the bed as I groaned internally. *Is sleeping in too much to ask for?* I waited a few more minutes, just enjoying the comfort and warmth of the bed before finally crawling out of bed and heading towards the ensuite to get ready.

As I entered the throne room, I noticed Lawrence was talking to some man whose back was to me. I couldn't tell who it was, even if I did know them. I made my way from the door to the center of the room where Lawrence and this mystery man were standing. When I was about a foot away from them the mystery man turned and bowed.

"Your Highness."

He had the brightest, most sincere smile on his face. His deep navy eyes sparkled as a lock of his strawberry blonde hair fell in front of them, he brushed it back with one hand while a slight blush formed on his beige cheeks. He was wearing one of the royal guards' jackets, navy blue, like his eyes, with the golden crest of Soluna embroidered on the left side of his chest.

"Your Highness, I have been looking for you." Lawrence bowed lowly as he spoke.

"Sorry, Lawrence, I was exhausted this morning."

He raised a knowing brow. "Yes, well that tends to happen when you sneak out to party all night long."

"Oh, you knew about that, huh?" I could feel my face get warmer and I couldn't help but avoid his gaze, as I answered.

"Indeed," Lawrence replied with the same monotone expression he usually had. "That is why I would like to introduce you to Benjamin." He gestured to the man beside him and Benjamin bowed again.

"It's nice to meet you, Benjamin," I smiled at him before returning my attention to Lawrence. "Lawrence, about yesterday, I—"

He cut me off before I could think of a poor excuse as to why I snuck off, I was half relieved as I had yet to come up with one.

"Princess Amara, if you are going to be leaving the castle grounds you will need a proper escort."

"I'm sorry. Wait, what? I'm not in trouble? And hold on, an escort?"

"Yes, that is where Benjamin comes in. He is one of the palace guards and has been assigned to be your new attendant, as your regular one, Wesley, has come down with something."

"Palace guard...but he seems so young?" It wasn't supposed to come out like a question, but it did. "Actually, Lawrence. I was hoping you had some time to talk. I feel as though this could be the perfect opportunity to ask you some questions I have been meaning to ask." I gave him a tight smile as my eyes flicked to Benjamin beside us, then back to Lawrence.

Lawrence opened his mouth to answer when another one of the palace staff caught his attention.

"Excuse me." Lawrence walked off leaving me alone with my new 'escort'.

Seriously? My fists balled in frustration as I watched him exit the room.

"So…" I nervously smiled up at Benjamin. He looked just as uneasy as I felt, fidgeting with the lapel of his uniformed jacket.

"Any big plans for today?"

At least he didn't ask me about the weather.

"Uh…not really. I was thinking about just relaxing today, maybe read a book, go for a walk in the garden." *Not like I can really do much around here.* "What about yourself?"

The tense expression on his face washed away and his smile was back, "Oh you know, just following you around."

I couldn't help but gasp. *What did he just say?*

He breathed out a laugh. "You know, it's my job."

"Oh, right!" I couldn't help but laugh and he joined in as well. He just had something about him that made me feel safe and comfortable, and not just because he was my new escort, which I assumed meant bodyguard. Honestly, I was surprised I hadn't had one sooner, but that was something I wasn't going to complain about.

"Well, I'm kind of hungry. Want to accompany me to get some food and we can get to know each other a little more?"

His eyes widened as he cocked his head slightly. "You mean, you actually want to get to know me?"

"Of course! I mean we are clearly going to be spending a lot of time together now."

"Sounds good to me." He smiled then bowed for a third time. "After you, Princess."

I found it a bit ridiculous that I was sitting in the grand dining hall at the large table by myself. Someone had brought me an assortment of cheese with other finger foods and six different drink options. Benjamin stood awkwardly behind me as I ate, not making a sound. At times I found myself glancing over at him to make sure he was still there. And he was, *of course* he was. I wondered what he must have been thinking about, so I tried out my weird, newfound powers. But alas, they never seemed to work when I wanted them to.

Was there any sort of training I needed to do for this? Am I supposed to be searching for some old master to teach me the ways of telepathy? Maybe I just need practice. Dammit Avery, focus on one strange thing at a time. I should invite him to sit, or have I waited too long now? Stop being a baby and be nice. Maybe he's hungry?

"You can sit down, you know," I finally said as I gestured to the seat next to me. I watched him as he nervously rubbed his neck with one hand and pulled out the chair with his other.

"Thank you, Your Highness." His shoulders slumped slightly. *"Why is this so awkward?"*

"Oh good, it's not just me!" I relaxed in my seat as well.

"Pardon?" He cocked his head.

"Not again." I palmed my forehead with my hand.

"Did I do something wrong?" He gulped.

"No, not at all," I tried to reassure him. "I'm just weird sometimes, it's hard to explain. And please, you don't have to call me 'Your Highness' or whatever."

"Well, I must admit, you're quite different from what I had expected."

"Oh? What exactly were you expecting?"

"Please do not take this the wrong way, Your—ugh—I mean, Princess." He cleared his throat before continuing. "You seem so much humbler than I thought. I always pictured you to be like most nobles, overly confident and conceited." I snorted a laugh at the comment as I pictured the nobles I had met thus far, and he wasn't wrong. "You just seem to be the opposite of what I had expected Princess." He finished and smiled brightly at me.

"Oh, well thank you. And you can just call me Av—" I coughed dramatically as I realized what I was about to say. *Crap! Not again.*

Benjamin stood up so fast he nearly knocked over his chair as he reached towards me. "Are you all right, Princess?"

"Uh, yes. I just had a tickle in my throat," I assured him, but my voice wavered. I stood up straight out of my chair as I tried to channel this more confident princess, he thought I was. "As I was saying, you can just call me Amara."

"All right, so what's next on the agenda today, Amara?" He smiled as he spoke but he still seemed unsure about calling me that.

I thought about what I wanted to do today, and the truth was I still hadn't had a chance to explore the castle as much as I'd liked to. "The weather is lovely out today. What do you say we take a walk to the garden, and you can tell me more about yourself?"

His head tilted to the side slightly, "If that is what you would like to do. After you." His arms gestured the way like Vanna White.

"Thank you."

As I made my way towards the door, I saw two all too familiar faces enter. I immediately noticed Xander was unhappy as I could already see his death stare from the fifteen feet between us. He crossed his arms as I approached.

"Oh, hi. Xander." I smiled, deciding I should greet him friendlier as I considered our truce. "This is Ben. Ben, this is Prince Xander." I turned to face each of them as I acquainted them with one another.

"Prince Xander." Ben bowed, though the smile that was there before had now vanished.

"Oh, I'm so sorry!" I turned back to Benjamin completely forgetting all formalities. "Is it okay if I call you Ben? I guess I should have asked if it was all right first."

"Princess, you can call me anything you like." Ben laughed. "And Ben is perfectly fine, Amara."

"And you can keep calling me Prince Xander." He scoffed and I glanced over my shoulder raising a questioning eyebrow at him.

Seriously?

He met my gaze and smirked. "And I'm also her fiancé."

"Yeah, whatever." I rolled my eyes. "Anyway, we are going out to the garden. I will be out there in a second if you want to wait for me in the hall, Ben."

"Of course, Your Highness." Ben bowed, yet again before exiting.

I waited before he was out of earshot. "Sounds like the arrogant Xander we all know and don't love is back."

"Could you try to *not* flirt with all the castle guards?" Xander angrily accused. "I mean we have to keep up this whole getting married act after all and you're making me look bad. Think of how it makes me look if my woman is out there flirting with everyone."

Even Erik gasped with me as Xander barked.

Not wanting to continue to be chastised by my future *fiancé*, I turned around and stepped out the door to meet Ben who was waiting for me in the hallway.

He whistled as he tapped his foot, admiring the artwork that was hung in front of him. Multiple photos of both the sun and moon lined the walls of this corridor.

"Ben," I called out, unsure if he had heard me enter the hallway. "Are you ready?"

"Of course."

Ben walked a few steps behind me the entire way, I assumed this was protocol, but I just found it weird.

I stepped outside to my new favourite spot; the cool autumn air kissed my cheeks and blew my hair all around me. I pushed my hair away from my eyes so I could fully take in the beauty around me. *I don't know how much longer I'll be here, but I'd love to see the leaves change colour if I'm still around.* Admiring the scenery, I noticed Chaz and Vivian standing over by the white rose covered gazebo again.

Great, why is he always here? Ben's familiar voice called from behind me. "Is everything okay?"

I put on my best fake smile before turning to face him. "Yup! Do you mind waiting here a moment?"

He nodded and I walked over to greet Chaz and Vivian, looking back to make sure that Ben was still where I left him a few feet away.

"Chaz, Vivian," I lifted a hand in greeting.

"What the hell?" I didn't doubt for a second that Ben could see Chaz's scowl from where he stood. I was glad my power decided to start working again now. I felt like Chaz was the perfect person to practice on.

"What are you doing here?" I asked, trying to sound like a general question about his location rather than a complaint about seeing his face.

"I could ask you the same thing," he mocked.

So much for trying to keep things civil.

"She never comes down here."

Maybe Amara doesn't, but I love it here.

"I know I never come down here but I figured I could use a change in scenery."

"Well, I liked it better when you didn't."

Wow, what arrogant ass.

Vivian's whiney voice chimed in, "Chazie! I'm going to be late for meeting Christina for our spa day!"

"You go get ready. I'll send the driver around the front to take you."

She blew him an obnoxious kiss and flipped her hair back before walking off. Chaz eyed me up and down while letting out an unpleasant grunt before following behind Vivian.

Well, that went better than expected. Ben was already by my side. "I'm sorry you had to witness that."

"I get it, His Grace is a royal pain in the, well, let's just say a royal pain." I couldn't help but laugh at his bluntness. "Lead the way." He smiled as he bowed down slightly, waiting for me to choose a direction to take. I decided to go right down the path. It led to an old stone wall covered in more vines and flowers and at the end of it was a wall of hedges creating a giant royal maze. I took a step inside and looked back to make sure he was still following me. He was a few steps behind me the whole way.

"You don't have to follow me, you know, Ben."

"Actually, I do. It's quite literally my job, Princess."

"I know, but what I meant was you can walk with me. It's less creepy."

"If that's what you'd prefer."

I waited as he closed those few steps between us, and we started walking beside each other in silence through the maze.

Okay, so still pretty creepy.

"So, Ben, tell me a little more about yourself."

"What do you mean? There's not much to tell." His brows wrinkled as he cocked his head again.

"Well, what do you do for fun?" I asked.

"I like to train." He shrugged slightly.

"Oh, like working out?" I guessed.

"Kind of, I mean I have to practice my sword skills and hand combat."

"You think that's fun?" *Sounds like hell to me.*

"I mean, I sort of enjoy it. I like to run and clear my head. What about you?"

"I love to read." *And watch movies and tv remakes of those books, among other things. But I'm still not sure if they have T.V. here.*

"Oh really? I love to read and write!" His smile beamed brighter than his already cheerful smile.

"Really? You write? What kinda stuff do you write?"

"Mostly poetry and short stories." His smile wavered as he whispered.

"That's awesome! I'd love to read something of yours sometime, if you'd like."

"It's fine. I'm not very good anyway and I'm sure you're very busy." He shoved his hands into his pants pockets as he hung his head.

I spun around; arms high in the air around me. "I've never been so unsure of what to do with myself." I wasn't lying.

"I don't have much time to write anymore really. Especially now that I'm actually training in the royal guard." His shoulders slumped in defeat.

"Did you always want to be in the royal guard?" I was genuinely curious.

"No, not really. My father and brothers were all in the royal guard so you could say it was the family business. I was born into it. I always loved reading and writing even at a very young age. I always dreamed of becoming a famous poet. But becoming a member of the royal guard is my duty and I have to uphold this great honour. Not everyone is chosen to become a member of the royal guard, as you know. I cannot let my family or kingdom down."

"But what about your dream?" I stopped dead in my tracks and he halted next to me. "You can't just give up on that. I believe you should always follow your heart and do what you love." He just plucked at the cuff of his shirt, nothing saying a word, so I continued, "You always have to find time to do what you love so if it's writing then find or make time for it."

"I-I don't know." His gaze was still at his feet as we continued to walk along the maze's path. "I always thought when the time came my dream would change and that I would love my position in the royal guard and give up on my silly dream of writing. However, now that I'm so much closer to it I don't know if it's what I really want. I enjoy it, and I'd give my life to protect you, but I never get time to do what I've always loved."

"I'll make you a deal. Every other day we'll come down here to the garden for a few hours and sit down so I can read and you can write."

"Really? You'd do that for me?"

"Sure! Why not? I would love to just sit out here and relax with a good book."

"You are too kind, princess, truly." I loved the way he smiled. It reminded me of a golden retriever after he brings you back the ball while waiting for you to throw it again.

We reached the end of the path which led us back to the castle doors. I decided to make my way back in and up to the royal chambers and of course I was escorted by my new bodyguard. He bowed one last time as I slowly closed the door. I breathed a sigh of relief.

I am exhausted and it's only noon.

"Maybe I'll take a nice long bubble bath!" I suggested to myself and jumped as I heard my door open again from behind me. *Maybe Ben forgot something.*

As I turned around to ask him if he needed anything, another voice spoke.

"Maybe I should join you." Not Zac's smug face was eyeing me up and down as he winked at me.

"What are you doing here?" I didn't even try to hide how annoyed I was. His face changed as his grin was gone and he was nervously looking everywhere in the room except towards me.

"I'm worried about you. I feel like you've been avoiding me."

No kidding. I could practically feel my eyes rolling to the back of my head. *Is he that oblivious?*

"I know things were only supposed to be physical between us but it has become more than that for me, I genuinely care about you Amara." He paused briefly, catching my eyes in his

106

gaze as he took a few steps closer. "I'm sorry for just assuming things would be the same, I know it's been a while, and well, I'm just sorry. If I made you feel uncomfortable in any way, I just needed you to know that wasn't my intention."

"Erik, whatever we had is over. This was wrong and I don't even know that my—I—I don't even know what I was thinking." *I can't believe I did that again.* He frowned; eyes crinkled as his eyes locked on me. "Whatever this was needs to be over now. Besides, what about Xander?"

A feeling of guilt washed over me. I knew I hadn't done anything and Xander could be a major jerk, but I still felt bad for the guy. This was his friend.

"Xander already knows." He shoved his hands in his front pants pockets.

"He does?" I asked, even though I already knew the answer.

Erik rubbed his neck with his one hand. "Well..." He dragged out. "Not exactly. But he obviously knows about your agreement. You made that pretty clear earlier, and he's with who he wants to be with anyway."

"Right." I bit out as a sudden lump formed my throat.

"Oh, did you not know about him and Victoria?"

"How could I forget?" I replied dryly.

"They've been together for a while now. Well, I will let you get back to your bath." He just turned and walked out the door as if it were nothing.

Could this day get any worse? I made my way back over to my bed instead and just collapsed.

I'd been laying in bed for who knew how long, unable to sleep as my mind filled with worries and doubts. *I am so sick of this place. I just wish I could go home. I don't even know where the hell I am. No one will tell me anything! Am I even still on earth? Am I in another world or dimension? Have I fallen and severely injured my head?* I screamed into my pillow to muffle the sound. *Pull yourself together, this is bigger than just you. But, do I really want to do this for some kingdom I don't even know? I want answers, sure I don't have much going on back home but they just expect me to drop my life like it's nothing?*

CHAPTER NINE

Amara

Everything is so dark; I can't see a thing. Wait, that's the Shadow Lord from my dreams!

They were standing in a dark lit room, the walls made up of stone. Their back towards me as they peered out the only window. Darkness engulfed them, making it even more difficult to see. I couldn't move or look away; it was as though I was seeing everything through someone else's eyes.

A long, thin creature hovered into the room as thick shadowy curls coiled around its body. Its beady blood red eyes glowed and were the only other distinctive features I could make out in the dark. It had no mouth and yet it somehow spoke.

"They're getting closer to us as well as the prophecy."

"Continue to keep a close eye on them and stop them at any means." Shadow Lord did not move or even glance at that creature as they left.

"Amara! Wake up!"

I screamed as I awoke abruptly, still surrounded by darkness. A set of strong arms tightened around me and squinted as I waited for my eyes to adjust. Wesley's face looked down at me. His arms tightened once more as he held me on the ground in his lap. His face now buried in my neck as he murmured incoherently.

"Where are we?" I asked as I slowly pulled back.

"Are you all right?" his familiar voice sang.

My head was spinning, as well as everything else around me. "W-what happened?"

"You tripped as you were walking down those stairs we found in the library, remember?"

"What?" I questioned as I rubbed at the throbbing pain in my head.

"You must have hit your head harder than I thought. We should go back up so I can check you out in the light."

"Wesley." He stared deeply into my eyes as if he were searching for something there. "I'm fine, honestly. I just had another creepy dream. I think it just frightened me a little at first. I'm okay now." I placed a hand on his reassuringly.

"What happened? You woke up screaming." Wesley blinked several times in disbelief.

"The cloaked figure was back, and he was talking to some creepy shadow-like creature. He mentioned something about the prophecy." I blew out.

"The prophecy? Wait, did you say again? As in you've had a dream like this before. Maybe someone is trying to tell you something." He stood up and held out a hand to help pull me up.

"As I said, it was just a dream."

"If it was *just* a dream, why didn't you tell me sooner?" His squinted face peered down at me.

"Because I said it was just a stupid dream, okay? Maybe you should go find some matches or something so we can see down this path."

"Maybe we should get your head checked out first?"

"Maybe you should do what I say, instead of questioning me." He jerked back as though I struck him.

"Right," he quickly replied before turning without even a second glance in my direction.

I knew I should have told him about the dreams sooner, but I just could not. I knew he would have worried too much and he already had enough to worry about. But, part of me wondered if he was right, what if someone was trying to tell me something?

I only had to wait a few minutes before I heard Wesley's footsteps descending back down the steps. A faint light illuminated and his face came into view as he held a torch already lit in each hand. He practically shoved one in my hand as he walked right past me without even a word or second glance. *I must have really upset him.*

I followed a few paces behind Wesley as we continued down the stone tunnel path in silence. Even with the torches it was hard to see more than a few steps ahead of us. Everything around me was dark, it was hard to see anything besides cobwebs, and more darkness.

After a while I finally broke the silence with a loud, obnoxious sigh. He did not even flinch and just kept looking straight ahead. *The least he could do is check back every once and a while to make sure I'm still here and no crazy creatures grabbed me.* I rolled my eyes.

We walked for what felt like forever in this silence, when a faint light shined at the end of the tunnel.

"Come on," he called, still refusing to glance back at me.

We slowly approached the opening. Wesley stopped as he reached it, and instantly tensed. "What is this place?"

I walked to his side. "I have no idea."

Avery

"Amara! Wake up!"

Jerking upright and screaming in fear, I opened my eyes, desperately trying to take in my surroundings. I was in Amara's room. Hazel stood a few feet away from me, her brows crinkled softly as she watched me with worried eyes. It had been just over a week since I'd even seen Hazel, or Xander for that matter. I'd pretty much just been going from my room to the gardens to meet with Ben aside from meals.

I tried several times to get a hold of Lawrence to talk and get some answers, but it was never 'the perfect time'. I wanted to push further and insist on those answers, but every time I tried or told myself I could do it, panic rushed in. Along with my lack of confidence I was never one to push for what I wanted. I avoided people and anything to do with conflict. That was another reason why I liked having temp jobs. I didn't have to stay with the same people too long and it wasn't serious enough to have a superior yell at me. My mom always told me I was a push over and needed to stand up for myself more, but that terrified me more than heights.

"Are you all right? What's wrong?" She inched closer but still kept some distance.

"Hazel, thank goodness it's just you!" I took a moment to control my breathing again. "I'm sorry I must have been having another nightmare."

"I'm so sorry. I shouldn't have just barged in here waking you like that."

"I'm fine but thank you." My heart rate finally began to slow.

"Well, if you ever want to talk about these nightmares you're having, I'm here for you. Anyway, I haven't seen you in a while, so I just came by to see if you wanted to get ready together." She wore the biggest smile as she held up a bottle of champagne with two glasses.

"Ready for what?" I asked.

"You're hosting a formal dinner tonight for everyone staying at the castle. Which is why we'll need these." She giggled before placing the glasses on a table, then started pouring the champagne.

"Of course, I am." I groaned internally while trying to stop my eyes from rolling.

"I'll take that as a yes." She cheered as she raised her glass. "And by the sounds of it you need this more than I thought."

I joined her and picked up the other class. "So, what should we toast to?"

"New friends, and new adventures!" We clinked our glasses together and she gulped hers down. Just as I was about to take the first sip out of mine there was a knock on the door.

"What now?" I complained. *Well, at least someone around here knows how to knock.*

"Come in," I blurted and my stomach turned as I thought about the possibilities of who it could be.

Luckily for me, Stella walked in and did her usual courtesy as she greeted me, "Your Highness." She stood back up and continued, "I was sent to deliver this to you." She handed me a letter in an envelope and turned to walk back out.

"Thank you, Stella," I called and she curtsied again before continuing out the door.

"Who's it from? What's it say?" Hazel squealed as she tried to peer over my shoulder to get the answers faster.

I pivoted back to face her as I proceeded to open and read the letter. "Xander. He wants to meet on the terrace tonight after dinner."

"Oooh, Sounds romantic!" she teased.

"Yeah, we'll see." There was no holding back my eye rolls this time.

"Now you have to look extra good for tonight! Show me all your best options!"

"Okay, okay!" I laughed as I headed towards the closet, wondering if Hazel knew the truth about her brother and my sisters' arrangement.

I walked in and Hazel waited outside in anticipation for me to come out. I could hear her squealing with the double doors shut.

"Hurry up!" She called.

I walked out in a royal black ball gown.

"What about this?" I was unsure of how I felt about this one, it was gorgeous but just didn't feel right. *Maybe this one is too much? Do I look like I'm going to a wedding or a funeral?*

"That dress is stunning on you!" Hazel admired the dress, but I still felt like it wasn't the right one for me.

"I don't know, let me try something else on." I turned and headed back into the giant closet continuing my search through the racks on racks of dresses. Hoping and waiting for something to jump out at me. *What, did she rob a bridal shop?*

"Do you want me to go grab some of my dresses I brought with me for you to try on?" Hazel shouted from the other room.

And that's when I saw it. I picked the hanger up off the rack and held it up in the air as I admired the intricate lace patterned design. I put the dress on, and it was even better than I could have imagined. Amara must have had it tailored to her exact measurements because it fit me like a glove. The bodice hugged my curves perfectly and as I glanced in the mirror I noticed tiny gems stitched into the laced pattern that sparkled like stars against the blue material. The horsehair skirt was a few shades lighter and fell flawlessly to the ground. I slowly walked back into the room where Hazel not-so-patiently waited, and her face was already beaming.

"You have to wear that tonight! All eyes will be on you!"

Is that even what I want?

Hazel must have sensed I was still uneasy about wearing this.

"Trust me, you look gorgeous!"

"Okay, this is the one!"

"You look amazing, you won't regret it! Do you want me to help with your hair and makeup?"

I studied her. "But we need to find what you're going to wear first."

"I forgot my dress! How about I go get changed and just meet you down there?"

"Works for me," I replied right before she ran off.

115

I walked over to Amara's vanity to curl my hair. I was rummaging through the drawer and found a beautiful jeweled crescent moon hair clip. I decided to clip half my hair up with it as it matched my necklace and dress perfectly. I styled my hair with long loose curls that fell out and around the hair piece.

I guess I should get this over with.

Ben was waiting for me just outside my door to escort me to the Grand Dining Hall. We kept our greeting brief and started down the hall. Once we made it to the grand staircase that led to the Great Hall, which we would have to pass through. The hall was filled with people. Everyone dressed in extravagant suits and dresses. It reminded me of another ball. Not only were the guests dressed elaborately, so was the hall itself.

Tapestries hung along the walls and from the ceilings. Blue and gold floral arrangements were everywhere, from the stair railings to the walls of the hall. Guests stood around small, bar height circular tables that were stationed throughout, with even more floral centerpieces on top. If this was just the Grand Hall, I wondered how excessive the dining hall would be.

As I continued to descend the stairs, three guests in particular stopped what they were doing and looked my way. I gulped as I recognized Xander, Erik, and Victoria whispering as I made my way closer to them. Of course, they had to be in my path to the dining hall, why wouldn't they be? I approached with a tight-lipped smile, unsure of how this interaction would go after our last over a week ago.

"H-hi, have any of you seen Hazel? She was supposed to meet me down here." My eyes shifted from them to the rest of the room in hopes she would just appear before us.

"I haven't seen her, sorry." Xander replied as a corner of his mouth lifted.

"It's all right." My gaze landed on his for a moment before I moved to head into the dining room.

"Hey, we kind of match." Xander's voice caught my attention and I turned to face him once more.

I scanned him up and down. He wore a blue dress shirt, almost the exact shade of mine, Solarian royal blue. He wore no jacket and had his sleeves rolled up to his elbows, with black dress pants. I tilted my head slightly in surprise. Sure, this was more dressed up than he usually was, but compared to everyone else in the room, he was dressed down.

Glancing over at Erik and Victoria, both wearing matching scowls on their faces, I noticed he was in tux, and Victoria in a stunning black velvet dress. The dress hugged her breasts and hips tightly before flowing seamlessly to the floor. It did not have any designs or sparkles, it didn't need to. On her, it was like it was made specially for her, and I didn't doubt that it was.

My eyes made their way back to Xander and I couldn't help but laugh a little. "Yeah, we kinda do. I guess I'll see you later." My heart skipped a beat as I thought back to his letter. I gave an awkward gaze, and an even more awkward smile as I turned to leave.

I walked up to the grand dining table where Hazel was already seated on the far end of the table. Just as I had imagined the décor inside was just as beautiful. The tablecloth alone was probably worth more than my bedding set back home. It was, of course, royal blue with a glistening gold pattern embroidered. There were large golden candle holders running along the length of the table and between each candle holder was an arrangement of blue roses. Similar tapestries were hung inside from the hall. They had even replaced the chandelier that normally hung above the center of the table with one that was five times the size of the old one.

"There you are!" I cheered when I finally made it to her.

"Here I am!" she teased as she turned to face me while flipping her hair back over her shoulder.

"You look amazing!" I stopped to admire her gorgeous floor-length burgundy gown. It was hard to get a good view of her dress while she remained seated but there was a lovely lace pattern along the bodice.

"I know." She grinned.

Wow, I love the confidence in this girl.

She continued, "Now, let's get this dinner part over with so we can skip to the dancing!"

"Oh great, there's a dance after this too," I complained as I pulled my chair out and slumped into it.

"Of course! Then we can find out what Xander wanted to talk to you about." She winked at me and my stomach tied into knots.

Great.

"Everyone please be seated; dinner is about to begin," an unfamiliar voice announced.

I sat down as the rest of the guests filled the room and the overly decorated table. Xander was one of the first ones to walk through the door. I turned back to Hazel to distract me.

"So, how was your day?"

"Pardon?" Her face squinted with confusion.

"I'm just trying to make conversation." I smiled awkwardly, hoping she'd take the hint.

"We've been together a good amount of the day and you're asking me this now?" she questioned me for a moment before a light went off in her head. "You're trying to make it look like you're already in a conversation, so he doesn't interrupt. Don't worry, I've got you."

I nodded while watching Xander in my peripheral vision. Hazel's lips moved but I couldn't hear anything. Everything around me fell silent, and I was suddenly all too aware at how fast and loud my heart was beating, wondering if anyone else could hear it as loudly as I could as he approached.

"Is this seat taken?" he asked.

Hazel and Xander both just stared at me expectantly, Hazel looking even more interested in my answer than he was.

"No, it's all yours." I gestured to the chair with a hand, and he sat. I quickly turned my attention back to Hazel.

Her smile was even bigger than before as she started teasing me with kissing faces. I elbowed her in the arm and gave her my best 'cut it out' stare. But as he sat down, I could feel the sides of my mouth lifting into what I could only imagine was the goofiest grin. *I probably look like the biggest idiot. Stop smiling!*

All I could think about throughout the entire dinner was what Xander wanted to talk to me about. I could barely even remember to eat the food in front of me. I kept trying to listen in on his inner thoughts to get some insight, but of course, nothing. Every once and a while I would glance his way just to see if he was doing the same.

After dinner was over, I went to ask him if he wanted to go talk. Before I got the chance, he excused himself and left without another word. *Maybe he has to make a pit stop? He did say to meet him there after all.*

Everyone else quickly fled from the table and moved into the ballroom for the dance portion. *Hard pass.* I figured I would get this talk over with, so I went straight to the terrace from the ballroom to wait for him. I waited, and waited, and waited. Over a half hour must have gone by as I waited out on the cold terrace for him, but he never showed.

"Is this some kind of sick joke?" I asked myself. "He knows how I feel about heights. Screw this and him! I've waited long enough for that jerk!" Storming over to the door, I reached up to turn the knob, but it wouldn't move. I began pushing the door but it felt like something was in the way blocking it.

What the heck is going on? "Hello? Is anyone there?" I desperately called. Panic sunk in as I continued to call for help, "Oh my God! I think I'm trapped out here!" I started to bang on the door again even harder as I sobbed, "Help! Hello? Anyone! Help me please!"

I was losing hope, unsure how much more time had even passed. The rain was coming down hard. The terrace was covered however, that did little when the rain came down sideways. I was shivering from the cold and gave up on calling for help at that point. No one was answering, my teeth were chattering, and my throat was horse. My back was to the door and slowly slid down, now seated against it, sopping. I wrapped my arms around myself to attempt to warm myself.

"Amara! Are you okay?"

Am I imagining his voice?

"There's something blocking this door, hang on!" Xander's voice shouted from the other side and was replaced by a scraping sound.

I slowly managed to pull myself up and backed away from the door seconds before it opened. I ran to Xander and practically jumped on him, wrapping my arms around him and continued to cry.

"Xander!"

"Amara! Are you all right?" he asked hesitantly before placing his hands on my back. *She's freezing.*

I was so happy to have the door finally opened; I couldn't help but hold him. I felt extremely safe and warm in his arms. Until I remembered he was the reason I was there.

"This is all your fault!" I interjected, pushing myself out of his arms.

"My fault? How is this my fault?" He jerked back, shaking his head.

"Are you kidding me? You were supposed to meet me up here forever ago!" I balled my fists as I tried to hold in the rest of the tears that were building up.

"I have no idea what you're talking about." His usual, arrogant tone was back.

"The letter!" I practically screamed.

"What letter?" He screwed his face up in confusion.

What? He didn't send me that letter? This didn't make any sense. It said it was from him, who else would have sent me a letter signed 'Xander'.

I watched him for a moment, but he genuinely seemed just as confused as I now felt. "If you never sent me that letter, then who did?"

"I have no idea what you're talking about," he grumbled as he jammed his hands into his front pockets.

So, he didn't want to talk to me. My stomach dropped. I must have looked and sounded so stupid. *How could I have thought he might actually want to apologize to me or even talk to me apparently.*

"I have to go," I mumbled underneath my breath still holding in some of the tears from moments ago. I started towards the door when he gently placed his hand on my arm stopping me. I slowly tilted my head back to him.

"Y-yes?" I stuttered.

"Amara, I don't know what you are talking about in regard to some letter but, I do want to talk to you."

Looking up into his eyes, hope must have beamed through them.

"I crossed a line earlier and I—" He paused as he blew out a harsh breath. "I'm sorry. I was rude and I made a mistake. So, I wanted to apologize."

The sadness in his face and tone quickly changed and his smirk was back. "Also, I wanted to tell you how beautiful you looked tonight." He held my gaze. *"Absolutely stunning."*

This was probably the most genuine smile I had seen from him. I couldn't help but to grin as he spoke those words to me.

Victoria came bursting through the door and practically knocked me over in the process of getting to Xander before tripping and conveniently falling right into his arms. *I don't buy this act for a second.*

"Vic, are you all right?" he asked as he steadied her.

"I am now." She smiled softly at him.

Barf.

"Huh?" Xander's face brows drew together and eyes squinted.

"Uh, I mean, ahh!" She groaned and grabbed her ankle, wincing in fake pain. "I don't think I can walk on my own. I need your help, Xand."

Xander hesitated for a moment. "Are you going to be okay, Amara? I can take you inside if you need anything."

"No, I'm fine. Thank you. It seems as though Lady Victoria needs you." I narrowed my eyes at her, easily seeing through this charade.

"Here, I'll take you back to your room." He put his arm around her waist to give her support and as they walked past me, she winked at me. *I can't believe he's falling for this performance.*

"Thanks, Xand, where would I be without you?" Her voice was as fake and phony as ever.

"I'll talk to you tomorrow, Amara," Xander added before exiting the terrace with icky Vicky.

"Seriously?" I asked myself before deciding to call it a night and made my way back to my room. Alone.

Amara

We reached the opening of the tunnel and were instantly blinded by a bright light. After a few seconds, my vision returned to me, and I gasped when I realized that there were torches lining the perimeter of the walls that were now somehow lit. Wesley still appeared to be dazed from the change of lighting.

We were still underground but as I glanced around the large open room, I noticed the stone circle that filled the majority. In the center of the stone circle was a large stone pedestal. Etched into all the stones were markings of the different phases of the moon and the sun. As I continued to look around in awe, the same markings were along the walls and floor.

The first thing to hit me was a sense of familiarity. I felt as though I had walked these floors a million times. I turned to see if Wesley was experiencing anything weird as well, but I was greeted by his shocked face, jaw hanging open. Before I could question what had caused such a reaction, I noticed that the engravings on the floor were glowing, moreover, that *I* was glowing.

"What the—"

I carefully made my way towards the pedestal, I felt drawn to it, like it was calling to me. As I approached, I noticed in the center were two, even more intricate markings of the sun and the moon. Only the markings of the sun had lit up around the room. The warm golden glow pulled me closer and closer to the pedestal.

"Wait! Amara, don't!"

A bright golden light shot out of the plinth and a vision overtook my senses.

Everything went black I couldn't see or feel anything. All I could hear was an unfamiliar voice.

500-some-odd years ago, lived a pair of twins like no other. One with hair as bright and golden as the sun itself, the other, a silver shimmering glow like the moon. They had powers like no one had seen before, they did not know where they came from or what they were. When they were young, they moved from village to village. As soon as the villagers found out about their powers, they would force them out, even though they meant them no harm and tried to live peaceful lives.

The voice paused and I could suddenly see everything that this mysterious voice was saying vividly as if I were pulled back to experience everything as it happened. I saw two young girls that couldn't have been more than eighteen years old. Aside from their hair colours, they were practically identical, both with long wavy hair and striking green eyes. They not only looked identical to each other, but to me and Avery as well. The voice continued.

During the day, when the sun shone, Cyra had the ability to see into the future. At night, when the moon's pale light brightened the dark sky, Calypso was able to control those around her with her mind. We now know that they were this world's first Celestials.

Though neither one of them had ever used their powers unless provoked or to help someone in need, most of the people of their village grew scared and hatred for the twins arose.

The village people began to try to hunt them down when they were most vulnerable and beat them. One day they decided to go after Calypso while she was alone during the day as her powers were useless while the sun was up.

Cyra saw a vision of her sister being cornered and killed by an angry mob of villagers and rushed to find her before it was too late. She found her just as the villagers had her surrounded. They all screamed and shouted as they closed in on her and Cyra lost sight of Calypso. She could hear the cries of Calypso as she begged for them to stop, but Cyra knew all too well what was going to happen next.

She pushed her way through the crowd as she tried to reason with them, but they just pushed her down to the ground as Calypso was, in their minds, their only real threat. Cyra sobbed as she picked herself up and pushed her way towards her sister screaming just in time as she placed herself in front of an arrow.

The villagers backed off after they heard the sound of her deadly scream as blood began to pool around her. They watched as Calypso wept over her sister's lifeless body screaming for someone to help but the crowd abandoned her and their plan.

A beam of light shot down upon Calypso and she was lifted into the sky by the bright golden glow and she was forever changed. When Cyra died her ability to see into the future was passed onto Calypso. Calypso was gifted with even more power than she could have ever imagined; she was able to use her powers whenever she wished and was also given the gifts of immortality and creation.

Some villagers gathered around as they began to worship Calypso. To reward them, she used her new power of creation to gift them with the celestial gifts she and her sister once shared.

Knowing that the celestials and the rest of the mortals would be in a never-ending war, she decided to create a safe haven within the magical world of Caelestia, the same world the original goddesses had once created. She named it Soluna.

After a few years of living in Soluna, Calypso's powers became too strong for even her to control and eventually a part of her soul split into two. This other half named herself Esmeray and carried all of her grief and hatred for their past.

Esmeray looked like a mirrored image of Calypso, except for her hair was a dark, deep brown. She took Calypso's ability to control others, leaving Calypso with only her ability to see into the future and power of creation.

Esmeray stole Calypso's grimoire, used it to raise shadow demons and used their new power to control them. Neither one of them could defeat the other and eventually Esmeray captured Calypso and locked her away. Calypso saw this coming with her powers she still had and so before she was captured, Calypso was able to steal the grimoire back and hide it. She then used her powers to look 500 years into the future to see her sister's soul would be reincarnated into another set of celestial twins.

Their magical powers alone would not be strong enough to defeat Esmeray so, Calypso relinquished her powers and sent them 500 years into the future so that the new set of twins would one day be able to unlock these extra abilities in order to defeat this great evil. Before Calypso was taken, she created the prophecy foretelling the future twins' destiny.

CHAPTER TEN

Amara

I opened my eyes and was standing in front of the stone plinth, I glanced back at Wesley, his mouth hung open and eyes wide, looking as shocked as I had felt.

Did he see that too?

"What the hell was that?" I could not help but question whatever that was.

Before he could even attempt to answer me, a strange shadowy smoke appeared behind him, quickly materializing into one of those demons from my nightmares. It's glowing red eye fixed on me, then instantly back on Wes before it lunged at him.

"Wes! Watch out!" I screamed in horror.

It knocked him to the ground with one hit. I ran towards Wesley, but now the creature stood directly in front of me. My instincts kicked in and I instantly took out my sword, unsure if I could even touch this thing.

Twelve years ago.

I was standing in my room wearing a pair of old ripped up, stain covered pants, a black tank top, and muddy boots. My hair was pulled to the side in a messy braid. I glanced at the time on my nightstand.

"I better hurry up before they come for me!"

I ran to the largest painting hung in my room which concealed the hidden door to the secret passageway, but when I was mere inches away, the main door opened.

"It's too late for that young lady!"

I could already feel my eyes rolling to the back of my head as she spoke. Prudence, my 'Royal Etiquette Instructor', felt more like my babysitter. I turned slowly to face her.

"You are not even dressed, this is not how a proper princess should look!" she snapped.

"Maybe I don't want to be a proper princess," I mocked. "And what is wrong with the way I'm dressed?"

"You look like you belong in the stables, not a princess who is supposed to one day rule!"

"Well, maybe I'd rather be in the stables."

"No! This is not what a proper princess should do. You have to prepare to be queen one day."

"And if I don't want to be queen?"

"Well, unfortunately for all of us, you are all that this kingdom has, you do not have a choice. Now, what have I told you about using contractions? Get dressed immediately and meet me in the classroom or I will have to inform the king and queen of your insolence."

"Yes ma'am." I saluted mockingly as I waited for her to leave the room. "As if." I snorted.

I continued towards the hidden door and followed the secret path that led almost directly into the stables. Once there, I noticed I wasn't alone. There was a young boy who seemed to be about my age. His clothes were even dirtier than mine and don't even get me started on his messy hair.

"Sorry, I didn't realize anyone else would be out here."

He jumped in surprise, then spun around to face me.

"Neither did I. I'll leave you alone." He smiled and started towards the exit.

"No wait!"

He stopped mid step.

"You don't have to go. What are you doing here anyway? I thought I was the only one who snuck out here."

"I didn't exactly sneak out here. I sort of work here." He blushed, his eyes shooting to the ground as he kicked his feet in the dirt.

"What do you mean, sort of?"

"Well, I was training to be a knight for the royal guard one day but—" A pained expression etched on his face.

"But what?" I asked.

He was hesitant but continued, "My father was captain of the royal guard. He was the best they'd ever seen so they knighted him and gave him the new title of Grand Master. He was my hero. I wanted to be just like him and I trained with him everyday he was home until the day he never came home."

He took a deep breath and his eyes shifted, "A few days went by from when he was expected to be home, we didn't think too much about it at first these things tended to happen, and then there was a knock at the door. I still trained so I could be a knight my father could be proud of until my mother found out. She only wants me to work in the stables. Now I have to practice alone in secret and have no one to teach me how to actually ride one of these things." He gestured to one of the horses.

"That-that's awful! I'm so sorry you had to go through that, uh, I'm sorry what was your name?"

"Wesley, but my friends call me Wes. Umm, at least they would if I had any."

"Hey, I'll be your friend! I'll even teach you to ride!" I beamed with excitement.

"I don't have any money if that's what you were hoping for, sorry." He turned to leave again but I grabbed his arm to stop him.

"I don't want your money." I smiled

"Then what *do* you want?" His arms crossed over his chest as he tapped his foot impatiently.

"For you to practice your training with me. And a friend," I mumbled the last part in embarrassment.

"Why would you want to train with me?" His head tilted to the side.

"I have my reasons." I waved a dismissive hand.

"Which are?" He raised a brow as he questioned my motives.

"Can't a girl keep any of her secrets?" I replied, shrugging a shoulder.

"I thought you wanted to be friends. Friends tell each other all of their secrets." Disappointment took over his face and I quickly gave in.

"Fine." I paused. "I want to learn how to fight."

"Well, I guess I can't say no to that." He smiled, extending a hand for me to shake.

I slowly reached up and took his hand awkwardly, shocked that was all it took; he did not question me further. His smile grew bigger and brighter once our hands met and it was infectious.

"I have to go, but let's meet here everyday at noon for training."

I started to make my way back to the castle and his voice called out to me.

"Wait! I never got your name." His hand brushed my shoulder to stop me. My eyes shifted from his hand then to his face.

"Amara." A mischievous grin formed on my face as his jaw dropped in recognition.

"P-p-princess Amara?" He stuttered before getting down on his knees, bowing low. I ran before he was even back on his feet.

Present day.

"Who are you?"

I screamed at this thing, still wielding my sword. It just stood there in a battle stance.

"Who sent you? What the hell do you want? Answer me!"

In the blink of an eye, it was gone. My eyes darted around the area as a smoke like shadowy fog crept in. It was hard to see anything anymore.

Where could it have gone? I looked back to see it standing in front of Wesley trying to finish the job it already started. I didn't know what else to do. It was too far away from me at this point.

131

"No!" I cried dropping my sword, but instead of it falling to the ground beneath me it flew towards this thing and Wesley, making direct contact with this creature. As soon as it hit this shadowy figure it disappeared along with the eerie fog. I spun around frantically trying to figure out if it had really disappeared. *It just vanished, just as quickly as it appeared.* I ran over to Wesley.

"We need to get out of here before that thing returns!" I pleaded with him, half pushing him as I tried to get the hell out of this place.

"How did you do that?" His eyes widened as he stared at me.

"I will explain everything but right now we need to get out of here!" I grabbed his hand and ran faster than I ever had.

Avery

Even though I had another one of those crazy vivid dreams, I woke up feeling well rested and not to the sound of my own screams.

I need to talk to Lawrence or someone about this. I guess I'll just have to add this to the list of many things I want but probably won't be able to talk to him about. This can't just be a dream, something weird is going on here. But who would even believe me? I sound crazy! Hey Lawrence, I have these weird visions when I go to sleep. Oh, and I can read minds now too! Yeah right, I'd be sent to an asylum.

I finally stopped my inner babbling long enough to breathe when there was a knock on the door.

"Come in!" I called.

Ben walked in and bowed. "Good morning, Princess."

"Good morning, Ben." I hoped that the twitching I felt in my right eye was not visible and I didn't look as insane as I felt.

"The Lord Regent has sent me to get you. Once you are ready, I shall escort you. He needs to speak with you in his study."

This must be it! The 'perfect time' to talk about everything and finally get answers. I've already been here for a couple weeks. School has already started, I hope I can get a refund. Might as well just take the semester off if I'm not leaving soon. Not like I know what the hell I want to do with my life anyways. Focus, I need answers, and today I will get them.

"I'm fine like this, lead the way."

We walked down the corridors that led to Lawrence's study in silence. I continued to think about how deranged I must be and questioned if any of this was actually real or if I was already locked up in some loony bin.

I always wanted my life to be more dramatic like in the movies and series I watched. Careful what you wish for, I guess.

Before I knew it, I was in front of the door to his study and nearly knocked over Xander who just happened to be standing outside of the door. It had been about a week since I last saw him.

"Oh shoot! I'm so sorry! I wasn't paying attention." I reached out one hand to help steady him, not that he really needed it.

Here comes some more of those theatrics I was just thinking about.

"Good morning, Amara." The one side of his lips tipped up into a subtle smirk. "And that's fine, don't worry about it, I'm sure you must have a lot on your mind." He looked down as he rubbed the back of his neck. "I will leave you to it, Your Highness." Ben walked back the way we came.

"So, listen I just wanted to—" Xander started but was quickly cut off.

"Princess, I really need to speak with you," Lawrence's voice chimed in from behind the door.

"I guess I'll see you later then." His full smirk was back as he walked past me.

"Yeah, see you later."

I reached for the door just as it opened from the inside. Lawrence stood there holding it open as he gestured me in and closed it again behind me. It was my first time in his study. He slowly made his way to his seat behind his desk. Everything was very neat and tidy. Neutral colours of beige and brown everywhere. His large wooden desk stood in front of the wall furthest from the door with a leather chair behind it and two smaller chairs on the side closest to me.

Okay, you can do this just ask him for the answers you rightfully deserve. I turned to Lawrence and my breaths quickened, my chest rising and falling too rapidly. *Stop being a baby and ask him!*

"You wanted to speak with me." I blew out. *That's not what I wanted to say.*

"Yes, Miss Avery. I have some good news and some bad news."

Famous last words.

"Okay?" I watched him carefully, waiting for him to continue.

"So, the good news is that Prince Xander is going to be going back to his kingdom for a few days. The bad news is that you will be going with him."

"What? Why?" I exploded. "Don't I even get a say or choice in this?"

"Tonight is Coldoria's Winter Moon Festival."

"What does that mean?"

"Every year on the first full moon of Coldoria's winter season there is a festival to celebrate it. The first Winter Moon stays up for a full twenty-four hours. Once the sun begins to set the festival begins and lasts the full twenty-four hours that the Winter Moon is up."

"Well, I guess that doesn't sound too bad. It sounds kind of pretty, actually. When do I have to leave?"

Lawrence placed his one hand on his forehead as he shook his head. "I'm sorry, Miss Avery. You only have an hour to get ready."

"What? Seriously?"

"Yes, and I suggest you dress warmly." He didn't look up from the papers on his desk as he spoke.

"I guess I better go get ready then."

Thanks for the heads up. Why couldn't I just ask him? All I ever get out of him are half answers or not now. I knew the real reason why, I've always been this way. I've always been too scared to ask for what I wanted, what I deserved. I clenched and unclenched my fists in frustration at not being able to just do or say what I wanted to.

My hair was down; loose curls fell to my lower back. A few pieces were braided from the front to meet together in the back and clipped with the stunning crescent moon shaped hair pin I had found earlier. I searched through the enormous closet, half expecting to fall into Narnia, when I found a door that led into a smaller closet. *Seriously?*

A bag sat to the side of the closet and I placed it in the center, loading it with clothes that would be deemed warm, as well as shoes, pajamas, and books, lots of books.

Checking the clock, I realized I was already late. I grabbed one of Amara's thick, plush cloaks and made my way out the door. One of the guards insisted on carrying my bags and followed behind as I rushed down the corridors to meet whoever I was supposed to be meeting.

When I got there, I saw both Ben and Xander patiently waiting at opposite sides of the room with the double doored exit between them. I hesitated, unsure of who was taking me to Coldoria.

"H-hey, guys," I stammered as they both looked up and smiled at me. Ben was the first one to walk up to me.

"Hello, Princess. Are you ready? Our carriage awaits."

A carriage again, seriously? What ever happened to that Impala?

I waited but Xander didn't come up to us, I followed behind Ben as he walked up to the exit and held the door open for me. I glanced back at Xander one last time and shyly waved as I walked through the doorway, but he just turned away.

As soon as I walked outside, I saw two white horses in front of a large burgundy and black carriage. I slowly stepped inside, it was covered in velvet and silk drapery and sort of reminded me of the inside of a genie's lamp. I sat down and the door opened, my eyes instantly shooting back to it just as Xander stepped in.

I guess he is traveling with us back to Coldoria.

He sat down beside me but avoided eye contact.

What did I do now?

Ben stepped in seconds later, sat down across from us and smiled. Xander huffed and pulled a book out of his bag and began to read it as the carriage started to move.

I must have fallen asleep quickly into the ride as I didn't remember any of it. The gentle movement of the carriage and the wheels moving below was the only sound I heard for a while as I kept my eyes closed. I sat curled up and leaning against the one side of the carriage.

Too afraid to let Xander or Ben know I was awake and let the inevitable madness begin. I listened as I pretended to still be sleeping but they both sat in silence, that or they just left me here alone while I slept.

Carefully opening one of my eyes, I peeked over at them. Xander was still seated next to me sat reading while Ben sat on the other side of the carriage staring out the window. I decided to actually get up and fully opened both eyes while slowly stretching and sitting up straighter. Neither one of them acknowledged my movement so I turned and gazed out the back window behind me.

Everything was covered in a thick blanket of snow. I guess this is why Lawrence said to pack warm clothes. It was like I fell asleep and woke up in the North Pole.

The sides of the roads were lined with enormous pine trees dressed in snow. Though the trees and road were covered, the snow itself was coming down in a light sprinkle. It had a magical feel to it. Winter was always one of my favourite seasons, though I imagined it was because I had more of an excuse to curl up with a blanket and read, that and the holiday Hallmark movies of course.

A smile tugged at the corners of my mouth as I took it all in and hoped I'd get time to go out and enjoy the snow. I love it if I don't have to drive in it. Suddenly, we came to an abrupt stop. I looked to Ben and Xander for an explanation.

"We are just about to enter the castle grounds. I just have to inform the Coldorian guards at the gate of our arrival," Ben announced before bowing and exiting the carriage.

"Coldoria is beautiful." I smiled in an attempt to make conversation with Xander.

"You ain't seen nothin' yet." He winked and I couldn't help but laugh like an idiot as my face heated.

The carriage jerked and I fell into Xander beside me, his arm reaching up to catch me.

"I guess Benny-boy isn't coming back in," he mocked.

"Benny-Boy? Really?" I didn't even try to hide the annoyance in my tone as I pulled away from him.

"Yeah, cause he's not a man, just a boy."

"Well, you're a man-child."

The carriage came to another stop and Ben stepped back in before either of us could say another word.

"All right, we're here. Did you need any assistance escorting yourself out, Princess?" Ben asked kindly.

"She's my princess, I'll escort her out." Xander stood up so he was level with Ben and wedging himself further in between Ben and myself.

"I'm nobody's anything! I can escort myself out, thank you very much."

I pushed them both out of my way as I tried to get to the door and tripped on the step landing face first into the snow below. Xander stepped out, not even trying to contain his laughter.

"Should've accepted my help," he continued to laugh as he literally stepped over me and made his way towards the castle doors.

"Oh, my goodness! Princess! Are you all right?" Ben yelled as he jumped out of the carriage and held his hand out offering me help getting up. I stood up on my own and brushed the snow off my face and body.

"I'm fine, Ben, honestly. And I told you, you can just call me by my name." I smiled trying to hide my frustration and how cold I was from that fall.

"Okay, well, Amara, are you all right?"

"I'm fine, thank you for asking." *At least someone did.* "Wow, this place is incredible."

I finally got to take in the true beauty that was around me. The light snow falling danced and glistened around the twinkle lights that were hung around the trees and buildings. Ice sculptures were carved and placed all around the courtyard, kids were running around making snow angels and having snowball fights. I hoped I'd be able to join in later.

The castle itself seemed as though it was made of ice. It sparkled, glistening brighter than any other structure around.

I wonder what this castle is really made of. It looks unbelievable.

"They are in the process of setting up for the festival tonight. I hope Prince Alexander is ready." Ben awoke me from my winter wonderland trance.

"What do you mean?"

139

"He's been in Soluna for a little while and I wonder if he has had any time to prepare for his big speech."

"What big speech?" I asked.

"As the crowned prince, he will have to give the big welcome speech and light the first lantern."

"What lantern?" I felt like a broken record.

"Each year the king gives his welcome speech. But this year Prince Alexander will be giving it. After the welcome speech it is Coldorian tradition for everyone to light a floating lantern, make a wish, and release it into the night sky under the full Winter Moon."

"Wow! That sounds beautiful!"

"It is. Are you sure you are all right and didn't hit your head? Maybe we should get you checked out."

"She must have hit her head worse than I thought."

"I'm fine. I think I'll just go lay down for a bit though."

"That sounds like a good idea. Let's go inside the castle and find Prince Xander or someone who can show us where we will be staying. After you, Amara."

I walked into the castle to see a crowd of people in the corridor. Xander was hugging a woman with a man whom I assumed to be his father, due to the ridiculously large crown on his head, standing behind them. Off to the side, slightly behind them by the stairs stood Hazel, Erik, and Victoria.

The castle itself was such a contrast from the outside. The inside was not made of the same ice-like material as the outside was. It was just like any other mansion you would find back in my world, not that I'd ever been in one. Painted walls with artwork hung and marble floors so white I wondered how often they had to be cleaned.

"Oh, honey, it is so good to see you!" the lady hugging Xander practically cried, bringing my attention back to them. "I have missed you so much!"

"Stop babying him," the man in the crown muttered.

"I have missed you, Mother," Xander said to the woman, ignoring the man's comment.

"Prince Alexander, good to see you again." The crowned man put out one hand for Xander to shake. However, Xander ignored the hand and instead rolled his eyes. "The feeling is mutual, Father."

"Prince Alexander, why don't you show our guests where they will be staying," his mother interjected.

"Why should I? I'm not the butler." He tsked.

"Xander, this is not how we treat our guests," she whispered softly to him but I was standing close enough by this point to hear.

Wow, he's even rude to his own father.

"Welcome, Princess Amara and guest," the queen greeted us, Ben bowed and I followed his lead, unsure of what else I should be doing. She continued, "Please follow Prince Xander to your quarters. Xander you may also want to show the princess around the castle before dinner as well."

I watched as he rolled his eyes yet again before stalking off while muttering under his breath. I smiled at the king and queen before following him.

He took us up the grand staircase and led us down a long dark corridor. I followed a few steps behind Xander, with Ben a few steps behind me. We all walked in complete silence, the sounds of our footsteps practically echoed. A few castle workers passed and stopped to bow their heads at us along the way, Xander didn't even acknowledge a single one of them. Xander began grumbling under his breath again, but I couldn't quite make out what he was saying. We finally reached the end of what must have been the longest hallway on whatever planet we were on. Two doors stood side by side.

"Here we are." He paused for a moment. "Amara, you're in the room on the right and Brent you're on the left." His jaw locked.

Ben just smiled. "I'm right beside you if you need anything Amara." He made his way into his room leaving me alone with Xander.

Xander took a step closer to me and smiled, as if mimicking Ben's genuine one, "Dinner's in three hours, you can show yourself around." He continued past me, I watched as he walked away without even a second glance.

I decided to go into my new-new room to compare, and let's be honest, what else was I going to do? Actually show myself around, hard pass.

Opening the door, I discovered my bags on the floor in the center of the room. *When did they have time to do this?* The room was a decent size, bigger than my one back home, but smaller than my one in Soluna. It had two large dressers, a king sized bed, electric fireplace, and my own ensuite. I took some time to unpack my bags and placed my clothes into the dressers.

There were several paintings decorating the room. Some of landscapes, others abstract. As I admired an elegant watercolour painting by the window, I noticed that Xander had joined the kids in the courtyard, he was actually laughing and running around playing with them. He looked up at my window and our eyes met, I immediately ducked. *What am I doing?* I closed the curtains and breathed a sigh of relief.

Maybe I should get some rest before dinner after all, and by rest I mean lay down, and read a book.

I was surprised by how warm the room was. The heat must cost them a fortune. The room was warmer than back in Soluna. I opened one of the dresser drawers I had just put my clothes into and pulled out one of my loose fitted white tops and decided I wasn't going to wear any pants because what is more comfortable than lounging around in your underwear with fuzzy socks and a good romance book? Nothing.

Turning on the switch to the main light, I waited for my eyes to adjust to the darkness before making my way over to the bed. The lamp on the nightstand lit a warm yellowish glow as I tapped it and curled up in bed with the thick warm covers. I opened my novel and internally laughed at the irony of reading a book about a girl starting her new life in a new city where she finds a new love.

Standing in the hallway of my room in Xander's castle, the dim lighting kept anything too far out of sight and mind. My hair had been pulled back and styled perfectly to go with the lilac gown that wrapped around my frame like it was made for only me. I looked up at the man before me, his attire just as nice and polished as my own.

Our eyes finally met, I couldn't help but stare at them, trying to decide if his eyes were more blue or green as they sparkled intensely down at me. My gaze made its way down to his lips and the one side lifted into his sexy smirk.

"Princess, you look beautiful tonight. I don't know how much longer I can hold back." Xander's words sang in my head as he placed one finger under my chin, lifting it slightly towards him.

"Then don't." My gaze flicked to his lips then back to his gorgeous eyes. "Kiss me," I breathed.

His hand slowly slid down my neck, then my back, stopping at my waist. He pulled me in even closer. His lips gently brushed against my ear as he whispered, "Amara?"

"Amara? Amara!" I nearly fell out of bed but caught myself as his loud screaming woke me.

"What the hell?" I yelled in horror.

Still in my room in Coldoria, the romance novel I had been reading sat on top of me opened, I sighed as everything played through my thoughts. *There's a reason why you shouldn't fall asleep reading these things.* Xander stood in the center of the room, his mouth snapped shut.

Great, don't tell me I was talking in my sleep or something.

"I came to show you around before dinner after all, but, uh—" He stopped mid-sentence.

"But what?" I questioned him as I slapped my book shut.

"Damn."

Remembering what I was wearing, my face began to heat up as I shrieked, pulling the covers up over my face. "Oh my God! Turn around!"

Without hesitation he spun around and mumbled, "Sorry, I didn't mean to uh, sorry. I—I'll just go."

"Oh, great. I can't stop picturing her like that now."

Just freaking perfect!

He continued to just stand there.

"Get out!" I screamed one more time. "I'll get dressed and meet you outside my door."

This can't seriously be happening right now.

He left without another word.

I can't believe that dream. Although, I must admit, it was a lot better than those creepy dreams I've been having lately.

Making my way over to the dresser once more, I scanned my options. The same lilac dress I wore in the dream was there. *I must have seen this earlier while I was looking for something comfy to wear.* I slipped into it and was glad this one didn't have zippers like some of the others I'd been wearing lately. I surveyed the results in the mirror and quickly straightened out my curls and tied half of my hair back, a few pieces at the front fell forward framing my face. *God, how can I face him after that?*

Xander was waiting for me in the hallway.

"Don't you know how to knock?" I grumbled as I bit at my nail, trying to avoid meeting his eyes out of embarrassment.

"I did! And if you must know, I was worried. You didn't answer when I was calling you and I thought something might have happened. Excuse me for trying to be a gentleman." His lips pursed.

"Oh please! You? A gentleman?" I laughed. "If anything were to happen to me, I'd be willing to bet that you'd be the source of it." I pointed an accusative finger in his direction.

"Whatever, let's just go to dinner."

He turned to leave but I placed a hand on his arm to stop him. "Xander, wait."

"What?" He shrugged out of my touch as he peered down at me.

"I thought we were going to go on a tour of the castle?" I raised a brow, trying to hide the smirk I felt pulling at the corner of my mouth.

He genuinely looked surprised as his eyes widened. "You've got to be kidding me."

"Okay, I'm sorry. Even though you were extremely rude, and don't know how to knock."

"Well, aren't you just the queen of great apologies."

"Don't roll your eyes at me," I said as I narrowed mine.

"I told you, I not only knocked but I called out and you weren't answering me." He was practically pouting at this point.

"Right, 'cause you were worried about me." My eyebrows elevated as I snorted.

"What? No!"

"You said you were. You care about me, don't you?" I teased, pushing his arm gently.

"No, I just couldn't let anything happen to you under my roof."

"Oh, okay. So, why'd you change your mind?"

"Change my mind about what?" His nose wrinkled with uncertainty.

"Showing me around."

"Shut up, let's just go before I change my mind again." A smirk replaced the frown he wore as he passed me and I couldn't help but feel triumphant.

I followed him through the castle, through the kitchen and out towards the back of the castle. We stepped outside, which I was not really prepared for as I was still only wearing a dress and heels, but I didn't want to bring that up since we were somewhat getting along, and by getting along I mean neither one of us had said a word to the other the entire time.

He led us to the edge of the large castle garden where the trees stood like a fence outlining the castle grounds. He turned to me and raised an eyebrow as he smirked. I gave him a

146

confused questioning stare, one brow arched and he lifted a branch from one of the trees as if he were opening the gate to this secret path that the trees were concealing. The snow continued to fall lightly as we walked along the narrow, snow-covered path.

"We don't have much time before dinner, so I'm just going to take you to the best place."

I didn't reply, unsure of what to say. *What could he possibly be showing me?* I hesitated before taking my next step but continued to follow.

It wasn't too much longer before he lifted another tree branch opening to a clearing in the forest. There were more twinkle lights strung around the trees, just like at the castle courtyard, but this time it seemed different, more private and intimate. Stone slabs formed a path that led to the center of the clearing where a stone bench surrounded by thriving white moon flowers stood. It was like magic.

How are they even surviving in this snow?

I slowly spun around trying to take everything in. Just beyond the bench was a pond completely covered in a layer of ice that sparkled like diamonds underneath the lights hanging above.

"This was my favourite spot."

I looked back over my shoulder at Xander before turning back to the pond before me.

"Wow, you really took me to your favourite spot?" I whispered.

"Yeah, I guess I did."

The sadness in his tone was evident. I turned to face him again to ask why he sounded so sad but when I opened my mouth nothing came out. I couldn't believe the sorrow in his eyes as he

147

slowly moved around the area, dragging his feet through the snow. *If this is his favourite spot, why does he look like he's about to burst into tears any second?*

I tried to focus on my own thoughts so that I wouldn't accidentally listen in on his, it just wouldn't be fair. This place was beautiful, it's hard to believe how anyone could've been sad here.

"We should go to dinner. You're probably freezing, I'm sorry."

So focused on Xander and my own thoughts, I didn't even notice how much I was shivering from the cold. He slipped his suit jacket off and handed it to me. I slowly took the jacket, my fingers gently brushing his as I grabbed it. I watched him carefully as he continued to avoid meeting my eyes. He started back towards the castle, I followed behind him once again in silence.

CHAPTER ELEVEN

Avery

By the time we arrived at the grand dining hall, everyone was already seated and waiting for us. Surprisingly, no one made any comments or even acknowledged us as we walked in. We walked up to our seats at the end of the table beside one another as everyone's conversations continued.

Once we sat down, I noticed Xander giving his father an intense death glare, his jaw clenched as the king spoke. I glanced around at the others sitting around the table. Ben sat across from me, momentarily smiling before resuming his conversation with Victoria and Erik. Is he seriously this nice to everyone?

Hazel sat in between what I assumed were two eligible bachelors. However, they seemed to be more interested in talking to each other than Hazel as she sat wedged between them, arms crossed. I continued to scan the table. The king and queen sat on the other side of Xander. There was a young woman on the other side of the king wearing a tight red, low-cut dress with bright brown eyes and braided chestnut hair. Does Xander have another sister?

After a few more moments of chatter, King Alexander stood, and the table fell silent.

"Now that all of our guests have arrived, I have an announcement I would like to make. Let us all raise a glass in celebration of not only the winter moon festival, but of the Engagement of my daughter, Princess Hazel and Lord Sterling of Alden." He raised his glass, and everyone hesitated briefly before joining.

"Hazel's getting married?" I whispered to Xander as his father took his seat.

"We'll see about that."

Xander leaned over towards the queen who sat between him and his father. My guess was as a buffer. The queen just sat there expressionless, staring at her food that was just placed before her. She didn't even touch it, like she hadn't even noticed it was there.

"Father, I thought we had an agreement? As long as I did what you wanted, Hazel wouldn't have to marry some prince or nobleman of your choice." Xander's voice was calm, but his shoulders were stiff and jaw clenched.

"Things have changed. She needs this, I can't have her running around the way she does. Even if she is a bastard."

I had to stop myself from doing a spit take. My eyes shifted around the table to see if anyone else had heard what he said but no one else even glanced in our direction.

"Are you kidding me?" Xander's voice raised.

"Watch your tone around me boy." The king's eyes narrowed at Xander.

"You can't do this; she doesn't deserve this."

The waiters continued to bring out more food as I looked around uncomfortably to see if anyone else was witnessing the awkward stare off Xander and his father were having.

"You know what, I was going to wait but now I have a much better idea." The king smirked before standing again.

"Prince Alexander had such a brilliant idea, I must share." He paused as he waited for all the voices around the table to fall. "As he has been staying in Soluna with Princess Amara, he suggested that Princess Hazel do the same. Princess Hazel will be moving to Alden first thing tomorrow morning with Lord Sterling indefinitely."

He stopped and before he could sit back down Xander had already jumped out of his seat and was screaming at him. "This is ridiculous!"

"Sit down!" The king slammed his fists against the table, pushing himself up once more. I flinched as the table vibrated beneath me.

"No, this is bullshit! You said if I agreed to this stupid arranged marriage Hazel would have the freedom she deserves!" Xander spat as he shook with rage. "You said you would stop setting up these courtships for her! Was that all just a lie?"

"I said sit down! I'm still the king around here and you will do as I say! Hazel will marry whoever I tell her to marry and that is Lord Sterling of Alden! She will leave first thing in the morning." The king slammed another fist down on the table, this time I wasn't the only one who had recoiled from the motion. Everyone at the table had their eyes on the king and Xander as they shouted at each other. I was honestly surprised that they hadn't been before, was this that common that they weren't even phased until that moment?

"So now she doesn't even get to stay for the rest of the festival? I'm already stuck in this stupid arranged marriage that neither of us want. Why the hell should Hazel have to go through the same torture I do?"

Torture? Ouch. I need to leave, this is awkward and embarrassing. I don't want to be here and nobody wants me here anyway.

I slipped out of the dining hall seemingly unnoticed thanks to the scene that had been unfolding before us. The hall I stood in was completely empty. Muffled shouts came from the other side of the wall where I assumed they continued their argument. I didn't want to go back to my room, the only other place I knew inside the castle was where Xander had taken me.

It seemed like a great idea to head there as he mentioned it was his favourite spot, but something about that just didn't seem right. It was just a beautiful place and I just wanted to be alone where no one could find me. The first place anyone would go looking would be my room so why not just enjoy the view for a while.

Sitting on the cold, snow-covered bench for who knew how long, I just stared out at the diamond-like pond alone with my thoughts. It was freezing, I should have brought a jacket or cloak, something, but it was too late for that. I thought about how little time I'd actually been here for. What seemed like months to me had only really been weeks. My life back home wasn't perfect, but it was mine and I missed it. I should've been going back to college and figuring out what I wanted to do with my life and I knew it definitely wasn't this.

I preferred when the drama was on my T.V. screen and I could turn it on and off whenever I chose. I know I shouldn't be upset, everything he said was true after all. Wasn't it? Hell, I wasn't even the one who was really engaged to him anyway.

Trying and failing to rationalize how I was feeling, I didn't know exactly *what* I was feeling. I was sad, I was cold and confused, and most of all, I was homesick. Footsteps sounded in the snow, creeping up behind me. I refused to look back at him, I refused to let him see me like this.

"There you are." He spoke so quietly I could barely hear him. He cleared his throat before continuing in a slightly louder voice, "Did I tell you why this was my favourite spot?" He paused again waiting for an answer that I was not going to give. "Even though it was once my favourite spot, I hate it now. I used to come here with my mom and Hazel. We would have picnics and play for hours. We were always happy here until—" He stopped again, but this time for his own sake as he took a deep, heavy breath.

"One night I came here, to our spot, to surprise my mom with some decorations for her birthday the next morning. But when I got here, I wasn't alone. I walked in on my father with another woman. She looked nothing like my mother, her skin was pale and hair a deep ginger red. They were kissing. She pulled away from him as soon as she saw me but the damage was already done at that point."

Xander stopped again, for a long time I didn't think he was going to continue. The only sound was his hard breathing as we sat in silence. After a while, he spoke again, his voice much more shaky than before. "He didn't realize it was me, he thought I was Hazel, the things he said about her and how violent he got with the woman. It was like I was seeing him in a new, darker light. Things were never easy with my father, but they got worse after that."

I ran and told my mother everything. She just hugged me, not at all affected by my story. She obviously already knew. Even though she didn't give birth to Hazel, she treated her with the same love and care that a mother should. Hazel and I had no idea that my mother wasn't Hazel's birth mother. She told me that she loved Hazel like her own and always would. Since that day my father was no longer discreet with his affairs and even brought on official mistresses. I never came back here again, until now." He paused again. "It was such a happy place but that feels like an eternity ago to me now. Now it just all seems like a lie. Especially with how much crueler my father became after that. I know you've heard the rumours."

I heard the heartache in his voice. He took another step towards me, and I turned my head the opposite direction.

"Amara, are you all right?" he asked, taking yet another step closer and placed a hand on my shoulder; I could feel the warmth of his fingertips on my cold bare skin. "Amara? If it's about what I said—"

"What? That this is torture for you and neither of us want this?" I snapped, finally looking up at him as I cut him off mid-sentence.

He hesitated. "Yes. I'm sorry, I didn't—"

"Don't be. You have absolutely nothing to apologize for. It's all true, isn't it? This is torture for you, we never asked for this and neither of us want it. I know I don't."

I could hear him calling to me as I walked away but refused to turn back. I just made my way back to my room where I could cry in peace.

The entire walk back to my room was a blur. The last thing I wanted was for someone to see me like this and ask, 'What's wrong?' or 'Are you okay?' Why does that always make things worse? As soon as I got back to the room and shut the door, the tears started to pour.

What is wrong with me? Why do I even care? I am being so selfish right now; I can't imagine how Hazel must be feeling right now. I need to go find her, pull yourself together Avery! I took a deep breath and wiped my eyes and the tears from my cheeks.

As soon as I stepped back outside the door, I nearly hit someone. I mumbled an apology before looking up. I instantly recognized him as the man King Alexander introduced as Lord Sterling.

"You have to stop this wedding!" I blurted.

His one brow arched slightly. "Do you really believe I want this marriage?"

"Don't you?"

"No, but I do not have much of a choice in the matter myself. Trust me I do not want to go through with this marriage any more than Princess Hazel." He breathed a laugh as he spoke.

"Hey, you could do a lot worse than Hazel."

"Yes, well, she is not really my type," he practically whispered.

"What? A beautiful, smart, independent woman is not your type?"

"Exactly." I waited for further explanation before it finally clicked as to what he meant.

"Well, then this is perfect! If neither one of you wants this, it can't be that hard to stop it from happening."

"Unfortunately, we do not get a say in the matter. You should know what that is like." He eyed me suspiciously before continuing, "However, I do have a different kind of proposal for her." He smiled and I hesitantly nodded.

We figured we would check the most obvious place to find her first, her room. I raised my arm to knock but she opened the door before I got the chance as if she were waiting on someone. She held the door open for us with a tight smile on her face. To be honest, she looked better than I did at that moment.

"Unfortunately, this marriage is beyond my control for now as it is my parents' wills. However, they do not care about what happens before the wedding so long as it happens. Therefore, you do not have to come stay with me in Alden before the wedding," he explained to Hazel.

"My mother was able to convince my father to allow me to stay for the remainder of the festival. But I can't stay here after, he would not allow it." Her smile faded.

"Then come stay with me in Soluna!" I insisted. "Your father will never know, Xander will probably be coming back to Soluna anyway, and I doubt Sterling will tell your father otherwise." Sterling nodded, forming our new alliance.

Hazel's face lit up, her smile big and bright. "In that case, I should start packing!" She winked. "I'll see you at the festival in an hour!"

"What? I only have one hour! I better go."

After rushing back to my room to clean myself up because I looked like a mess, I decided to take a long soak in the ensuite tub. It ended up taking more than half the time I had to get ready. When I finally got out, I styled my hair and put on some warmer clothes considering the festival would be held outside all night. I made my way through the castle corridors, the sound of children laughing and music playing echoed from outside.

I guess I took longer than I thought to get ready, sounds like the festival has already started. I tried to hurry but quickly became lost in the huge empty castle. I should have taken Ben up on his offer to escort me earlier.

The sound of footsteps crept up behind me, I quickly looked over my shoulder but there was nothing there. I took a deep breath and continued forward in the direction I was going but then suddenly, everything went black.

I slowly opened my eyes as I rubbed the back of my head where I felt a jolt of pain. It took a minute for my eyes to adjust, everything was dark, and the smell of mold and mildew surrounded me. I tried to take in my surroundings as I lay on the cold, wet stone ground. My chest tightened as panic rushed in. I was in some sort of jail cell or castle dungeon. There were no windows, the only light was a dimly lit lantern on the other side of the metal bars, too far for me to reach. I started pulling and shaking the metal bars as I screamed for help.

Muffled murmurs of voices rang from somewhere around me. Frantically trying to figure out where the sounds were coming from I noticed cracks in the ceiling. Something wet splashed my face, water dripped in from the ceiling. *A leak?* Examining the ceiling from where I stood, I tried to figure out exactly where the water dripped from. It was so dark and I was too short to get close enough to see anything.

"Hello! Can anyone hear me?" I cried but the whispers quickly changed into loud cheering. "What the hell is going on? Am I underground? How did I get here?"

The cheering died down just as I heard his familiar voice speak, "I want to thank everyone for coming to celebrate Coldoria's Winter Moon Festival. This year I wanted to especially thank someone special to me."

He briefly paused before continuing, "The—uh—Winter Moon marks the beginning of our longest and darkest nights. We light these lanterns here tonight as an offering to the Winter Moon so that she may grant us what we wish for most and that she may give us light and warmth this dark and cold season. We are asking for her to lend us her energy so that we may project our hopes and wishes into the universe. So, if you could all join me in lighting a lantern, making your wish, and let the Winter Moon Festival commence."

Another tear fell down my cheek as I listened to Xander's speech. I quickly wiped it away with the palm of my hand and continued to look around the tiny room for a way out. I felt around the stone walls and more tears began to fall.

"This is hopeless!" I cried.

Falling down to my knees I sobbed, head in hands. *Why is this happening to me? I never should have come here, to Coldoria, to Soluna! None of it! Why couldn't I have just stayed back home. I liked my simple life; I was never trapped in a dungeon or on a terrace!*

"Princess Amara! Watch out!"

My head shot up as Ben ran towards me while pointing behind me. I spun around, a distorted dark figure floated in the corner, slowly making its way closer to me. It blended in with the shadows so well as if it were a part of them. It's beaty red eyes bore into me. Screaming in fear, my eyes widened. Quickly wiping away the tears that formed in my eyes to clear my vision. Ben had drawn his sword and was chopping away at the lock on the dungeon door.

The creature loomed before me, its glowing red eyes were the only thing I could make out from it. Its body was practically non-existent, more like smoke that just swirled around. The same type of smoky-shadow that swirled around its body now whirled around the rest of the dungeon.

"I've seen this before!" I shrieked as I stood frozen in fear.

It was that same thing that followed me, lurking in the shadows the night I left for Soluna, the same thing from my more than creepy dreams. Ben swung the door open and jumped in front of me, placing himself in the middle of me and that thing.

"What are you?" He yelled as he waved his sword through the shadowy smoke of its body, it just swirled around his sword.

His voice grew louder, "I said what the hell are you?" The creature's glowing eyes faded as the smoke dissipated.

"I'm not crazy?" I mumbled more to myself than Ben. "That thing was real?" I didn't have time to process before Ben grabbed me by the wrist and started running.

"We need to get out of here!" I nodded as I ran behind him still in shock. "I'm sorry Princess, but I do not think it is safe for us to stay here any longer."

I hesitated briefly. "You're right, we will leave first thing in the morning."

We finally stopped running once we made it outside. The festival was in full swing, I felt much safer surrounded by so many people. Ben continued to look around cautiously as we walked through the crowd. We made our way back to my room as I wasn't really in a celebrating mood.

"How did you find me?" I asked

"I noticed you weren't at the celebration, so I went up to your room to escort you, but you weren't there. Luckily, the inside of the castle was pretty much empty so I went searching for you. I heard you calling for help, which led me to the dungeons."

"Well, thank you."

We arrived at my door, and I immediately started balling, unable to hold it in any longer.

What if he never found me?

I crashed into Ben, hugging him tightly as I sobbed into his chest.

"Thank you," I whispered once more before running into my room.

I couldn't stop the tears from pouring out. It wasn't just tonight's terrifying encounter, it was everything. Tonight, Xander, being away from my real home. This was just too overwhelming for me and now there was some crazy creature out there after me.

I started to pack up my things in an attempt to take my mind off of everything when I heard yelling from outside my door. I ran towards it and swung the door open to find Ben and Xander arguing.

"I told you, she needs to rest." Ben's voice lightly raised.

"What is going on here?" I questioned them both.

"It is my duty to protect you Princess. Prince Xander was trying to disturb your slumber." Ben's usual tone was already back.

"I was worried when I didn't see you at the festival and Brian here wouldn't let me in!"

"The princess needs her rest, we are leaving first thing tomorrow."

"What? She can't leave! We just got here!"

"Hello! I'm standing right here!" I interrupted them as I placed myself between the two like a barrier. "What is wrong with you two?"

Ben lowered his voice and bowed before me. "Princess. Prince Xander was trying to disturb you. I told him you needed your rest before we leave tomorrow morning."

"And I told you, we just got here!"

"Thank you, Ben, for doing your job but Prince Xander can come in for a moment." I narrowed my eyes at Xander before turning back into my room as I waited for him to follow behind me.

"See yeah later, Bruce." Xander chuckled to Ben as he strolled past him through the door's threshold. His smug smirk instantly faded as the door closed and he gazed down at me.

"Where were you? I was searching the crowd for you while giving my speech, but I didn't see you. I'm sorry—"

"I heard every word of it," I whispered as I cut him off from his attempt at an apology.

"Then where were you? I didn't see you afterwards either, I couldn't find you anywhere." *"I was worried about you."*

His thoughts surprised me. *He was worried about me? Me? Can I really trust him though?* I could see the hurt and sorrow in his eyes.

"I know this is going to sound completely insane but something attacked me. It was something, well, I don't really know what it was. It had scary, narrow glowing eyes. It came out of the shadows in the dungeon."

"The dungeon? Why were you in the dungeon?"

Right, 'cause that was the most bizarre part of what I just said. I rolled my eyes and continued, "Yes, I was walking down the hallway towards the courtyard for the festival when everything went black. When I woke up, I was locked in the dungeon. I think someone attacked me and trapped me down there."

I couldn't help as my eyes started to water again. I was shocked when he wiped away one of my tears with his thumb before handing me a handkerchief out of his pocket.

"Th-thank you." I took a deep breath, but before I could finish explaining, he spoke.

"So, you're leaving tomorrow then? I'm sorry I wasn't there to protect you and as much as I don't like Bryce, at least he was able to save you."

"Right, well goodbye I guess."

"Okay, good night. I will see you in the morning." He turned to leave.

"No," He stopped and glanced over his shoulder at me. "I mean no you won't. I'm leaving extremely early, so you'll probably still be sleeping."

"I'm going back with you." He smiled.

"You can't. This festival is too important for you."

"Your safety is more important to me." He winked and walked out the door and I retreated to my bed to attempt to get some rest.

Amara

We had been running through the maze of underground tunnels for what seemed like hours. We finally slowed down as we tried to find a safe way out. I closely watched Wesley as I followed behind him. He never even glanced back at me once. I imagined all the questions he must be thinking about asking but never did. *How long have I had these powers? What other powers do I have? Why didn't I tell him?* I waited for him to ask me but he didn't.

"Wes." I broke the silence.

"Friends tell each other all their secrets."

I could hear the sadness in his voice as he continued to look forward instead of back at me. A cold chill of guilt tugged at my heart as I remembered those same words from when we first met. I took a deep breath, already regretting what I was about to say as I had to focus on the more pressing matter before us.

"We have more important things to worry about right now. For example, how are we getting out of here?"

"We could try retracing our steps and getting out the same way we came in through the safe house. I doubt that thing is still there waiting for us."

A loud buzzing noise sounded in my ears just as a sharp pain shot through my body. I could no longer see or hear Wesley. I screamed in pain, falling to the ground as my hands clutched my head. A warm muscular body caught me before I hit the ground.

"I—I see her," I stuttered.

I tried to focus my eyes. I could see Avery in a dark room with that same thing that attacked us earlier creeping towards her.

"Avery! Watch out! Behind you!" I cried, but she didn't move. It got closer to her. *Why can't she hear me?*

"Princess Amara! Watch out!"

Avery's head shot up as one of the palace guards ran in. The guard drew his sword and was trying to get to her. Everything faded, I blinked and Wesley's face was all I could see as he held me in his arms.

"Avery's in trouble."

CHAPTER TWELVE

Avery

Shrouded in darkness, my body shivered from a cold night's air. Slowly, I was able to see more and more and quickly realized I was outside in a dark, decaying forest. There was no sign of anyone, and I wondered where I was and how the hell I got there. Wet droplets gently touched my cheeks as wet snow fell all around me.

"Hello? Is anyone there? Xander? Ben? Anyone?"

The wet snow swiftly switched into a heavy downpour of SOUL. I ran, frantically trying to find shelter to hide in to stay dry. There was nothing around me but darkness and trees. I spotted a large tree with lots of branches and hid beneath it. It was too dark, an ominous fog rolled in making it even more difficult to see anything beyond two feet in front of me.

Where did this fog come from? I squinted my eyes as if that would actually help my vision. The sound of branches rustled behind me and I jumped in panic.

"Hello?" I called, hoping to hear a familiar voice respond, but was only answered with an eerie silence. "Don't cry." I told myself as I wiped a mixture of tears and rain from my face.

A cracking sound came from behind me, I spun around to see what the source of it was but as I did, I heard it again from my right. This time, I slowly turned and came face to face with that same shadowy figure from before. Only it didn't have a face, even as it stood inches before me, I could only make out its glowing red eyes, somehow clouded in smoke and shadows.

I screamed in horror and tried to escape but was somehow frozen in place. I opened my mouth again to scream but this time, nothing came out. Tears built behind my eyes as I continued to move but was unsuccessful.

The fog cleared and was replaced by hundreds of the same shadowy figure as the one that stood before me. They were slowly closing in around me as I stood frozen in place. I tried to call for help or run away once more, but it was no use. I closed my eyes as the tears continued to fall and thought, this is it, this is how I die.

I jolted forward, finally letting out a scream and opened my eyes, but I wasn't in the forest. I was in the carriage on my way back to Soluna. I studied my surroundings as I tried to slow my breaths. I was soaking wet, probably from sweat but again, that dream seemed too real and I was literally drenched.

"Amara, are you all right?" Xander asked in a panicked tone with a genuinely concerned expression on his face.

"What happened?" My eyes darted around the carriage.

"You fell asleep. I didn't want to—uh—disturb you." I wondered why he seemed so nervous. Then I realized just how close I was to him and noticed the wet spot on his shoulder. *Did I fall asleep on him?* I quickly slid over to distance myself from him.

"Thank you," I said while turning my gaze out the window, but my eyes quickly wandered back over towards Xander, who just sat there staring at me.

"What?" I asked, a lot more rudely than I probably should have.

"Nothing," he said as he rolled his eyes and scoffed.

We rode the entire way back in silence, briefly exchanging glances before looking away from one another again. At some point I must have fallen asleep again because when I awoke, we were back inside the castle walls of Soluna, but Xander was gone.

Jeez, he just left me here? What a jerk. I slowly rose from my lying position just as Ben opened the door to the carriage.

"Oh, Princess, you're awake!" he said with his usual cheery tone. "Prince Alexander left but I wanted to make sure you were all right and escort you back to your room." He smiled.

"Thanks, Ben, but that won't be necessary. I think I'm going to go for a walk around the castle." *And clear my head.* I smiled, as I took his hand as he helped me step out of the carriage. Just before Xander walked through the castle doors, he stopped for a moment and watched me exit before turning back and walking inside.

I smiled and thanked Ben before making my way towards the castle to do some more exploring. *I just realized, with everyone still at the festival in Coldoria, this could be the perfect opportunity to look around and see what I can find out about this place and my family.*

I walked around aimlessly for a few hours; it became pretty dark with no more natural light coming in through the windows. The halls were dimly lit with the candles hung along the stone walls. I walked to the end of the corridor and was met by a set of giant dark wooden double doors. They had intricate carved designs sketched throughout them. I lightly traced the designs with my fingers as I admired the beauty of them. I glanced around me to ensure I was still alone before opening the doors. They made a low creaking noise as I struggled to push the heavy doors open.

"Hello?" I called out but was only answered by my own echo.

The room was even darker than the corridors, but luckily it has a light switch. Most of the rooms have electricity in the castle, and the entire town has electricity and yet they keep the hallways lit by candle only. It's like they were trying to make it extra creepy.

I flicked the switch and watched as all the lights in the enormous room began to turn on one after the other. The walls were made up of bookcases from floor to ceiling. *This is like a dream come true. Why didn't I find this library sooner?* I slowly walked around the room in awe, I had never seen so many books in one place my entire life. *This puts Indigo and Chapters to shame.* I laughed to myself.

As I walked around admiring the library, I remembered something. *Isn't this where Amara said she found a secret passageway to that study?* I continued around the room pulling out random books off the shelves, hoping for anything that could possibly be the entryway to this super secret study she found before.

As I explored the library I found many books that piqued my interest, 'History of Soluna', 'Sunna and Selene', 'Warriors with Wings'. The list went on and I started to pull some off the shelves, half hoping it would trigger the opening to the secret study while the other half of me just wanted to get a pile of books to take back to my room to read later.

This is impossible, I complained as I dramatically melted into one of the overly plush cushioned chairs at a table. I glanced over at the pile of books I collected on the table beside me. *Well, one chapter couldn't hurt. But which book should I start with?* I read all the titles again and decided on 'Warriors with Wings'.

Before I knew it, I was 174 pages in and had to force myself to put the book down. *Hmm, I wonder if there is anything I could use as a bookmark around here.* A loose piece of paper was sticking out from underneath one of the bookcases nearest me. I bent over to pick it up and noticed that it was about half an inch above the floorboards compared to the rest of the bookcases on either side of it.

This must be it! I started to examine every book on the shelf and noticed there was a book called 'Defenders & Descendants' that was noticeably less dusty than the rest. I started to pull the book from the shelf but it was attached along the bottom. *This is it!* I heard a click as the bookcase slowly began to open. I moved out of the way to allow it to open fully.

I carefully stepped into the small study, I stumbled around in the dark for a few moments until I was finally able to find a light switch. It was just as Amara described. Small photos hung up all over the walls, a tiny desk with unorganized papers thrown all over it. The room had a faint mildewed smell that I tried to ignore.

I felt a slight smile tug at my lips and my eyes started to water as I got closer to the photographs; I realized this was the first time I'd ever seen a picture of myself as a baby. I slowly reached for one of the photos and took it down to get a closer look.

There we were. Two identical and adorable babies. Our hair was a much lighter blonde than it was now. We had such big smiles on our faces, as did our mother as she held us both in each of her arms. Turning the photograph over I checked to see if it had any writing on the back like Amara had mentioned, but there wasn't. I flipped the photo back again. I just wanted to look at it a little longer. Then I noticed something strange. I pulled the photo closer to my eyes to really look at something blurred in the background.

I gasped and I dropped the photo. "It can't be, this is crazy!" I slowly bent down and picked the photo up off the ground to examine it once more and there it was. That same shadowy figure that I kept seeing. It was a lot more transparent in this photo than the last few times I've seen it, but there was no mistaking it's piercing, glowing eyes, it was the same creepy creature I'd been having nightmares about.

I investigated the room around me, completely paranoid that I was being watched or followed, but there was nothing there. I took a deep breath as I tried to calm myself down.

"This can't be happening. It doesn't make any sense! I must be going insane! It's the only explanation!" I slowly pulled the photo back up, hoping I was imagining things. The shadowy figure was gone, as if it just vanished from the photo or as if it were never even there to begin with.

"It's gone! It can't be, I know what I saw!" I searched around the room again. "Screw this!" I ran out of the study and library as fast as I could. *I'm going back to my room, or somewhere with actual people so I can confirm my sanity. What the hell is going on!*

As I hysterically ran down a corridor, I slammed into something hard and practically fell on my ass.

"You need to watch where you're going." Xander extended a hand.

"This is a first."

"What is, you falling for me? I don't think so." He smirked.

I scoffed, slapping his hand away and helped myself up. "I meant you actually offering to help me up, but there you go again ruining it by opening your big mouth."

"Here, you dropped this." He laughed as he bent over to pick something up.

Oh no! The picture! I quickly snatched it from his hand, hopefully before he could get a good look at what it actually was.

"Jeez, why do I even bother trying to be nice."

"This is you trying to be nice? I'd hate to see what you're like around someone you really hate."

"Whatever," he said as he pushed his fingers through his hair and started to walk away in the opposite direction I was headed.

"Wait!" I called out before I could even realize what I was doing.

"What now?" He turned back towards me.

"Uh, it-it's nothing," I stammered and turned to head back to my room.

"No, what is it?" His tone completely changed. He almost sounded worried.

"I just, I'm still a little torn up from my dream earlier, do you think you could maybe walk me back to my room?" I asked while nervously chewing on my bottom lip. I figured he'd say something rude or snarky back, but I really was scared after everything that had happened lately.

"Sure." He slowly stepped towards me.

"Thanks."

We slowly walked towards my room together. I kept glancing up at him but he just looked straight the whole way.

"So, do you want to talk about it?"

"Talk about what?" I asked, even though it was pretty obvious what he was asking.

"About your dream."

"Not really, to be honest."

"Okay."

His response surprised me yet again. He didn't push for more information, he didn't laugh, there were no snarky remarks about me being a baby for still having nightmares. *I just don't get this guy. One minute he is the rudest jerk on the planet and the next he's human? It just doesn't make sense.*

"Well, good night, Princess." He pulled me back from my inner babbling as I realized we were already standing directly in front of my bedroom doors.

"Good night, Xander." I replied but he had already started to walk away. "Wait!" I called to him again and he turned around once more. "Thank you." I smiled.

He didn't say anything, he just smiled before continuing his walk back to wherever he was headed before I bumped into him.

"I really am ready for bed." *I just hope I can sleep through the night without any more creepy nightmares.*

I slowly brought the picture, that was now crumpled up in my hand closer to my face, my hand was shaking as I was readying myself to take another look at it. There was nothing in the background. *Maybe I'm just over tired and seeing things. I'm stressing myself out, I just need some rest. Yeah, sure that's it!* I assured myself as I walked over to the nightstand beside my bed and opened the top drawer. Amara's journal was at the top and I decided it was as good a place as any to hide the photo for now.

"Maybe once Lawrence gets back, I can ask him more about this photo and my past." I put on one of Amara's elegant silk and lace nightgowns and pulled back the giant covers to crawl into bed. *You just need to sleep this all off, Avery.*

Amara

"Avery's in trouble."

"What are you talking about? Are you okay?" Wesley practically shook me in his arms.

"What I mean is, that same creature that just attacked us, is going after Avery, too."

"How could you possibly know that?" His eyebrows crinkled in concern. "Is this another secret you've been keeping from me?"

"No, this has never happened before." He looked more confused than ever. "I don't know how to explain it. I just saw her and she is in trouble."

"Well, maybe you didn't really see her. You say this has never happened in the past. So maybe that thing freaked you out and now you're just worried about Avery."

I searched his eyes as I thought about what he just said then pushed his arms off me and picked myself back up.

"I know I sound crazy, but it felt too real. We have seen weirder things, even before today. Maybe that bright light from earlier did something to me."

"I guess it's possible. You are right after all. Why not add magical psychic powers to the mix, you clearly have other powers you've been hiding for who knows how long." His voice dripped with sarcasm.

"We have much more important issues to worry about. We need to get out of here and we still need to find the prophecy. And if that was not enough, some creepy thing is after us and we have no idea how to defend ourselves against it! As much as I do believe that Avery needs help, we can not afford to go back just yet. She will be okay; she has to be." I took a deep breath and decided to continue forward.

"Where are you going?" Wesley called as I walked away.

"Forward."

We continued to walk in silence as if the last few minutes never happened. *He cannot be that mad at me for not telling him.* I glanced back over my shoulder at Wesley, his gaze fixed on the ground as we continued walking through the tunnels.

I was unsure where these tunnels would lead us next, or if we had already come this way or not. They were all the same; dark, dim, and gloomy. We eventually came to a larger opening with two different tunnel pathways. *Left or right?* I thought to myself quickly before Wesley had a chance to catch up, he continued to trail behind me the entire way.

I glanced back at him before making my final decision.

I continued forward and firmly said, "We're going right."

"After you," he practically whispered.

After walking for a while longer, a small light appeared ahead. *What is that?* I began to slow, Wesley hurried to my side.

"We need to be careful. We don't know what could be ahead," he said as he put his arm up in front of me as if trying to protect me from something.

"Right, because we knew what was ahead of us throughout this whole tunnel maze," I said as I pushed his arm down and continued to walk ahead of him towards the light.

Wesley let out a small chuckle before continuing to follow behind me. A small smile formed after hearing his laugh. *He can never stay mad at me.*

The tunnel soon began to widen and change into more natural looking stone and dirt-clay walls. The ground was uneven with large stone boulders randomly placed around, they had moss growing on them. As I continued an earthy scent filled the air around me.

"I think we're in a cave." Wesley said, now by my side once more. As we made our way closer towards the light, we hit a cave wall.

"Great, we're trapped." My voice echoed back at me.

Wesley walked up to the wall lifting his hands up, feeling around the wall. He slowly approached the side of the cave where we saw the light shining through.

"No, we aren't! There's a small opening here where the light is coming through and I think we'll be able to squeeze our way out." He looked back at me.

"After you." I motioned towards the tiny opening.

I waited and watched as Wesley wiggled his way through the little opening until I could not see him any longer and the faint shining light was all I could see.

"All clear!" He called out before I made my way through the opening.

As soon as I was out of that cave, I immediately felt the warmth of the sun shining on my face like a familiar friend peeking through the tall trees above us. We were surrounded by tall, thick, pink coloured trees. The leaves, which looked more like flower pedals than leaves, danced in the small breeze as they fell from the treetops. The ground was covered in green grass and the fallen leaves from the trees above. I did not realize how long we must have been in those tunnels as the sun was now clearly up.

"This place is beautiful!"

A rustling noise beside me made me jerk in response, Wesley was digging for something in his pockets. He pulled out a map of Soluna and wore a puzzled look on his face.

"What's wrong?" I asked.

"We've explored everywhere within the Kingdom of Soluna as well as most of Caelestia, but I have never been here, have you?"

"Well, no." I replied.

"Exactly! It's not even on my map. So, where are we?"

"I do not know." I tried not to let my worry shine through, but Wesley was right. Between the two of us, we have been everywhere inside and surrounding my kingdom, so where exactly were we now.

"I have an idea." Wesley reached back into his pocket and pulled out a compass. "Let's continue south." He pointed in the direction I assumed was south and we headed that way.

We made our way through this gorgeous forest, but I soon noticed everything began to change.

"What is happening?"

It was as if everything around us was dying. The once stunning trees were now rotting. The tops of the trees were bare, and the sun was hiding behind dark grey clouds. The beautiful leaves that danced around us had become wilted and black, covering the ground beneath us.

The deeper we went into the woods the more withered and decayed it became. The little bit of sun that shone through was gone, as if the forest were wrapped in shadows. I shivered as the once gentle breeze had now become a harsh unsettling wind. I could hear the eerie rustling of trees and branches breaking around us as though something were watching us.

A crackling sound came from behind us. Jumping, my hand instinctively clenched onto Wesley's. His smile was warm and calming.

"It's okay, I won't let anything happen to you. Besides, you're a lot scarier than anything we could find here."

I threw him a soft smile before worry consumed me again. I shuttered thinking about that thing we saw in the tunnels. *What if it followed us here? What if we are in its lair? What if there were a whole nest of them here just waiting to attack?*

Wesley squeezed my hand. "Like I said, it will be okay."

I painted on a smile, attempting to mask my fear and we continued further into the woods.

CHAPTER THIRTEEN

Amara

We had barely taken two steps when a whisper sounded. Before I even had a chance to look in the direction it was too late. Wesley was thrown to the ground and covered in shadows. I screamed as I removed my sword from its scabbard and swung it at the cloud of shadows above Wesley.

This one was similar, yet somehow different from the one we saw in the tunnels. When I swung my sword, it made contact, like this one had a more physical form. As soon as the blade tore into the creature it let out a deafening screech. My sword dropped as I instinctively covered my ears.

The shriek must have been a cry for help as more of these things materialized from the shadows surrounding us.

Wesley reached for my sword, "Amara! Catch!" He cried, tossing it towards me.

I reached forward grabbing my sword in midair by its hilt and spun around to ward off the creatures from getting any closer.

Wesley had pulled out his own sword and stabbed that thing before him, it immediately vanished.

I quickly ran to his side and held out a hand. "Are you okay?"

"Never better." He smirked as I helped him to his feet. We stood back-to-back with our swords out as we tried to fend them off.

"There's just too many of them," I whispered.

"We'll just have to try to clear a path and make a run for it."

"Are you sure we can even outrun these things? They seem to appear and disappear out of thin air."

"We don't really have any other options."

He's right. I tried to find the easiest way to escape and of course, it was the way we were already headed; further into the woods.

"Follow me!" I yelled as I ran, sword swinging.

Wesley followed close behind as we attempted to fight our way through. As we approached the creatures in front of us, they began to disappear. *Something is wrong.* I turned my head back and noticed they were still close behind.

I slowed down and soon stopped running altogether, Wesley nearly ran into me.

"What are you doing? We need to get out of here!" He panted as he grabbed my hand and tried to pull me with him.

"Wait, look!" I pointed at the demons that were chasing us moments ago.

"What? We need to move!"

"No, seriously look! They are not chasing us anymore. They are just hovering there. What the hell is going on?"

"You've entered the barrier." An unfamiliar voice called out.

Wesley and I quickly turned in the direction of this mysterious voice, our swords once again raised.

"Who the hell are you? Show yourself!" Wesley demanded.

A pale young woman with short wavy auburn hair stepped out from behind a broken stone wall that was falling to pieces. That was when I realized we were no longer in a forest.

"Where are we?" Utterly confused, I noticed we somehow ended up in some sort of deserted village. Everything was falling apart and the village was in ruins.

"How did we even get here?" Wesley looked as bewildered as I felt.

"As I mentioned," The strange woman continued. "You've entered the barrier." As she spoke, she slowly made her way closer to us, arms raised high in surrender. "You can lower your weapons; I mean you no harm."

Her clothes were tattered. She had a scar that went through her right eyebrow down to just above her icy blue eyes.

"It's more than I can say for those shadow demons." She gestured to those things that led us here.

"Shadow demons?" I asked.

"Yes, those creepy things out there are known as shadow demons. Don't worry those ones can't get to us."

"Those ones?" I gulped as I asked, fearing I already knew what she was about to say.

"Unfortunately, there are plenty of other creatures in here that can. We should probably get out of sight as soon as possible." She headed back behind the stone wall.

"Wait, why are you helping us?" I shouted.

"And why should we trust you?" Wesley quickly added.

"Hey, you could always take your chances with the other demons." She called back as she continued to walk away.

Wesley who was already looking back at me. We both shrugged and followed her, trying to keep up with her fast pace.

"You never answered our other questions, who are you?" Wesley questioned her again as we stepped into an old building. There were holes in the exterior walls and half of the roof was missing. "We have a lot of questions." He added when she did not reply.

"Okay well firstly, you can call me Ophiuchus. What are all these other questions you have for me?" She peeked back over her shoulder and winked at him.

We continued through the broken building. Stepping and climbing over fallen rocks and other debris that covered the floor. We stopped in front of a dirty torn cloth. Ophiuchus pulled it back unveiling a wooden door with strange rune markings carved into it. She gently knocked on the door three times before a small slit opened at eye level.

A low raspy voice spoke, "Password."

"Constellation." Ophiuchus mumbled under her breath.

We waited a moment before the runes on the door began to light up like fire, I watched in amazement as they quickly disappeared as if it had never even happened. The door slowly opened, and Ophiuchus entered. My eyes darted to Wesley once more, worried at what we were about to get ourselves into. He shared a similar skeptical look with me seconds before I felt the warmth of his hand brushing against mine, it slowly slid down until our fingers intertwined.

"We're in this together. Whatever the hell this is." His smile reassured me.

I checked behind the door to see who opened it, but there was no one there. We both took a deep breath and then followed Ophiuchus through the door and down a flight of dark creaky stairs.

"Watch your step," she called from the bottom.

Wesley leaned in close to me. "How the hell are we supposed to watch our steps? It's too damn dark to see anything." I nudged him and gave him a look I was not even sure he could see.

There was a light at the bottom of the staircase. As we reached the bottom, it opened up to a large underground tavern filled with people. Everyone stopped to stare at us. They all resembled Ophiuchus in the sense that they were covered in cuts and bruises, their clothes torn and covered in dirt and blood.

Ophiuchus turned to Wesley with her scarred eyebrow slightly raised. "Now I'll answer your questions."

Wesley did not speak for a few moments as he watched her like he was analyzing everything about her. He opened his mouth to finally say something, but I cut him off instead. "What were those markings on the door?" His eyes shifted to me, then back to her.

"Those markings are keeping us safe and hidden down here." She answered my question but kept her eyes on Wesley.

"Safe from what exactly? And where are we?" Wesley did not hesitate this time.

"As I mentioned earlier, although that barrier is keeping those demons out, there are others here stuck inside the barrier with us."

"Where are—"

"What do you mean stuck inside?" I cut Wesley off again.

"That barrier doesn't just keep the shadow demons out, it keeps us in. We're trapped here and now so are you." She turned to Wesley, then added, "I'm sorry, I never caught your name."

"Wesley. My name is Wesley."

"Well, Wesley—" She smiled. "Sorry to break it to you but you are stuck here in the Shadow Lands now."

"We are not trapped here and where exactly are these Shadow Lands? I do not remember seeing them on any map. What happened to the forest?" I interrupted.

"The Shadow Lands are hidden deep within the forest; the barrier keeps it hidden. You can't see it or enter it from the outside unless they want you to. And by then it's usually too late, you're trapped inside."

"We can't be trapped here, there must be a way out!" Wesley blurted.

"We've tried. Some of us for centuries. There is no way out," she insisted.

"Who are they? And centuries? How does that even make sense?"

"They are the one who created this barrier and the Shadow Lands, Shadow Lord."

Shadow Lord. A shiver went through my entire body as I heard that name.

"There are other demons and followers of Shadow Lord within the barrier, searching for us and hunting us down. Shadow Lord has full control over all the demons and anyone without our special gifts."

"Special gifts?" Wesley asked.

"Yes, most of us have some type of special gift. Flying, teleportation, talking to animals, the list goes on."

"Celestials," I whispered to myself without realizing. Ophiuchus eyed me suspiciously and I cleared my throat. "Sorry, please continue."

"Even with these gifts, we can't escape. We think they are capturing us to take our gifts for themself."

I felt a warm feeling in my chest. "We cannot stay here. We need to find a way out. Come on Wesley!" I ordered.

"Right." He followed.

"Wait! It's not safe. We're trapped but if you want to discover that for yourselves, I won't stop you. All I ask is that you stay here for the night and wait until morning. The demons are much stronger at night," Ophiuchus warned us.

Wesley looked at me, and I nodded in approval. "We will stay the night and leave first thing in the morning." I declared.

"Then tonight we drink in hopes you will find something we have not!" Ophiuchus raised a cup as the crowd cheered and joined her.

"Wesley, we should really try to get some rest so we can be more prepared for the morning," I whispered, trying not to draw too much attention from the cheering crowd.

"If that is what you wish, milady. However, one drink for their hospitality could not hurt."

I glared at Wesley, then he added, "Some might call it rude even."

"One drink," I said and he gave me a knowing smirk.

Ophiuchus was a few steps away at the tavern's bar and waved us over. "I guess—" Before I even noticed Wesley was already walking over to the bar.

How is this getting us any closer to the prophecy? I groaned and followed behind him.

"Please meet Orion. He is a very skilled swordsman and archer. He also has incredible strength." Ophiuchus introduced us to the man behind the bar as he handed me and Wesley drinks. Orion had deep brown, wild unkempt hair. His eyes were as grey as the skies outside yet not as uninviting. He winked at me, and I almost choked on my drink.

"Careful, Beautiful." He smiled.

"She is not beautiful; she is Amara." Wesley interrupted. "I mean, not that she isn't beautiful of course, I just meant her name."

I looked at Wesley with surprise, one for his comments but also the fact that he was quick and smart enough to not mention that I was a Princess.

"Anyway, Wesley, can I give you a tour?" Ophiuchus had already grabbed onto his hand and started pulling before he answered. Our eyes met briefly before she pulled him off too far and I downed the rest of my drink.

"So, Miss Amara. Can I pour you another drink?" Orion teased.

"Please."

Avery

Just as I closed my eyes there was a knock at my door. *I guess that's for the best. Who knows what kind of crazy dream I'd have this time?* I unraveled the layers of plush blankets and silk sheets from around me and pulled myself out of bed. I slowly made my way to the door and opened it, to my surprise Xander was standing in the doorway.

"What are you doing here?" I asked.

"Well, I uh—" I didn't understand why he was at a loss for words until I followed his gaze back to me. I looked down to see that I was still wearing Amara's nightgown. I instantly wrapped my arms around my body trying to cover myself up.

Why does this keep happening to me?

"Sorry." Xander politely turned around as he apologized.

That was unexpected.

"And the reason I came back was because I thought maybe you'd want to do something to take your mind off of your dream. I know you said you didn't want to talk about it and I respect that but I thought even if you didn't want to talk about it maybe you still didn't want to be alone either. I don't know, it's stupid, I guess. I'll just go." He started to leave.

Why the sudden change of heart?

"This was a mistake, she hates me."

"Xander wait, don't go."

He slowly turned back towards me. We just stared at each other in silence for a few moments. I didn't exactly know what I was supposed to say.

What is he thinking?

"I can't believe I used to hate her so much."

Used to?

"Um, will you give me a few minutes to change and I'll be right out."

185

"Sure."

"Okay." I slowly closed the door with the biggest grin on my face, glad he was still turned away and couldn't see it. I waited a few moments longer, leaned against the door after I had closed it.

"She's nothing like I thought she was. She seems so humble and introverted."

My smile grew even bigger and I felt my face begin to heat up. I finally removed myself from the door and made my way over to the closet to change.

I quickly threw on some comfy and less revealing clothes, then looked at myself in the giant mirror while I fixed my hair.

I opened the door half expecting Xander to be long gone, but there he was, still facing away from the door.

"Ready," I said and he slowly turned back towards me.

"I like your shirt," he stuttered.

"Wow, I sound like an idiot. But it does really bring out the colour in her eyes."

"No, you don't," I assured him.

"What?"

Crap.

"I mean thank you. You also have a nice shirt." My compliment sounded more like a question. "Hey, I'm hungry! Are you hungry? Let's get something to eat shall we!" I pulled his arm as I swiftly walked towards the kitchen. *I sound insane.*

We made our way to the kitchen and it was completely empty.

"I guess the kitchen staff must have the day off with everyone still in Coldoria. Should we go into town?" Xander asked.

"Why? I can just make us something. What are you feeling?"

"*You* can cook?" He looked surprised.

"Obviously. I make all my own food," I said proudly.

"Seriously?"

Shit.

"I mean not all my meals of course. But you know, some. So, what do you feel like?"

"How about dessert."

"What?"

"Oh no! Not like that I mean, not that I wouldn't. No, I just meant, how about a cake or something."

"Oh right, of course that's what you meant, what else could you mean?"

"Right."

"Right."

"So, what about a cheesecake?" I asked.

"Cheesecake sounds perfect."

You're perfect. Shit! No, he's not! I looked back up into his bright ocean eyes. *What the hell am I doing? Get your mind out of the gutter Avery!*

I watched him as he sat down on one of the bar stools at the kitchen's island.

"So, do I just sit here and watch while you bake or something?"

"I guess I could teach you how to make it if you'd like."

"That'd be pretty cool. I mean, it's not like I have anything better to do."

"Right." I narrowed my eyes as I continued to watch him jump off his seat and walk over to the fridge. *What is he doing now?*

"What ingredients do we need?" He called with his head stuck inside of the fridge.

I laughed as I walked over to him as I listed out the ingredients needed. We looked around but couldn't find everything needed for it.

"What about pizza?" I asked.

"Pizza sounds even better."

"Then pizza it is!"

He grabbed the readymade dough out of the fridge along with cheese, pepperoni and other obvious ingredients needed for a pizza. He passed them to me, and I brought them back to the kitchen island. I broke the dough into two smaller balls and started rolling one of them. He looked at me and I just nodded my head and gazed towards the second ball of dough.

Xander slowly walked to the island and watched me for a moment before mirroring what I was doing.

"This is a lot easier for a first lesson anyway," I mentioned.

"First lesson?" He leaned closer and raised one brow. I immediately felt flushed and looked back down at the pizza dough. "Maybe we can do the cheesecake for our second one then." He grinned.

"I'd like that." I tried to hide the grin I felt forming on my face.

"Good."

"Good."

"Great."

"Great." I glanced over and noticed he was trying to hide the same goofy smile I was.

"So, what exactly do you want on your pizza? And please don't say pineapple," I teased.

"Please. Pineapple doesn't belong on pizza. It doesn't belong on anything, really." We both laughed as if in agreement.

"So, then what do you like?" I asked again. He leaned in again, even closer, his eyes held mine and my heart started racing.

"These." He pulled up a pack of pepperoni and bacon in between our faces.

"All right, well grab the tomato sauce and I'll look for a cheese grater."

I swiftly turned away from him and towards the kitchen cabinets along the walls. I began rooting through the drawers until I finally found what I was looking for. I made my way back over to the island where Xander was waiting for me with the tomato sauce. I placed the cheese grater down and started flattening the pizza dough with the palms of my hands. Xander started to mimic what I was doing again with the second ball of dough.

"Great! Now pinch the edges to make a lip for the crust of the pizza."

"Whatever you say. You're the professional." He laughed.

"More sarcasm from Xander? Shocking."

"Okay, so now what?" he asked.

189

"Now we put the sauce and the rest of our toppings on." I grabbed the cheese grater and started to shred the cheese, occasionally glancing over at Xander, who was just standing there staring at me.

I know he is watching me to learn how to make a pizza but does he seriously have to stare at me with those mesmerizing eyes? I mean I'm just shredding cheese not painting the Mona Lisa!

"I'm just shredding cheese you know."

"I know, obviously. I just didn't know what else I could be doing."

I looked back up into his eyes. *They're like a sea green, shimmering under the sunlight.* His eyes narrowed and I realized how long I must have been staring into his eyes.

"Right well, let's put the toppings on and throw these babies in the oven!" *These babies? What is wrong with me?* I shook my head to myself as we put our toppings on. I took the pizzas and placed them on a pizza stone and into the oven.

"What should we do while we wait?" Xander asked.

"It doesn't take that long. We can just wait here and talk I guess."

"Talk? About what?"

"I don't know. I guess I should thank you."

"Thank me? Thank me for what? You're the one showing me how to make pizza." He shrugged.

"Thank you for coming here."

"It's not a big deal, I was hungry anyway."

"Not for coming to the kitchen moron, for coming back to Soluna with me. You didn't have to; you could have just stayed in Coldoria for the rest of the festival, but you didn't. So, thank you."

"Right, well it's not like I could have just let you come back alone after what happened." Xander turned his face away from me and shrugged while he ran his fingers through his hair.

"Well, I wouldn't have been alone, Ben came back with us too, remember?"

"How could I forget?" he muttered under his breath.

"Right."

"Did you want to talk about your dream?" I was surprised by his gentle tone. He seemed genuinely concerned.

"I've had a few. Bad dreams, that is. It's become a lot more common than I'd like it to be." I knew he was the one who asked about them, but I still felt weird confiding in him like that.

"How often are you having them? Do you think it means something?"

"Shit, I hope not," I blurted out a little too honestly.

"We do still have that truce of ours, so if you ever need to talk to someone you could always come talk to me."

He lifted an arm towards me and I looked up at him. As our eyes met, his hand stopped and just hovered inches above my shoulder for a few seconds before promptly pulling his arm back down to his side.

"So, do you think the pizza is ready yet?" he quickly changed the subject.

"Oh, yeah, right. The pizza. It should just be a few more minutes."

"Cool. I'll go look for some oven mitts."

He started digging through different drawers and cupboards. By the time he finally found them the pizza was ready. I took the mitts from him and opened the door to the oven. The smell of the pizzas instantly filled the room. *Mmm. I love pizza! This smells incredible.*

I took in a deep breath, allowing the smell to consume me. I didn't think I'd have it again until I got back home. My real home. *Do princesses even eat pizza? Well, this one is about to!*

I took the pizzas out and placed them on the stove top. I opened the drawer next to the stove and immediately found a pizza slicer. *That was easy!* I cut our pizzas and placed several slices on two separate plates and walked back over to Xander at the island with the plates in hand.

"Dinner is served." I smiled.

"I'm going to take this to go. Thanks."

"I need to get out of here."

What did I do now?

I watched as he ran off without looking back or a second thought.

CHAPTER FOURTEEN

Amara

It has been over an hour since Wesley left with her. Where could they possibly have gone? This place is not that big. I looked down into the bottom of my empty glass and sighed.

"How about another, Amara? On the house." Orion slid an already poured glass my way across the bar before I had a chance to answer him.

"Aren't they all on the house?"

Loud obnoxious laughter sounded from the other side of the tavern. I looked over to see Wesley and Ophiuchus coming around a corner giggling to one another.

"Ugh, seriously?" I downed the entirety of my new drink and before I could slam the glass back down on the counter Orion had already slid me another. I looked at the drink and then up at him. I smiled and then tossed that drink back as well.

I looked back over at Wesley and Ophiuchus. I couldn't help but stare at their needless flirting. Just then the beer bottle in Ophiuchus' hand exploded.

"Ouch!" she cried as she inspected her finger.

"Are you all right?" Wesley pulled her hand closer to him as he examined her cut.

This is all my fault! I can't believe I just did that! I need to go to bed, I think I've had too much to drink.

"You don't happen to know where I am supposed to be sleeping considering we are forced to stay here tonight do you?" I asked Orion.

He laughed. "Actually, we have already prepared a room for you and your boyfriend to stay for the night."

"He, umm, he's not really my—"

"Please, follow me." He laughed again and cut me off before I could finish.

I followed him to the far side of the tavern. There was a hallway with many curtains hung along the walls. We walked down the hallway to the second last curtain on the left. I looked at him questioningly. He raised the curtain with one arm, revealing an opening to a small cave-like room.

"It's not much, but it's a heck of a lot better than being out there with those demons." He smirked.

"I appreciate it, thank you." I entered the room, then looked back at him.

"My pleasure." He smiled before dropping the curtain door.

Seconds later Wesley stormed into the room.

"Is everything okay?" he blurted.

"Everything is fine," I assured him. "Why wouldn't it be?"

"Well, I just watched you run off with the bartender and you seemed pretty out of it."

"Oh, you weren't too busy with your new friend?" He just looked at me with his face wrinkled up in confusion. "I'm fine. I've just had a few drinks." I stumbled past him on my way to the bed, not exactly helping my case.

"You should get some rest." He caught me as I stumbled again and helped me to the bed.

"Why do you think I came here? And I'm fine, honestly. It's just been a while since I've drank."

"Right, well, get some rest. I'll take the floor." Wesley grabbed a blanket that was draped over the end of the single bed and started unfolding it to lay it on the ground.

"Don't be ridiculous." I placed my hand over his, stopping him as he waved the blanket in the air to unfold it. "I suppose we could share the bed." I quickly pulled my hand back. "But don't get any ideas!"

"I wouldn't dare." He grinned.

I got into bed first, steadying my breath as Wesley climbed in next to me. We lay side by side facing one another in silence. I tried to look away but could not. As I glanced up at Wesley, he looked back at me as though he was trying to memorize my face. His gaze slowly made its way up from my lips until our eyes met once again.

"Well, good night then." I quickly spun around, turning my back to him while I let out a deep breath I had not realized I was holding in.

The bed shifted, at first I thought he had also turned over until the warmth of his arm slid around my waist and pulled me in closer. I peeked back over my shoulder at him and opened my mouth to object, but nothing came out as I met his gaze once more.

"For tonight, can we just pretend? Pretend we're different people. You're not a princess and I'm not your attendant. Tonight, we're just Wes and Mara."

"I don't know." I breathed as my heartrate quickened as he held me, his breaths warm on my neck.

"I just want to hold you once, like I won't have to ever let you go." He whispered in my ear.

I nodded. "For tonight." It took everything inside of me not to turn back over and kiss him… taste him… feel him. I knew if I did there would be no going back. Things would never be the same for us and he deserved more than what I could give him. So, I closed my eyes. I was being selfish, but just for the night, I needed to be. Just once.

Good night, Wes.

Avery

There was a knock on my door. *Is it Xander again?* I walked over to the door and opened it to see Ben standing in the doorway.

"Hi, Princess. I-I mean Princess Amara. Uh, I mean, Amara."

"Hi, Ben." I laughed.

He smiled back at me. "I was thinking since we're back in Soluna, maybe you would like to go to the garden and do some reading and writing? We don't have to worry about running into the Duke or Duchess of Caelia."

"Hmm. I never thought of that! Let me just grab a book and we can head over."

I walked over to the desk Amara had on the left side of her room. It was more of a vanity than an actual desk, but I used it for late night reading. The lights around the mirror were great for that. I looked at the pile of books I had left there from the library before picking up 'Warriors with Wings' and heading back to the door.

"All right, let's go!" I said as I closed the door to my room and started towards the garden.

Ben quickly caught up to me.

"So, I've been working on a few things recently and I would love for you to read one of them. If you want to, of course."

"I would love to!"

"Really? Great!" His smile beamed with excitement.

Ben seemed very eager for me to read his work. I practically had to speed walk just to keep up with him the rest of the way to the garden. Once we were there, Ben started towards the big gazebo before I stopped him.

"It's such a nice day out. Why don't we sit under that tree instead?" I asked.

"But I didn't bring a blanket or anything for you to sit on."

"That's fine, we can just sit on the grass."

"But aren't you afraid you'll dirty your clothes?" Ben's face was filled with concern.

"Not at all. Come on." I pulled him by his arm as I ran over to the giant willow tree and sat down.

"So, where's that poem or story you wanted me to read?"

"I—I brought a poem." His usual smile was gone, his gaze fixed on the grass where he sat. "It's just a rough draft though. Probably not very good anyway, you should just read that book you brought with you instead."

"Don't be silly! I want to read it! Now come on, hand it over!" I teased.

"Okay, here." He fiddled around in his pocket before pulling out a folded up piece of paper. He hesitated before slowly giving in and handing it over to me.

"Like I said, I would love to read your work. But only if you're ready and want me to. No pressure," I assured him.

"It's okay. I just haven't had anyone read any of my work before. You'll be my first." He continued to stare at the grass and started biting at his fingernails.

"Well, I'm honoured."

I unfolded the paper and began to read his poem. It was handwritten and he had surprisingly good penmanship. As I read the poem I would occasionally look over at Ben. He seemed extremely nervous. He still wouldn't look at me and was now picking at the grass.

"This is really good!" I exclaimed.

"You're just being nice." He sighed.

"No honestly, it's really good, Ben!"

"Really? You mean it?" His face shot up with his signature smile as bright as ever.

"Of course!"

"Thanks," he whispered as he pulled out a notebook and pencil and started writing on the notepad.

He is really talented, he just needs more confidence in himself. I know what that's like. It's much easier being confident when you're trying to be someone else. That way if anyone is judging you or doesn't like you, it's not the real you. I sighed. Maybe I should practice this weird mind reading thing on Ben and see how bad his confidence really is to see if there's anything I can do or say to help him, plus I could use the practice.

I watched Ben and really tried to concentrate on what I wanted. Nothing. *Why isn't this working?* Squinting my eyes, as if that would have helped, I cleared my mind of all thoughts and focused on Ben and what I wanted to happen. But again, nothing.

Why are his thoughts so hard to read? I don't even have to try to hear Xander's, they just pop into my head without me even trying. Hmm. Maybe I should just let him be. He seems like he's in the zone. Maybe this is just all in my head anyway, I don't understand any of this.

I pulled out the book I brought with me and opened it up. As soon as it opened, I heard a ringing sound in my ears. I clutched my ears and closed my eyes to try to soften the loud ringing.

Everything was dark. I was surrounded by shadows and darkness. But this was different, I could see myself from a distance. As if I was watching myself in a movie or T.V. show from somewhere up above. I was in that same dark, decaying forest. Those things were closing in on me again, but this time as I was watching myself, I wasn't frozen in fear.

A glowing silver blue light radiated off of me. I raised my hands and screamed. That same light that luminated off of me shot out at those things and as the light hit them, they disappeared.

"Amara! Amara! Please wake up! Amara!"

I opened my eyes and rose in a panic, panting as I tried to catch my breath. I frantically looked around in complete confusion. I was laying in Amara's bed with both Ben and Xander standing next to me.

"Thank heavens you're all right!" Ben cried.

"What happened?" The last thing I remembered was reading Ben's poem.

"Yeah, what the hell happened? How could you let this happen to her?" Xander scolded Ben.

"We were sitting under that tree. I was writing while you read. Next thing I knew you were screaming and then you just collapsed. I carried you to the infirmary and they told me to bring you here. They've been in and out checking on you. I'll go let them know you've woken up!" Ben ran out of the room with tears in his eyes.

I looked to Xander. "How long was I out?"

"About an hour." His jaw clenched as he looked back at the door.

"I'm fine, you know. It's not his fault."

"He was there with you; he should have protected you!"

"Protected me? He brought me here, didn't he? I was probably just lightheaded or something. I'm fine honestly." I tried to convince him as well as myself. I could feel something in the pit of my stomach. That dream, if it was a dream, didn't feel right.

"You had another one of those dreams, didn't you?" He sat down at the foot of my bed.

"Yes."

"What happened?"

"It was like before. In that dungeon. Except, this time I was in a forest and there wasn't just one of those things. There were hundreds, and they were all after me."

All the lights in the room went dark. The only thing I could see was the tiny sliver of light from under the doorway out into the hallway.

"Xander!" I reached out and grabbed his hand with mine.

I heard a creaking coming from the hall. A shadow appeared on the other side of the door blocking that little light we had shining through. The door slowly began to open.

"Xander!" an annoying yet familiar voice called.

The lights suddenly flickered and then were back completely. I looked up at the doorway to see Victoria standing there.

Xander jumped up and was now standing beside the bed again. Victoria sprinted over to him and threw her arms around him.

"Oh, how I've missed you!" she screeched.

"Vicky, what are you doing here?" he asked as he unwrapped her arms from around his neck.

"Well, there's no point in being back in Coldoria if you're not there!" She grinned as she attempted to hug him again. "As soon as I heard you left, me and Erik made our way back to Soluna as well."

"Oh, Erik's here, too. Great."

Is that really what he was thinking? Shouldn't he be happy about that? Maybe I am just imagining things and hearing what I want to hear after all.

CHAPTER FIFTEEN

Avery

Hazel came running into my room and practically knocked Icky Vicky over as she literally ran through her and Xander to hug me.

"Amara! Are you okay?"

"I'm fine, thank you." I smiled and pulled away from our hug. I noticed that Erik must have also slithered his way into my room after Hazel as he stood by the doorway. I ignored him and looked back at Hazel. "What are you doing here? I thought you were able to stay for the rest of the festival now?"

"There was really no point in staying anymore after you guys left."

"So now we're all stuck here," Victoria complained.

"No one is stuck here. Feel free to leave." I glared as she continued to try and hang onto Xander like an accessory.

"Gladly, but not without Xander." She tugged on his arm as she attempted to pull him out of the room.

"I'm sure we can find something fun to do tonight," Xander said but was quickly cut off as the healers from the infirmary walked back in with Ben. "No one is leaving Soluna. However, we will leave your room and let the healers check on you." Xander smiled at me while he escorted himself, Erik, and Victoria out of my room.

"I feel fine, honestly. I probably just needed something to eat," I explained to the healers as they examined me.

"You do seem fine, just get something to eat and get some rest," the one lady said before she exited the room.

Right, like I don't get enough rest around here already.

Ben and Hazel looked at me with very concerned looks.

"Like I said, I'm totally fine. You guys need to relax."

"If you say so." Ben tried to fake a smile for my sake.

"Maybe we should just have a nice quiet girls' night. We could have a slumber party if you want?" Hazel suggested.

"I have a better idea." I smiled, Ben and Hazel looked at each other and then back to me.

"If we can't be at the Winter Moon Festival, we'll bring the Winter Moon Festival to us!" I exclaimed.

"But how? It's not winter here," Ben asked.

He's right. I never really thought about it before but the seasons are so weird here. It was fall back home before I left but in Soluna it feels more like a spring and yet in Coldoria it's winter. I don't understand at all.

"That's not the point. The point is we should celebrate and I have the perfect idea. But I'll need your guys' help to pull it off."

"This sounds great! I'm in, whatever you need!" Hazel cheered in excitement.

"Great! Hazel, I need you to make sure everyone is dressed up and meets us all in the garden tonight for seven. Ben and I can hopefully handle the rest!"

"Ohh, I can't wait to see what you have planned! I will see you at seven!" Hazel giggled as she ran out the door.

"Ben, I need you to find some staff that can help organize, decorate, and work at an outdoor ball tonight! We'll need twinkle lights, music, food, tables and chairs, the whole works!" I exclaimed.

"I'm on it!" Ben headed for the door but I stopped him.

"Wait! Is there a certain place we keep all the decor for our balls? Like a storage room or something?"

"Yes, in the grand ballroom."

"Awesome! I'll find it, now let's get to work!" I advised and Ben smiled once more before exiting the room.

I made my way down to the grand ballroom without seeing a single person along the way.

Wow, I really hope Ben can find some staff members and we can pull this off.

I entered through the main entry way into the grand ballroom. There were not many doors inside, so it wasn't hard to find the storage room. The room was dark but enormous. I found the switch and turned the lights on which helped but it could definitely have used a few more light bulbs.

I looked around and found candles, twinkle lights, tables and chairs with multiple linen options, and a few other decor pieces I thought might be able to work outside.

Now I just need help to bring some of these out.

"Need a hand?"

I turned around to see Ben with about eight other people all wearing castle staff uniforms.

"Perfect timing! We need to bring this all outside to the garden to set up. But we'll also need something for the music."

"No need to worry I've spoken to our usual live band for our balls and they will be here at six to set up." Ben assured me.

"Wow, that was quick!"

"It was easy, really!"

"Well, thank you!"

"We can take care of the rest, we're used to this; you go get ready and we will see you at seven, princess." Ben practically shooed me out of the room.

"Thanks again."

I swiftly made my way back to my room. I looked at the time on the large clock hung on the wall in the small seating area in the bedroom. *Five o'clock. I've only got two hours to get ready and meet everyone, I really hope this all works out.* I headed towards the bathroom for a quick shower, then applied my make up, and styled my hair before making my way to the closet to pick my outfit.

I walked into the giant closet and looked at my many options of dresses hung along one of the railings on the wall. As soon as I saw the dress, I knew I had to wear it. *I completely forgot about this dress.* I picked the hanger off the railing and held the dress up as I took another good look at it.

It was the stunning burgundy dress that Xander had bought and sent over to me for our engagement party I refused to wear. *I mean, why let such a beautiful dress go to waste? Right?* I held the dress up against my body as I looked in the mirror as an uncontrollable smile formed on my face. I put the dress on and looked for a pair of heels to wear with it.

Stepping back into the main room in the bedroom, I noticed the time. *Ten to seven. Crap! I've got to go!* I took one last look in a full length mirror, attempting to fix any imperfections before I ran out and to the garden.

Once I arrived, I quickly noticed everyone else was already there including the band who had already begun playing. I looked around and was surprised at how many people were here enjoying themselves considering most people were still in Coldoria. I couldn't believe how amazing it had all turned out in such a short amount of time. The lights were hung from tree to tree and paper lanterns were sporadically placed and hung with the twinkle lights.

This is even more beautiful than I had hoped.

"May I have this dance?" His voice startled me, I turned around to look at him, standing there with his hand out waiting for mine.

"Of course!" I spoke a little too loudly as I placed my hand in his. I looked up at Xander's face hoping he didn't notice as I simpered.

His already radiant smile gleamed brighter under the lights and stars above us as we walked hand in hand over to the makeshift dance floor Ben and the rest of the staff must have created.

We stopped in the center of the dance floor and I nervously placed my free hand on his shoulder as he placed his around my waist. We slowly started to sway to the music as I concentrated on not stepping on his feet this time.

"Nice dress." His smirk pulled at the corners of his lips.

"Yeah, well I figured if we are here celebrating Coldoria I might as well wear their colours," I teased.

"Right. Well, it looks like I was right after all."

"Right about what?" I asked.

"How you'd look in that dress." That smirk I kept seeing more and more of made an appearance as the right side of his mouth tipped up.

"Completely captivating."

My face warmed as we stared at each other for a moment before both looking away. As I gazed out into the crowd, I noticed Victoria looking around. It was obvious who she was searching for. As soon as we locked eyes, I swear her face turned green with envy. She marched onto the dance floor and over to us.

Lovely.

"Oh, there you are, Xander." She smiled at Xander before quickly narrowing her eyes at me. "I'm here to save you."

"I don't need saving." He shrugged a shoulder, keeping his one hand on my waist and the other in my hand.

"You don't need to dance with her to save face. No one important is here that doesn't already know how you really feel about her." Victoria reached up to try and grab Xander's hand from mine, but he jerked away stopping her.

"Listen, Vic, I asked her to dance. I'll just meet up with you and Erik later. She did all of this for us, you know."

Is that the only reason he's dancing with me?

Victoria stormed off and Xander and I continued our dance.

"How you really feel about me, huh?" I muttered under my breath unsure if I wanted him to hear what I'd said and even more unsure if I wanted an answer. "You can go dance with Lady Victoria if you'd prefer. I don't mind, really. I know about you two," I said slightly louder.

"What are you talking about? She's not—We're not—We've never. It-It's not like that."

"It-it's not?" I felt like a weight I didn't even notice until now had been lifted.

"I mean, we're just friends. Why would you think that?"

"It just seemed obvious. You're both so close."

"We are close, but not like that. Aside from Erik and my sister, she's my only real friend. But since our truce, I just feel like things have been changing between us," he whispered, pulling me in even closer.

"You do?" I asked hopefully, refusing to pull my eyes away from his.

"Yeah, I mean, I feel like we're becoming friends, maybe." He smiled.

"Right. Friends." I said, finally breaking eye contact as I watched our feet, waiting for the song to end. *Friends. Just like him and Victoria. Do we even keep dancing for the next song? What is he thinking? Now would be a great time for these powers to actually work.*

Before even getting the chance to attempt to read his mind, he pulled away.

"I-I have to go!" he stuttered then ran off.

What was that about? Maybe he was lying and really did want to go see Victoria. I wondered as I made my way around the garden looking for Hazel or Ben or literally anyone else who wasn't Icky Vicky or Not Zac.

Everyone seemed like they were having a good time. The castle staff especially, I'm sure they don't get to do this kind of thing often so I'm glad they are enjoying themselves. Laughing mixed with music filled the air. Tipping my head back I noticed how clear the night sky was. As beautiful as this party and sky were, a part of me felt like something was missing.

Maybe I'm getting home sick?

After a few more minutes and laps of wandering around I decided to go for a walk on my own. I made my way down the path. This was the furthest I had actually been able to go before. I usually only made my way as far as the gazebo or the hedge maze.

The path led to a small pond covered with white water lilies and the reflection of the stars and moon above. It was quiet and peaceful. The perfect place to clear my head. I could still hear the faint sound of music and people laughing in the distance. I sat down in front of the pond admiring its tranquility.

"There you are."

So much for clearing my head.

I turned my head back to find Xander walking up to me.

"I have a surprise for you, I went to get them but when I came back you were gone." He continued towards me, both hands held behind his back.

"That's why you left?"

"Yes, why else would I have just left like that?" He asked, head tilted slightly to the side as he continued to close the distance between us.

"I wasn't sure," I practically whispered, unsure if he even heard.

"Close your eyes and hold out your hands." This time both corners of his mouth lifted.

"Sounds like some kind of trick," I taunted.

"It's not, you have my word." He placed a hand over his heart, his smile widening.

I did as he said, practically squealing in excitement. He placed something in my hands before he spoke again. It was thin, and resembled paper, but had a slightly heavier weight to it.

"Okay, open your eyes." Opening them, I found two flattened paper lanterns in my hands.

"What are these for?" I asked, meeting his eyes.

"Well, I felt bad about what happened back in Coldoria, like it was somehow my fault. And because of that you missed what, in my opinion, is the best part of the festival. So, I went to go find these lanterns after our dance so that you could have the chance to make your wish and we could light them together."

"That's so sweet of you."

"No, it's nothing really." He pulled out a match from his pocket and took one of the lanterns back.

Xander took the match and lit his lantern, then mine. "Make a wish," he said as the flame from the lanterns flickered in his eye. He gently pushed his lantern into the sky and let the night's cool breeze carry it away.

I wish to stop having these creepy dreams. I watched the lanterns take to the sky until they disappeared and joined the stars above us before looking back at Xander. *And maybe dream of something better.*

"So, Amara, what did you wish for?" His eyes still seemed to burn with the flame of the lantern, even though I knew that made no sense.

"I can't tell you that or else it won't come true," I teased. "What about you?"

"I better not tell you; I don't want to risk it not coming true."

"I wished for us to continue getting closer."

"Come on!" Pulling Xander by the hand, I ran closer towards the pond.

Taking his other hand and placing it on my waist, I started to playfully dance under the moonlight to the faint sound of music in the distance. He laughed before joining in with me.

"Princess! Princess Amara, are you all right?" Ben's voice overpowering the music as he neared the pond. "There you are!" Ben popped out of the covered pathway smiling. "I was worried when I noticed your absence from the party after what had happened back in Coldoria."

"Well as you can see, she's clearly fine. So, you can go now, Beck," Xander shooed at Ben.

"I really am okay, but thank you for worrying about me." I looked over at Xander while loudly correcting him. *"Ben."*

"Of course, it is my job to worry about you. I will leave you to your dancing. Just call if you need anything I will ensure not to wander too far." He bowed and made his way back through the pathway.

"Why do you always do that?" I looked back at Xander with narrowed eyes.

"Do what?" he lifted a shoulder in a half shrug.

"We both know you know what his name is."

"Do we? Do we really?"

"Yes, we do. Ben is like the nicest guy I know. I don't understand why you don't like him."

"Exactly!" Xander proclaimed.

"Exactly what?"

"He's too nice," he huffed.

"How can someone be too nice?"

"He just is, okay?"

"Whatever. I'm just going to go get some rest. Everyone is going to be back tomorrow." I walked away before giving him a chance to get another word in. I started towards my room, trying to take a path that didn't involve having to pass by everyone else at the party. I wanted them all to enjoy themselves a little while longer.

CHAPTER SIXTEEN

Avery

After laying there for several hours, tossing and turning, I finally accepted the fact that I was not going to sleep. I looked up at the ceiling, my eyes wide and restless as I sighed to myself. *Why can't I just fall asleep? It's not that hard, I do it all the time! I know I'm more of a night owl but this is ridiculous!* I rolled over and looked at the clock on the nightstand. Three *a.m. seriously?* I turned fully over, my face in my pillow and let out a muffled scream.

I climbed out of bed and began pacing around the room. I looked at the stack of books on my makeshift desk. *I could read a book.* I thought. *But then I'll get too invested in it and never go to sleep. Maybe a late-night snack? Maybe some popcorn and a movie! Hmm, do they even have movies here? I haven't seen a T.V. since I got here.* My pacing continued.

I guess I'll just go for a short walk outside. Maybe it will calm me and help me sleep. I walked over to the closet to grab a robe to throw on and help cover up a bit more in case of a cool night's breeze and made my way out the door. It was so quiet, not only had the castle been extra quiet because almost everyone was still

213

in Coldoria until later this afternoon, but the few people that were here in Soluna would have been sound asleep.

I walked back into the garden; all the decorations had been put away as if the party earlier hadn't even happened. I might as well enjoy this view again before Chaz and Vivian return and claim it as their own again.

As I walked along the path, I began to feel a few water droplets hit my face. I looked up and smiled as the rain slowly began to fall around me. The rain looked so peaceful with the stars above. I began twirling around with my arms out wide like a child dancing in the rain laughing to myself.

I was so lost in my own little world until I was pushed over into a big puddle of water. I blinked several times to clear my vision and was shocked when my face became even more wet as it was being licked by a wet dog standing over me.

"Stark!" a voice called out. "Stark, what are you doing! Get off her!"

The dog immediately got off of me and stood next to me as it wiggled its entire butt in excitement.

"I'm so sorry! Are you all right? He gets a little too excited around people." Xander stood above me with his hand out in offering, which I accepted.

"It's fine, I love dogs! I prefer them to people actually," I joked.

"Me, too." He gave a breathy laugh.

"But where the heck did he come from?" I asked. *This dog hasn't been here the entire time, has it?*

"He's mine from back in Coldoria. I never got to see him while we were there since I had so much going on and we left so quickly. I kind of missed him. Hazel surprised me and brought him back with her, but I decided to keep him hidden just in case.

214

He'll only be here for a few more hours. I promise he will go back once everyone else comes back to Soluna."

I had to admit I was only half listening to what Xander was saying as I had already bent back down and was petting Stark as he proceeded to give me more wet kisses.

"He likes you." I looked up to see Xander smiling down at us.

"Well good because I love him, yes I do!" I continued to pet him as I started babbling in baby voices to Stark while Xander let out a small burst of laughter before bending down next to me and began petting Stark.

"I really do love dogs. He can stay here you know; I don't mind. I would love it actually."

"Thanks, that would be awesome actually. I have really missed him."

"Well dogs are supposed to be a man's best friend!" I joked.

"He really is my best friend and most loyal." He mumbled the last part under his breath and a feeling of guilt had my stomach in knots. I knew exactly what he was referring to.

I just wanted to scream, *That wasn't me! I would never betray you like that!* But I couldn't. He thought I had, and I still felt guilty.

"Like I said, he is more than welcome to stay here as long as you are here. Or longer even, I wouldn't mind," I attempted to lighten the mood again.

"I'm actually surprised you even like dogs, especially big wet ones like him."

"One, it's not his fault it's raining. And two, what kind of sick person doesn't like dogs? Do you really think that low of me?"

"I mean, I guess I did before. We never really bothered to get to know each other until recently."

"I-I'm glad we did." I smiled softly at him as we were still squatting down next to Stark.

"Me, too." He smiled back as we looked into each other's eyes. "'Cause you know, now we're friends." His gaze shot back to Stark.

"Right. Friends." I stood up. "Well, friend, I should get back inside, dry off and try to hopefully get some rest."

"Good call. Your silk robe is becoming a bit see-through from the rain. And wait, why are you up so late anyway?"

"Oh, I couldn't sleep so I came out here to—wait what?" I shrieked in horror and spun away from him. "My robe is see-through! Why didn't you say anything sooner?"

He laughed as if this were all too amusing to him. "I don't know. I guess I thought you knew. Who comes out here dressed like that and doesn't realize it?"

"Someone who expected to be alone and didn't expect it to start raining! Now if you'll excuse me, I'm getting cold and will be leaving!" I stalked off.

Glancing back over my shoulder briefly, checking if he was watching me as I stormed off. "Ugh!" Shouting as I buried my face in my hands, a little less cold than I was moments ago as my cheeks began to warm.

Amara

Waking up alone in the tiny bed, sitting up slowly as I glanced around the cave-like room. Wesley had not only left the bed but left the room altogether. *Where could he have gone?* He knew we were going to be leaving early this morning and it really was not like him to forget. *Knowing him he is probably preparing for our venture off again.*

I got up and quickly threw on my boots and grabbed my cloak and satchel from the ground. As I bent over, I felt a wave of pain and nausea hit me. This is why I don't drink anymore. Well, that and the fact that it is not what a proper princess should be doing.

Just then, I heard a loud and very annoying laughter coming from the other side of the makeshift door that hung above the whole in the wall. *As if this headache was not bad enough already.*

I slowly made my way over to the sheet debating if I should listen to what she thought was so funny or make myself known. *You are better than this,* I told myself before lifting the sheet up. The laughter immediately stopped as our eyes met.

"Milady." Wesley smiled and Ophiuchus laughed again.

"You're too funny." She giggled as she pushed his shoulder.

"He is not that funny actually," I blurted.

"Excuse me?" Ophiuchus looked at me.

"I think what Amara is trying to say is that this is not a laughing matter and it is time to be serious," Wesley intervened. "We were actually just discussing our plans for finding a way out of here."

"You should have woken me sooner. We can be on our way now."

"Oh, please we can't go just yet. I've actually prepared breakfast. We'll need the energy." Ophiuchus cheered.

"I'm sorry, we?" I asked her as my eyes shot over to Wesley.

"Yes, well, Ophiuchus has so kindly offered to be our guide. I thought it was a great idea considering she knows a lot more about this place and the creatures living here."

"And if you somehow do manage to find a way out, I would like to know about it so we can all escape," she added.

"Well, I cannot argue with you there." I painted a smile on. "Please show me where this glorious breakfast is that you prepared."

"Right this way."

She led us back down the hall and to the main room in the tavern. She had already had a table set with food and drinks. I sat down at the table and started to eat eggs and the mystery meat that was in front of me.

I heard a noise coming from the bar and glanced over, Orion was cleaning up the counter. He shot me a soft smile and I immediately looked back down at my plate. Before I knew it, he had walked over to our table.

"How is everyone doing on this fine morning?" he beamed.

"We were just getting ready to head out. They seem to think they can find a way out of here that we haven't tried so I decided to join them," Ophiuchus shared.

"Great, I'll grab my cloak." He smiled again and made his way back over to the bar before anyone could object.

We followed Orion and Ophiuchus out of the hideout and back into the ruins above. As soon as I felt the sun hit my skin, I felt a sense of warmth that I had not realized until that moment I missed.

I looked around again to really take in where we were. It was still very much a forest however unlike outside of the barrier there were remains of homes and other buildings. *What*

218

happened here? I thought as we made our way through the ravage of this place.

"You get used to it." Orion's voice sang from behind me.

"Excuse me?" I asked as he quickly closed the few steps that were between us.

"Of course, I want us to find a way out of here, but I wouldn't get my hopes up too high if I were you. It's not like we all just decided we liked it here and wanted to stay." His voice saddened.

"Well, I suppose you are right. However, I cannot afford to be trapped here." I insisted.

"I mean I would like to get out of here as much as the next guy but having you here with us now wouldn't be the worst thing."

"Oh, but it would! As I mentioned, I can not afford to stay here. I have duties and responsibilities. I must find a way out of here and fast."

"Well, I will try to help you in any way that I can." His goofy grin widened.

"I appreciate that. Thank you." I looked behind me where Wesley and Ophiuchus were laughing again.

Maybe I should not be so harsh. She is trying to help us, and he looks happy. As happy as he can be in this place anyway. I sighed internally as I continued to step over who knew what.

We reached the border of the barrier where Wesley and I had entered from yesterday. I reached my hand up slowly. As I gently touched the invisible way I was half expecting to be electrocuted or burned, instead the air where I had touched rippled like a pool of water. I pushed harder once the rippling had stopped but could not push through. It felt odd, like solid air.

"It circles around for miles. We could walk around the perimeter if you'd like," Ophiuchus suggested.

"Good idea." My tone was a lot less sarcastic than it had been earlier.

Wesley took out his sword and aimed it at the barrier.

"We tried that too." Ophiuchus added.

Wesley attempted to cut his way through anyway. His sword bounced back as if it were made of rubber. "It was worth a shot." He smirked as he placed his sword back into its scabbard before running his hand through his hair.

We began to walk and as we did, I slid my hand against the barrier hoping to see if there was anywhere that seemed different or felt like it might give way.

Suddenly, a jolt ran through my hand that knocked me down. The last thing I remembered seeing was Wesley catching me in his arms before everything went black.

An unbelievably bright light shined suddenly, I squinted to keep my eyes open. The light finally began to fade. Everything was different. I was alone, the only thing around me was this mysterious light that gleamed all around me, like I was staring straight into the sun and nothing else around me existed anymore. *Where did Wesley and the others go?* The light began to dim, only slightly as a figure seemed to emerge from the light. A woman stood in the distance, like she was not only in the light, but she *was* light. She slowly made her way towards me, floating as if she were weightless.

"Hello!" I called to the woman.

Once I finally got close enough to see her there was no mistaking her. It was the same woman from that weird vision Wesley and I both had in those tunnels. The same woman that had looked identical to me. The only differences were our clothing and our hair. Her hair was longer and messier, and the colour of shimmering silver as it glowed with the rest of her body.

"Who are you?" I asked.

"I think you already know."

CHAPTER SEVENTEEN

Amara

"Why am I here?"

"I brought you here because you need to leave the Shadow Lands at once." The woman responded.

"What do you think I am trying to do? I know I need to leave; I need to find the prophecy and return to my kingdom."

"That is the other reason why I brought you here, you need to go back and ensure nothing happens to either you or your sister. She is in more danger than you know and it is crucial that no one finds out who Avery truly is. We made certain to do things differently with the two of you so that the prophecy can not come undone," Calypso demanded.

"What the hell does that even mean? No one can even leave this place! It's impossible, how am I even supposed to get to her?"

"You can."

"What do you mean I can? How?" I begged.

"You just have to find it within yourself."

"You have got to be kidding me! How am I supposed to do that?"

"Only you have the power to break through this barrier."

"Great, so I just have to figure out your weird riddle and we can all leave."

"Only you." She began to fade.

"Wait! What about the prophecy? I still need to find it!"

Her voice sang in my head:

Affection grows,

A forced marriage fails due to temptation.

The world becomes shrouded in shadows,

A mysterious evil shall bring forth an age of death and destruction.

Through it all one must abide,

From her past she shall share her wisdoms,

It shall be then, when sun and moon collide,

The chosen ones and true heirs shall bring the rise of two kingdoms.

I closed my eyes as the same bright light from earlier shot towards me. When I opened my eyes, I was back in Wesley's arms on the ground.

"Oh, thank gods! You're awake!" Wesley cried.

"Where is she?" I asked in a panic.

"Where is who?" Ophiuchus asked.

"C—" I stopped myself as I looked up at her. "Never mind." I lifted my hand to rub my eyes but was surprised when I realized there was something already in it. I slowly opened my hand to see a small glowing orb that fit perfectly into my palm.

"What is that?" Wesley asked in awe.

I grinned instantly as I knew exactly what it was. "The prophecy." I looked up at Wesley, still laying in his arms, and his smile matched mine.

"Come on, we're getting out of here!" I cheered as I picked myself up off the ground.

"How?" All three of them asked in unison.

"Only I can get us out of here." I grinned as I looked back at them all and winked.

I lifted my hands, with the prophecy still in one, up to the barrier, closed my eyes, and thought about how much I wanted and needed to leave. I felt a warm sensation in my hands and fingers, when I opened my eyes my hands were glowing as bright as the sun above us. I touched the barrier and just like that I was able to walk through.

"Come on!" I called.

Wesley ran to me as if he were about to pick me up and swing me around in the air when he hit the barrier hard, knocking him off his feet.

"Wes!" I yelled as I ran to him. "Are you all right?" This time he was the one on the ground in my arms.

"Yeah, I'll be fine. But what the hell? I thought you said you could get us out?"

"I can! She said only I could."

"Who did?" Orion asked as he helped Wesley back to his feet.

"That's not important. What *is* important is that I can clearly break through the barrier. I just need to figure out how to get you to come with me. Maybe if we were holding hands or something as I walked through."

"It's worth a shot."

Wesley and I intertwined our fingers as we attempted to walk through the barrier. But again, he was stopped and only I was able to go through as our hands stopped where the barrier began.

Only you. Calypso's words sung in my head. "Oh no," I whispered.

"What? What happened?" Wesley asked as I walked back up to him with tears in my eyes as I finally understood what she meant.

"She did not mean only I could break the barrier. She meant only I could leave." I hugged Wesley tightly. "So, we just have to find another way out of here." I wiped my eyes. "All right, let's keep looking." I began to walk in the direction we had been going before my bizarre vision when Wesley grabbed my wrist bringing me to a stop.

"No. You must go on without me. You finally have what you need."

"I need you," I cried.

"No, we both know you don't. I'll be fine. I'll be waiting here for you to come back and then we will find a way out, unless of course I find a way out before you come back." He tried to play it off as a joke.

"Wes, I can't just leave you here!" I looked down at his hand still holding onto my wrist.

He pulled me into another, tighter hug. "But you must. We both know that the kingdom must always come first."

The sun suddenly vanished as storm clouds filled the skies. I looked around in a state of shock as we were unexpectedly surrounded by something I had never seen before. They had horns on their beast-like heads and wings as they flew all around us. I quickly realized that it was not dark storm clouds above us but these creatures swarming the skies. They had a more humanoid upper body with human-like arms and hands that held weapons of their own. While their bottom halves were more animal with hooves as feet and long swift tails that whipped around them. Though they had the same red glowing eyes as the shadow demons we had faced before.

"You're not going anywhere," one of them hissed.

"They can speak?" Orion bawled as he and the others pulled out their weapons.

I shook my head trying to pull myself together before dropping the prophecy into my satchel and grabbing my sword.

"What the hell are these things?" Wesley wailed.

"We told you there were other things that plagued the Shadow Lands during the day," Ophiuchus roared as she began to fight them off.

"Go!" Wesley yelled as he gestured towards the barrier. "We will fend them off for you to escape."

"Are you kidding? I need to stay here and help you guys fight!"

"No! You must go, don't worry about me!"

"How could I not worry about you? I know I joke about being so strong but I need you! I can't do this without you!"

"I know you can." He smirked as we continued arguing while fighting off these new demons.

"What about you? I can't just leave you here!"

"I'll be fine, I know you'll come back for me." I froze as I watched him fight. "Amara!" He called out as he sliced through them to clear a path to me. I looked up to see one of them charging towards me with a club in each hand. My sword fumbled in my hands as I tried to ready myself. Wesley jumped in front of me taking the blow from both clubs with his sword before taking out a dagger and stabbing the demon in the chest.

"W-Wesley, you saved me," I cried as he gently held my face in hand, his thumb brushing the line of my jaw.

"Now go and save the rest of the kingdom, then come back and save me."

His lips crashed into mine. I wrapped my arms around him pulling him closer and deepening the kiss. His hand slid from my face into my hair. Heat rose from my stomach to my chest, the feeling of his body against mine like a black hole pulling me in like gravity, lost to his touch alone. His hands began to trail down my back, sending shivers everywhere he touched. They stopped as his fingers squeezed at my hips, pulling me even closer briefly before quickly pushing me through the barrier. It was too late once I realized what he had done.

"Wesley!" I shrieked, still somehow able to watch from outside the barrier as those creatures covered the three of them in darkness.

"You have to go, don't worry about me! I'll be here waiting for you, milady," Wesley's voice called from the swarm of darkness.

I scrambled to my feet as I readied my sword but none of the new demons had made it past the barrier and then, just like that, I was no longer able to see into the Shadow Lands. I looked up at the sky and could see the sun trying to peek through the clouds and treetops above. I was back in that decaying forest we had been in just before we entered the barrier.

"I will come back for you Wesley. I promise." I wiped the tears from my eyes once more and warily turned back the way we had come the day before.

Avery

I met with Ben in the corridor outside my room early that morning, even though I was running on next to no sleep. We made our way out to the garden and were met with a beautiful sunshining day. I wanted to meet earlier so that I could speak with Lawrence as soon as he returned from Coldoria.

We sat under the tree again and enjoyed the serene silence of the gorgeous garden. I was unable to focus on reading the book I had brought, I kept on reading the same line about five times before I finally gave up and let out a loud sigh.

Ben looked up from his notepad. "Is everything okay, Princess?"

"Yes, sorry I truly didn't mean to interrupt your writing. I just—I don't know. I guess I just have a lot on my mind and can't focus on this book." I sighed again. "Hey! I have an idea; do you have anything new you've written that you would like me to take a look at and we could discuss?"

"Trust me, whatever I have written would not come close to anything you're reading. If you cannot focus on that, there is no hope with mine," he teased.

"Don't say that! You're very talented, honestly. I just thought maybe the discussion part of your work would help distract me."

"Well, if it is just a discussion you are looking for we could talk about anything." He smiled.

"Ha, I suppose you're right."

"Would you like to talk about what is troubling you?" he asked.

Where the hell am I? Can't really ask him anything like that. Hmm I guess I could talk to him about that figure I kept seeing in that photo. But then I'd have to talk about said photo. Ugh.

He broke my inner babbling. "Or we could talk about something else."

"Did you have fun last night?" I asked.

"Yes, it was very nice of you to put something like that together for all of us still here at the castle. Thank you. I'm not quite sure if I had properly thanked you. It was the first time I was actually able to have fun at an event like that."

"What? Seriously?"

"Well, yes. It is my duty to protect you and I must always give you my full attention."

"I know it's your job to literally follow me around and protect me but you have to live your life too you know," I tried to reason with him.

"I live only to serve this kingdom and to protect you," he quickly added.

"Look around." I paused for a moment while we did just that. It was quiet and peaceful within the garden. The only other sounds were birds chirping and leaves blowing in the gentle breeze. "Do you see any danger?"

"Well, not right now but that is why I have to be prepared and ready for anything. Think of the whole reason we are here in the first place. We should be in Coldoria and yet we are back here." His face turned grim. "I failed you."

"You didn't fail me, you saved me." I placed a hand on his shoulder, attempting to cheer him up.

"No, you should not have even been taken in the first place. I have been doing a horrid job. I should be with you at all times and guarding your door when you are sleeping." He sat up straight as he proclaimed what sounded like an overly excessive new plan.

"That sounds like a bit much, when would you even sleep. Plus, I like to have my privacy."

"This is how it was supposed to have been from the start. With night and day shifts but I thought I could handle this on my own. You are so nice and treat me as though I am not just your attendant, but your friend."

"You are my friend."

"That is kind of you to say, but I must put your safety first and above all else," he insisted.

"Things really are different here," I muttered.

"Pardon me?"

"Oh—uh—nothing."

I guess I got used to the idea of him being more like a friend than some bodyguard. I do love spending time with him, but do I really want him around all the time? Seeing everything I do. I guess things are different here, sometimes I forget I'm just playing the part of a princess. It feels so natural being around everyone here sometimes I get lost in the role. It makes sense but I just thought twenty-four-hour surveillance in my own castle was a bit much. Maybe I'm getting a little too used to the people here. It feels like I've been here forever but really, it hasn't been that long at all.

Ben interrupted my inner monologue once again. "Lawrence and the others should be arriving soon. You mentioned you needed to speak with him as soon as he returned."

"Yes, walk me back to my room first? Not like you have a choice I guess." We laughed.

Pacing in front of Lawrence's study, I tried to collect my thoughts before knocking. *This is it; I am finally going to ask him everything. Perfect moment or not, I need answers. But what do I want to know? There's just so much that I don't know. I mean what do I even know about this place, really? Okay, just breathe Avery, you can do this!* I took one more deep breath before finally knocking on the door.

"Come in," his voice chimed.

I gulped as I slowly opened the door.

"Miss Avery," he said after I closed the door behind me without even looking up from his books, "What can I do for you?"

"Lawrence, I think it's time you finally tell me everything." I tried to sound regal and not too demanding.

"Ah, yes. I was wondering when you would come to me again for more answers. Please, sit." I walked over to the leather seat facing his desk and sat down. He put his books and papers down and looked me in the eyes as I sat. I hesitated for a moment wondering if I should ask him something or wait for him to start.

I opened my mouth to speak first but was interrupted as he began, "First, let me ask you something, Miss Avery."

"Okay." My face nervously squinted, confused as to what he could possibly want to ask me right now.

"Since you have arrived here in Soluna, have you felt anything different or strange?"

"What do you mean by that?" I asked.

"What I mean to say is have you felt yourself begin to change at all?"

Aside from this weird power I'm still trying to figure out how to use?

"I—I'm not sure," I stuttered.

"Has anything happened to you or have you seen anything you cannot quite explain? Something you might think is too unbelievable to be true?" he asked, looking as serious as he always did.

"What? You can read minds too?" I blurted before covering my mouth with both hands.

"Ahh, so it is the gift of telepathy that you possess."

"What? No! That's crazy! It was a joke, obviously. Ha-ha!"

"Miss Avery. Let me tell you a story. Long ago there lived two twin girls with astonishing powers. Some called them witches or sorceresses, some called them aliens, and some called them Celestials."

"Wait. Celestials? I've heard that before. The twins, one of them sacrificed herself to save her sister."

"Yes, how did you know that?" He looked shocked, which was surprising for his usual emotionless face.

"I had a dream about that. I thought it was just some weird crazy dream I had like all the others."

"What others?"

"I've had quite a few about a hooded figure named shadow-something."

"I believe these to have been more than just 'weird crazy dreams' Miss Avery. Magic is real here. At least it used to be. The celestial that sacrificed herself for her sister, part of her soul lives inside of both you and Princess Amara. We knew you would be the prophetic twins we have been waiting for and we knew you would each share extraordinary gifts."

"What does that even mean? Magic is real? We both would share gifts. Wait, does that mean that Amara—"

"Yes, Princess Amara has gifts as well. You are the only ones left with these gifts now."

"Why? You just said that magic was real here? Wherever here is," I muttered.

"Caelestia. A parallel world split into realms, much like the world you were raised in but magical. Magic has always lived here and so the Celestials came here and created Soluna within Caelestia. They created it for other celestials like yourself."

"Like me?" I laughed bitterly. "I'm no 'Celestial'. I'm just trying to figure out what I want to do with my life, my regular, ordinary, mundane life."

"You are anything but ordinary. Once we found out about the two of you being the prophetic twins your parents tried to keep it quiet. They told the people of Soluna that they had lost one of the twins during delivery and tried to hide that there were two of you from everyone except a select few trusted individuals." He paused for a moment before continuing, "It did not work. These dark shadows kept coming for you."

"You mean for us?" I grimly asked.

"No, you." His eyes shifted and he spun his chair around as his back was now towards me, he continued again, "Your parents gave you up to protect you."

"How would leaving me all alone protect me?" I scoffed.

"I brought you to the mundane world. A world where magic did not exist. The world you call home. We thought it would be best if the king and queen did not know exactly where you were as it would be hard for them to know and not go see you. However, I would check up on you to make sure you were safe."

"So that's how my mom knew you? You what? Just left me with her and would randomly check in to make sure no demons attacked us?" I couldn't hide my anger and frustration any longer.

"I knew the demons would not get to you there. Until recently which is why I came to get you. Your sister found out about you and asked me to find you. Of course, I already knew all about you and where to find you but I waited. I knew you were safe until that night when I came to get you and one of those shadow demons had been following you."

"So, I guess I wasn't so safe after all, huh?"

"Maybe it's best if you go take a breather and we can pick up with this conversation tomorrow." He suggested.

"No! I want to know everything, and I want to know now."

He let out a long exhale, "If that is what you would prefer then I will tell you the rest of the story." He swived back to face me again. "Calypso, the celestial twin that had survived, would speak to your mother in her dreams like it seems she does you. She had told the queen that this great evil was coming and gave her a protection spell to use on herself as she already knew that it could not touch Amara."

"Well, I guess it didn't work," I mumbled.

"No, because she did not use it on herself, she used it on me."

"What? Why?" My eyes sharpened like knives as I watched him.

"Because I was the only one who knew where you were. They killed everyone with the ability to use magic and altered the minds of everyone else. My memories remained intact due to the protection spell and because we do not possess the ability to wield magic, we could not use the spell on anyone else. I am the only one not only in Soluna, but all of Caelestia who remembers magic really exists and our true history."

CHAPTER EIGHTEEN

Amara

I had been walking around trying to retrace my steps back for who knew how long. I stopped and looked up to the sun. I was rather good at getting an estimated time by looking at where the sun was in the sky but unfortunately for me, the clouds and trees were still concealing most of it.

"I want to be out of this forest before nightfall. Those demons may have been able to follow after me through the barrier, and if not, those shadow demons might come back. I need to get out of here." I stopped again to look around for anything that might seem familiar.

"All these damn trees look the same!" I paused once more to look above. "Maybe if I climb one of these trees, I could get a better look at the sun's position and maybe even see a way out of this forest and back towards the cave that leads to the underground passageways."

I walked over to one of the largest looking trees I could find nearby. I took a deep breath and braced myself for what I was about to do. I leaped up grabbing hold of a sturdy branch with both hands. I struggled to pull myself up but finally managed. I sat straddling the branch with one leg on either side.

"Great, only about a hundred more to go." I reached up to the next sturdy branch that was about eye level and pulled myself up. Glad that this one was a lot easier and hoped the rest would be just as close together.

I was pleasantly surprised to find there were a lot more branches as I got higher up the tree. I took advantage of them and began to climb the tree with a lot more ease now that I had much better hand and foot placement options to climb.

My momentum began to slow once I was closer towards the top of the tree as fatigue washed over me. I stopped to catch my breath and give myself a small break before I attempted to climb the rest of the way. My grip felt like it could give at any moment. I reached around to the other side of the tree where a thicker branch hung and pulled myself over so I could straddle the branch and give my hands and arms a break as well.

Peering down below to check if I could see anything from my current height, all I could see were more trees and dirt. I drew in a long breath and held it for a moment before releasing and began to climb again, this time I was determined to make it to the top without stopping.

As I neared the top of the tree, I began to feel a warm breeze brush against my skin. The sun was still trying to peek through the clouds above though I was able to get a better idea of its placement. *It's late afternoon.*

I looked ahead in the direction I was traveling but could not see much other than the same old decaying trees. I squinted, trying to focus in on the area before me. Then I noticed a faint pink line in the distance.

"The pink flower trees!" I cheered. "Whoa!" I caught myself just in time as I began to wobble on the treetops. I clung to the tree trunk to steady myself. "I think I can definitely make it to the bright forest before nightfall if I can get back down and hurry."

I had my plan, now I just needed to follow it and hope I did not run into any snags along the way. I began to shimmy down the tree with even more ease than the way up. I did not take a single break and made it down in record time.

If Wesley were here, we would have made it into a competition. Who could have gotten up and back down the fastest? Definitely me, but I'm sure he would have given me a run for my money. A tear escaped my eye as I thought about my dearest friend and his fate. *Relax. Everything is going to be okay. I am going to make it back to the castle, save Avery and my people and then come right back and save Wesley. I must.*

I wiped my tears and started running towards the faint pink line I saw from above. As I made my way through the forest, darkness suddenly took over. *How could it have gotten so dark so fast? There is no way it could have been this late.*

Met with more darkness, I attempted to see anything beyond a few inches in front of me. The trees around me rustled, met with eerie whispers, quickly filled the air around me. I readied my sword and slowly rotated around in a circle as fog crept in, making it even more difficult to see more than a foot in front of me.

If only I had some light. That's it! Light! I need to get that bright magical light back from earlier, but how? How did I make it appear before? I just wanted it to and thought of warm happy thoughts. Think of Wesley.

I thought back to when things were so much simpler. When I did not have so much pressure to be perfect, to be something I am not. When I could just be who I wanted to be and not who I am obligated or needed to be.

Two years ago.

I climbed up the side of the stables to get onto the wooden support beams running along the inside ceiling. *This is a great place to scare him!* I took a deep breath as I held my arms out on either side of me to keep my balance as I walked across to the center of the beam. I straddled the beam as I waited for him to show up for today's training.

"Hello?" He called, walking into the almost empty barn. I watched as he looked around for me. "Mara, are you here? Hello?" I stifled a giggle as he continued to search for me. "I guess she isn't here yet." He shrugged and I waited until he stood directly under me.

"Guess again!" I yelled jumping off the beam and tackled him to the ground while he screamed in horror. "You're dead! And you're such a baby!" I laughed as I hoped up and offered him my hand.

"I'm not a baby, you're just crazy! Who does that?"

"It's called a surprise attack and you clearly weren't prepared." I teased.

"Prepared for what? My psychotic best friend to come flying out of the sky and attacking me? You're right, I would have never expected that," he complained.

I placed my hands on his shoulders and leaned in closer to him. "You have to expect the unexpected." I looked into his eyes for a brief moment.

He leaned in even closer and whispered in my ear, "Like this?" Before I even had the chance to process what he'd said he swiped my legs from under me, knocking me to the ground.

"Okay, now we're even." He laughed this time offering me a hand up that I gladly accepted.

"I knew I'd find you here playing in the mud like some sort of swine." Her voice dripped with disgust.

"Prudence." I spun around to face her as I mimicked her fake smile.

"Not only have you skipped your princess lessons yet again for today. We are now late for a meeting with the king and queen."

"How can I be late for a meeting I know nothing about?"

"If you bothered to attend your lessons, you would have known about this meeting."

"Let's make a run for it." I lowered my voice for Wesley's ears alone. Unfortunately for me, she must have had the hearing of a bat from hell.

"Do not even think about it. Now, follow me. We do not even have time for you to change first." She rolled her eyes and grabbed me by the wrist. I looked back at Wesley as he mockingly waved goodbye. I reached out and grabbed his waving hand and pulled him right along with me.

Present Day.

Avery

"So, hold on a second. There was magic in Coldoria and other places in this world too?" I asked.

"Yes, and everyone has had magic erased from their memories. We still have some magical items in our worlds of course. For example, that car I used to use to travel to the mundane world to get you. However, due to the spell that was cast people do not even question how these magical items work. I do try to limit the use of magical items until everyone can somehow regain their lost memories, but some things I cannot hide, especially in other kingdoms."

"Like flowers growing in the snow?" I asked.

"Yes, that would be quite magical I suppose." Lawrence's eyebrows furrowed.

Just like that garden in Coldoria, I thought before asking, "Is there any way to break this spell? I mean, there has to be, right?"

"I am sure there is, but we do not know how to break it. I am hoping that once Princess Amara finds the prophecy there may be a clue or something in it to help us break it. That and prove that she is the true heir. That you both are."

"I'm not interested in becoming a queen, Lawrence. Amara can have the throne all to herself like she has always wanted."

"That is not something she has always wanted and that is yet another reason why it is so important for her to find this prophecy. She never wanted to be queen either and many people believe she is not fit to rule because of her past."

"What past? You mean Miss Perfect Princess wasn't always so perfect?" I laughed at the thought of how much she could have changed. She was a princess after all, aren't they supposed to be prim and proper?

"She was not always this way, Miss Avery. She used to be such a free spirit and full of life. She wanted nothing to do with being queen or a princess for that matter. She wanted to work for the royal guard, actually." He smiled slightly to himself as he must have been thinking back to a much younger and different Amara than I imagined her to be.

"She would always say, 'If I have to be a princess then I will be a warrior princess!'" His smile was gone just as quickly as it had appeared. "That all changed once your parents died. She was forced to grow up fast. I stepped in as regent and helped as best I could but something in her had changed. She stopped letting many people in and her once carefree ways were gone. She devoted herself to being the perfect crown princess that you thought her to be. Afraid to make any mistakes and tarnish your parent's great legacy.

"It was difficult for her. Everyone had an opinion on what she should be like. How she should act, dress, who she should and should not associate with, whether she was fit to rule. She put on a great act, but there were still a select few of us that knew deep down, she just wanted to be that carefree girl once more. Sometimes she would show that side to those of us she was still closest to but as I mentioned she had closed herself off to so many. She puts up a good front, but I know that the things people say and what they think bother her and I too wish she could just be that free spirit she once was."

Wow, I can't even imagine. She hides it well." *Not that I really even know her, I've only met her once and it was very brief, but I wouldn't have guessed.*

"I think that is enough for today, Miss Avery. If you have any other questions, we can revisit this topic another time," Lawrence said.

"It's fine. Thank you for telling me all of this." I smiled before leaving the room.

Damnit! I forgot to bring up that picture. Oh well, I guess it would be better if I were to bring it anyway. And it's not like I have seen any weird shadows since we've been back or on that photo again. Maybe the thing in the dungeon is getting to me and I just imagined it on the photo. I hadn't been looking where I was going but somehow managed to make it back to my room in one piece.

CHAPTER NINTEEN

Amara

Two years ago

We entered the throne room where my parents were expecting me. As usual, I was instead greeted by Lawrence. Prudence finally released my wrist as she curtsied to the Royal Advisor.

"I am so sorry, Princess, but the king and queen could not wait any longer. They have instead left me to explain."

"This is why you should never skip your lessons." Prudence glared at me but I just ignored her and spoke to Lawrence directly.

"Explain what?" I asked.

"Well—"

Before Lawrence could even start his explanation three people entered the throne room from the only other entrance. The eldest male and the only woman, both wore crowns. All were dressed in black, burgundy, and gold lavish attire. The youngest man, who looked like he could not be more than twenty years old, avoided eye contact with everyone in the room as he scowled to himself. Prudence and Lawrence both bowed immediately after they approached us. Wesley and I shared a confused look but followed in their lead.

"King Alexander and Queen Desiree of Coldoria, welcome to the Kingdom of Soluna. We are so pleased to have you here. And of course, Prince Alexander," Lawrence greeted them.

"We will be looking around the castle to ensure this is a good fit for Coldoria. Prince Alexander, you stay here and get yourself acquainted." The king left just as quickly as they arrived.

"Prince Alexander, is there anything we can get you?" Prudence chimed in.

"Xander," he muttered.

"I beg your pardon?"

"Please call me Prince Xander," he responded, still refusing to make any eye contact.

"That's nice, why is he here?" I asked Lawrence, still waiting for my explanation on all of this.

"Princess Amara, please forgive me. The king and queen believe it best for you to marry someone of nobility."

"Marry? I'm too young to get married!" I insisted.

"Yes, they would like you to start your courtship immediately and after your twenty-first birthday you shall be wed." Lawrence's gaze waivered.

"You can't be serious! I don't want to marry some guy I don't know! I want to marry for love!"

"Ha," Prince Xander scoffed.

"Excuse me?"

"True love doesn't exist." He spoke and I glared at him as our eyes finally met for the first time. It was loathe at first sight.

"So instead of marrying for love, I'm being forced to marry someone who doesn't even believe in it? I don't want to be in a loveless marriage! I've heard the stories about King Alexander, he has more mistresses than brain cells." I heard Wesley chuckle from behind me and I struggled to hide my own.

"I do not believe in love, but I am not my father," Prince Xander blurted.

"Oh please, you even have the same name. Prince *Alexander.*"

His face wrinkled as if in disgust. "Oh? And you think I have not heard all the stories of the wild, rebellious princess of Soluna? No wonder you want to find love since your parents do not even love you."

"You know nothing about me or my parents!" I snapped.

"Neither do you, Princess. You're just some immature child rebelling against her parents to get their attention."

"Well, you're a-a—"

"A what?"

"I don't know! I just know I will *never* marry you!" I stormed off and Wesley was not far behind me.

"Ugh! Can you believe that guy?"

"Well, uh, actually," Wesley stammered.

"We hate him!"

"Okay, we hate him. But relax, it'll be okay." Wesley tried to calm me down as he took my hand in his.

"They just expect me to marry some random prince for our kingdoms. Just like that? I want to marry someone because I love them, because of the way they make me feel, because—" I stopped as my hand, along with the rest of my body suddenly became very warm. *Because of how one simple touch can make me feel.* I looked into Wesley's eyes, my gaze slowly lowered to his beautiful smile.

"There. Feel better now?" He smirked.

"Much." I smiled. "Besides, I refuse to marry him. What are they going to do, drag me down the aisle?" I laughed. "I won't even let it get that far; I will do anything to stop this arrangement."

"Forget about him and this silly arrangement." He paused for a moment. "Come on, I have the perfect idea to cheer you up!" He playfully pushed me then started running.

"What are you doing?" I called out to him.

"You best keep up!" He laughed and I chased after him instantly.

He was fast, but I was faster. I consciously stayed a few paces behind him to make him feel better, even though he was only doing this to make me feel better. We ended up back at the stables.

"The stables, really? This is supposed to cheer me up?"

"Hang on!" he said right before charging towards one of the exterior walls. He jumped and pushed himself up as he used a windowsill to climb up onto the roof.

"Are you mad?" I asked.

"No seriously, hurry! We don't have much time," he said as he held out a hand to help hoist me up. We slowly and carefully climbed to the top of the roof.

"Okay, so what's the surprise?" I asked. "And I already had one big surprise today so I don't know how you can top that."

"Just look," he whispered and sat down, looking out at the horizon.

"It-it's beautiful."

"Isn't it?"

I sat down next to Wesley and laid my head on his shoulder. He wrapped one arm around me while we watched the sun set and the sky change from different shades of pink, yellow, and orange.

Avery

Present day.

I made my way down the corridor after leaving Lawrence's office and soon came face to face with Xander and Hazel.

"There you are!" Hazel cheered. "I've been looking everywhere for you!"

"Here I am." I laughed awkwardly for a second before looking back over at Xander. "Hi, Xander."

"Hi, Amara." He responded with a soft smile.

"There's no way you guys aren't—" Hazel started but was quickly interjected.

"Aren't hungry. I'm hungry, what about you?" Xander bumped into Hazel as he spoke, and I gave them both a questioning look. I focused on Xander. *"Shut up, Hazel, why do I even tell her anything? She better not make things weird or awkward."*

"Right, no way you guys aren't hungry. But I just ate so I'll leave you two alone to go eat. Alone. Just the two of you." Hazel grinned at Xander.

"Okay, well bye!" Xander nearly pushed Hazel away as she started off back down the corridor. *I swear I'm never telling her anything ever again."*

"Wait!" I called back to her.

"Yes?"

"Didn't you say you were looking for me?" I asked.

"Yes, well, I just hadn't seen you since last night. We'll catch up later." She winked, then left.

"That was weird," I mumbled. *And what did Xander tell her?*

"Hazel is a weird one, what can I say?" Xander answered. "So, are you hungry?"

"I guess, I could eat."

"Great. I'll pick you up in an hour."

"An hour?"

"It'll be worth it trust me; I'll see you soon!" He ran off before even giving me a chance to get another word in.

Well, that was weird. Must run in the family. Or maybe he doesn't even want to have a truce anymore let alone be friends. He probably just used 'see you in an hour' so he can make up an excuse to get out of it.

Back to my room I figured I had time to kill and decided I might as well get ready. After having one of the fastest showers of my life, not washing my hair because it would not have had enough time to dry and style it I made my way over to the vanity. I reapplied my makeup and re-curled my hair before heading to the closet. *What should I wear? Are we just going down to the* kitchen? *I mean where else would we go? Still, I am supposed to be a princess. I might as well dress the part, right?*

After trying on multiple outfits and shoes, I realized I only had ten minutes left before he said he would have been there. Deciding on an off the shoulder sheer mint dress, I snatched it off the hanger and stepped into it just as a knock sounded at the door.

"Just a minute!" I yelled. *Crap, he's a little early. Okay I just have to zip this up. It's fine.* I tugged at the zipper but only managed to get it about halfway up my back. *You have got to be kidding me! Should I change into something else? I mean, maybe a dress is a little too much?*

"Are you okay? Do you need more time? I can come back." Xander called from the other side of the door.

"It's fine, I just can't get my zipper up all the way."

There was an awkward silence for a moment. *Ah hell. Why did I tell him that?*

"Do—uh—do you want my help?" He faltered.

"S-sure." I walked over to the door, let out a deep but quiet breath and opened the door.

"Wow."

"Thanks." My shoulders tightened as my chest rose and fell with rapid breaths.

"Pardon?"

Right. He didn't actually say that.

"Thank you for offering to help me." I quickly turned to face away from him before he could see my face turn any pinker than I imagined it already was. I chewed on my bottom lip, hoping that would help stop anymore stupid comments from leaving them.

"You're hair. It-it's kind of in the way," he said before clearing his throat.

"Oh, sorry." I brushed then held my hair up with one arm as he slowly zipped up my dress.

"All done."

"Great. Thank you, again," I said then turned to face him.

"Anytime." He smiled. *"Why did I say that? That must have sounded so creepy. Hey, call me anytime you need help putting on your clothes."*

I laughed at the realization that he sounded just about as embarrassed as I felt.

"Are you ready to go then?" he asked.

"Yes, after you."

Instead, he opened and held the door open for me. We walked side by side down the corridor and down the stairs. I started to veer left but he had turned the opposite way.

"What are you doing? The kitchen is this way." I gestured with my thumb in the direction.

"We aren't going to the kitchen or the dining hall. Come on, before anyone sees us." He took my hand and we rushed out the door.

There were guards all around the courtyard. Xander leaned up against the doors and pressed his finger to his lips.

"Where are we going?" I whispered.

"It's a surprise." His signature smirk was back.

Just then, I saw Hazel walk over towards the guards and trip. One of the guards caught her just in time before she actually fell. All eyes were on her.

"Come on!" He took my hand again and we dashed past them and out the gates.

This is crazy! What if we get caught?

"I figured we could use another night out. It's been a while." He didn't let go of my hand even after we stopped running and made it past the guards.

We headed down a short, simple path. The sun had already set, the moon glimmered as the stars glistened around it. I just stopped and stood there taking it in. I held my head up and closed my eyes and felt as though it were recharging me. I opened my eyes and smiled wide, not a care or worry insight.

CHAPTER TWENTY

Avery

We made our way to the village. It was a lot less crowded than I'd have thought it would have been for the time of evening. But that was probably a good thing. People kept their distance, not many even looked in our direction or paid us any attention. There were a few that I would catch giving us a quick glance but that was it.

I was surprised at how much they must have respected me, or rather who I was pretending to be to keep their distance and give us privacy. If this were back home, there would have been paparazzi everywhere if a queen and king to-be were out roaming the town.

I leaned in closer to Xander and whispered, "I'm glad that no one is paying much attention to us."

"That's probably because they don't even recognize us. Especially you."

"What do you mean, especially me? It's my kingdom, isn't it?" I realized I probably shouldn't have asked as Amara would have already known but it was too late at this point.

"I'm not sure to be honest. Even before we met, I had never seen what you looked like before. You should really be the one telling me." He laughed. "You're the one that hides your appearance." He paused again briefly. "What else are you hiding?" he asked as his smirk tugged at the corners of his mouth.

"Me? Hiding something? Of course not!"

He laughed again. "I'm kidding. It is not that uncommon for villagers outside of the castle walls to not be able to recognize you. It's a common practice for safety reasons."

"Right," I agreed as if I had a clue.

"Come on, it's this way!" He grabbed my hand and led me further down into the streets of the village.

I was glad he was able to navigate throughout the village, I couldn't remember a thing from my one night down here with Hazel before we ran into him and his friends.

"Here it is!" He smiled and made his way to the door of some regal restaurant.

I followed closely behind him. When we reached the door there was a gentleman standing there opening the door for us. *Is that his job? To just open doors for people coming and going out of the restaurant?*

There was a woman standing inside the door waiting to greet us as well. Xander went up and spoke to her, but I couldn't quite hear what was said. She smiled and then escorted us to a table. The place was not terribly busy, there were four other couples occupying the other tables. Once we reached the table Xander pulled out a chair for me to sit. The lady handed us some menus then lit the candles at the center of our table.

The restaurant was very similar to the type of extravagant ones we would have back home, not like I would have ever actually gone to one unless I was on a date with some guy who was trying to impress me. *Wait a second, is this a date?* I glanced around at the other couples, most seemed intimate, sitting close together, gazing lovingly into one another's eyes, holding hands from across the tables.

This can't be a date. We said we were hungry and going to get food. He is a prince after all, he's probably used to these types of restaurants. I peeked over my menu I was pretending to read at Xander to see what his facial expressions were like, or to see if I could hear his thoughts. Nothing. He looked completely unphased by this place. *Like I thought, he probably goes to places like this all the time.* I exhaled a sigh of relief and began actually reading the menu.

A third person came over to take our orders. They took my order first and I watched and smiled as Xander placed his. He handed the menus to them and then looked back at me.

"What?" He laughed.

'What do you mean?" I asked.

"You were just—never mind." He grabbed his glass, awkwardly shifting his eyes to the side. My face began to flush as I realized I'd still been staring at him with some goofy grin on my face.

How embarrassing.

"What should I say? Am I making things even weirder between us?"

I looked back over at him, and our eyes met.

So, do you like cheese? Is what came to mind after I heard his thoughts and I couldn't help but laugh.

"I love when she laughs." He smiled briefly. *"Oh no, is she laughing at me? Do I have something in my teeth?"* He placed

254

his hand over his mouth nonchalantly and I could see him smiling back with his eyes.

"Sorry, I was just thinking about something else."

"Does she not want to be here?"

"No, it's nothing. I just—" Then I remembered he didn't actually ask me that question. "I-I'm just nervous."

"Why?" he asked. *"Does she think this is a date?"*

So, it's not a date. I felt a sinking feeling in the pit of my stomach. *Did I want it to be?* "Oh, like I said, it's nothing. I just haven't been out in a while. Oh look! Here comes our food! Yum yum yum!" I rambled. *Yum yum yum? What the hell am I saying?*

Our food was placed in front of us by our waiter. "Enjoy."

"Thank you," Xander and I both said in unison. We looked from the waiter to each other and my cheeks started to warm again. I smiled slightly and then looked down at my plate as I began to pick at it.

Of course, this isn't a date. We are barely even friends. He 'hated' me not too long ago.

I casually glanced back at him again and noticed he was staring a little too intensely at another couple a few tables down from us.

"Do they look familiar to you?" he whispered as he jerked his head in their direction.

I looked over at the couple but couldn't get a good look at their faces as they had books covering them. Not menus, books. They were peering over their books at us. Once our eyes met, they pulled their books over their faces again covering their eyes.

"That was creepy," I said as I looked back at Xander.

"Yes, it was." He waved the waiter over and whispered something to them. The waiter nodded quickly and then left.

"Are you ready?" he asked.

"For what?"

"This!" He practically pulled me out of my chair and raced towards the door. Before I knew it, we were already outside, I looked back at the couple as we dashed past the window. They had already jumped up and were making their way to the exit. The waiter that Xander had spoken to was conveniently blocking their way out.

"Who are those people? What's going on?" I stopped and gasped as I attempted to catch my breath.

"I don't know but I don't really want to stick around and find out either." He began running again but stopped when he realized I didn't immediately follow.

"I don't think I can keep running like this." I continued my heavy breathing as I thought about how out of shape I must have been.

"Do you need me to carry you?" he asked as he made his way back towards me.

"What? Carry me? That's a little much don't you think?"

"Not really. I'm just trying to keep you safe."

"Oh. Well, thanks but I'll be fine."

"They're coming this way! Quick!" He shoved me into a dimly lit alleyway.

Wedged in between Xander and a cold stone wall, we stood so close together I felt the warmth radiating off of him. I looked up into his eyes. He had his one arm leaning against the wall around me and the other brought up to his face. His finger was pressed against his lips, warning me to keep quiet while he kept his eyes on the street we'd just come from.

"I think—" I started but was quickly cut off by Xander. His eyes shot down into mine as he towered over me, he had moved his finger from his lips to mine.

He leaned in closer and whispered, "I hear someone coming."

I gulped and nodded.

A shadow figure appeared from around the corner slowly making its way to where we were hiding. My hands grabbed hold onto Xander's shirt as if on instinct, pulling him even closer than before, his chest pressed against mine.

The shadow was nearing, then I saw it. The same type of demonic creature that attacked me in the dungeons and invaded my recent dreams. It creeped around the corner, slowly inching its way closer towards us. I froze. Xander looked from the creature and back to me.

"Stay behind me!" he roared then intently looked around us. "I can't find anything to fight it off with. You need to get out of here!"

"What? What about you?" I cried.

"I'll be fine, just run!" he shouted without even looking back at me.

"It won't matter, we both need to run. You can't make any physical attacks against these things!" He looked further down the alley way and his eyes widened. I followed his gaze. There were more of them, they quickly surrounded us.

I heard footsteps from the street, they were getting louder and faster as if they came our way. Ben and Hazel came running around the corner, now standing behind these demons. I could see Ben and Hazel well through these demons, like they were nothing more than smoke or fog around us.

"What *are* those things?" Hazel cried.

Ben ignored her. "We need to find something to fight them off with."

"Because physical attacks don't harm them, remember?"

The demons paid no attention to Ben or Hazel and continued inching closer towards us.

"Here!" Ben called as he threw a large stick to Xander. He immediately caught it and started swinging at the demons but again, it did not make any contact with them.

"What do we do?" Hazel asked desperately.

Ben fiddled inside his pockets before pulling something out. It was small and I could not make out what it was. He threw it to Xander. A match. Xander watched as Ben picked up another large stick and match and lit the top of the stick to make a torch then followed Ben's lead.

"Good thinking!"

They started waving the torches at the demons and they vanished as soon as the fire was close enough to them.

"What-what just happened?" I asked

"I had a thought. They are like shadows or something. No physical attack has worked and they only appear in the dark. What gets rid of shadows and darkness better than light?" Ben explained. "So ever since the incident in the dungeons I've been carrying around matches in my jacket."

"That's genius!"

"Wait a second," Hazel interjected. "You guys have faced these things before?"

"Yes, one attacked Amara. That's why we left Coldoria so suddenly. Wait a second, where did you guys even come from? Not that I'm not grateful for the save." Xander shot them a confused look. "Don't tell me you guys were the ones in the restaurant!"

"What? Us at a restaurant? Of course not!" Hazel had a devilish grin painted on her face. "Okay, okay! I wanted to see how your date went."

"Date? It wasn't a date," I insisted.

"Forgive me princess but I had to come. It is my job to protect you after all," Ben stated.

"It's fine. Let's just go home."

We all started back except for Xander. I turned back to see him still standing there with the now unlit torch in hand.

"Are you all right?" I asked as I walked back towards him while Ben and Hazel waited several feet ahead of us.

"I-I just can't believe this. I know you told me about this before but hearing it and seeing it are two different things."

"I know. Thank you." I smiled softly.

"For what?"

"Saving me."

"But I didn't really. It was all Brett. I wouldn't have been able to do anything without his help tonight."

"Ben," I emphasized his name, "was a great help and I'm glad they showed up. But even before they did you tried to save me. You told me to run and leave you here. You didn't have to."

"Of course, I did!"

"Why? We both could have ran. We were just about to try before more showed up."

"I needed you to leave. They are clearly after you and I wouldn't have been able to forgive myself if something happened to you."

"Right. Because of how would that make you look."

"No," he whispered as our eyes slowly met.

"Are you guys coming or what?" Hazel shouted from the street.

Xander exhaled loudly. "Yeah, we're coming."

CHAPTER TWENTY-ONE

Amara

Frantically gasping for air, my eyes shot open and darted around as they tried to take in their surroundings. Treetops, grey skies, and shadow demons, hundreds of them, all around me. A faint golden glow was the only thing keeping those things from reaching me, like a barrier. I was levitating within a sphere of pure light. A light that radiated off of me. The forest beyond the barrier grew darker and more decayed. *I need to get out of here.*

The demons kept their distance, it seemed as though they were unable to penetrate my barrier. A familiar warmth seemed to touch every inch of my body just as a demon loomed closer.

The same light that radiated off me seemed to tear through the demon from the inside out. It exploded as the golden light burst out of them, leaving them as nothing more than ash and dust blowing away with the wind.

The radius of the barrier was slowly shrinking. *I don't know how or why this barrier is protecting me, but I need to get away quick. I don't know how much longer it will stay up. Wait a second, why haven't I ever thought of this before? I can move stuff with my mind! Why have I never tried levitating myself? I can make myself fly!*

The faint pink line in the distance called to me. As I started to make my way towards it, my movements became erratic.

Screams burned my throat as I plummeted. *Concentrate!* I closed my eyes and took in a sharp breath while I continued tumbling through the skies. Exhaling, I opened my eyes. *I can do this, I can fly.* Three feet from the ground I froze. I let out a nervous laugh as I dangled in the air so close to the ground."

Swooping back into the air my laughter became almost moronic. "I can't believe it! I'm actually flying!" Whipping and swirling around in the sky, I finally made my way back up to the treetops so I could get a better view.

The golden glow around me stopped shrinking as well. *I must be getting a lot stronger than I was before. I never knew I could do anything other than move a few smaller objects around. Then again, I never tried.*

I made it to the pink forest in what seemed like no time at all. *This can really save me time! This is so much faster than travelling on foot, or by horse! Oh no, the horses! I hope they are okay!* From there I could see what looked like the safe house far off in the distance. *I could go straight there and settle in for the night then make my way back to Estrella in the morning!*

The sun shone on me through the window, it's warmth all consuming and familiar. It was somehow already morning. I managed to sleep through the night at the safehouse alone. I went downstairs hoping that that would not be the case, that I had dreamt everything and when I got downstairs, I would see Wesley's goofy grin looking back at me, but I did not. I was completely alone. Even the horses were gone when I arrived last night. And worst of all, Wesley and all those other people were still trapped in the Shadow Lands.

As soon as I stepped outside the sun warmed my skin once again and I heard a familiar voice, much like my own, whisper in my ear. "Trust your instincts. Trust nothing, and no one else."

Whirling around to find the source of the familiar voice, I found nothing. I was still alone. *Where had that voice come from? Had I imagined it?* Glad that I had gotten a good night's sleep, I knew I needed all the energy I could get. Closing my eyes, I thought about what I wanted to happen.

You can fly.

Before I even opened my eyes again, my feet dangled above the ground. The corners of my mouth tugged and I could not help but to smile. Flying higher and higher I passed the tree tops, the roof of the safehouse. I soared with the birds and danced and twirled around in the free open air. Then headed north-bound back to Estrella.

Avery

I had woken up earlier that day and met with Ben in the garden. If I was being completely honest, I was hoping to run into Xander there. It had been a few days since our not a date—date and I couldn't tell if he was avoiding me or if I was the one doing the avoiding. *I'm being ridiculous. What would I be avoiding him for anyway?*

I let out a sigh as I reread the page I was on in my book since I hadn't really been paying attention to what I was reading the first time around.

Voices came from the hedge maze and my eyes instantly shot to the exit hoping it would be him. But it was not.

Chaz and Vivian exited the maze together and her cackle echoed in my ears. *What could have been so funny? I don't believe Chaz has a funny bone in his body.*

"The duke and duchess of Caelia are back unfortunately." Ben barely breathed the last word as I stifled a laugh.

"Where were they?" I asked after realizing I probably should have already known.

"Back in Caelia. They were there for a while before and after the Coldoria festival. It is where they live after all. But you know them, they like to stay here as much as they can hoping that they can one day live here instead."

As king and queen. I won't let that happen.

"But don't worry, that could never happen." Ben smiled at me before diving back into his notebook.

I got up from under the tree we were sitting under and walked straight towards Chaz and Vivian with no actual plan as to what I was going to say or do.

Chaz noticed me first and I could see his eyes practically rolling out of his head as I reached them. Vivian turned and furrowed her brows as she looked at me.

"Why are you here?" I demanded.

"We had to be here for tonight," Chaz replied while his eyes narrowed into slits.

Oh great, was there some other party or ball going on tonight that I didn't know about?

Before I could reply, dark clouds filled the sky out of nowhere. Thunder and lightning rippled through the sky. Heavy rain began to pour around us.

Vivian yelled, "My hair!" She ran towards the castle doors to take cover, the rest of us followed close behind.

We all managed to make it inside without getting too drenched, although Vivian would have disagreed. She was still pouting about her hair as she ordered some staff and guards to get the rest of her things and she marched up the stairs to her quarters.

I waited a few minutes, so I wasn't too close behind her before I followed up the stairs but headed towards my room which was luckily in another wing of the castle.

Finally making it back to my room after a slight detour to the kitchen, I practically harassed the staff until I could find something to snack on. *What I'd give for a big bowl of buttery popcorn and a movie night right about now.* I sighed.

I went to turn the handle, but the door was already open. *Was someone in here?* The lights were still out. I turned on the lights and looked around the empty room.

"Hello? Is anyone in here? Ben?" I called out in case this was someone's idea of a joke.

The lights in the room and hall flickered before completely going out.

"H-hello?" I called again. *This is how horror movies begin.* I gulped. *Not the kind of movie night I was hoping for.*

I ran back to the main corridor where they had torches lit. At least it wasn't pitch black there. I slowly walked down the long hall but there wasn't a single other person. No staff members, no other lords or ladies. I decided to sit down under one of the torches at least I'd be able to see and be close to fire or a light source if one of those creatures decided it wanted to come back for me again.

I need to keep my mind off of those things and this black out. Besides, I'm sure it's just the weather. My mind instantly went to Xander and how much I wished he were there with me. How he tried to save me from those things even though he had no idea what they were. And most importantly how he just believed me about them back in Coldoria without even seeing one first.

Am I actually falling for him? This is crazy even if I do have strong feelings for him now, it doesn't matter. It can't. He thinks I'm someone else. I'm going to have to eventually leave this place and go back to my simple, boring life. He couldn't trust me either and why would he. The person he thinks I am, had betrayed him. I feel so guilty when I'm with him, I just want to shout 'It wasn't me!' That's probably why I'd been avoiding him, even though I didn't want to admit it at the time.

CHAPTER TWENTY-TWO

Amara

I opened the door without even knocking. I did not have any time to waste, and I knew he would be in there. When I opened the door, he was sitting alone at his desk going over all his paperwork. He looked up at me as if he had to do a double take when he noticed it was really me.

"Princess Amara, is that really you?" Lawrence asked as he jumped out of his seat.

"It is. And I have so much I need to tell you."

"Did anyone see you? Your sister is around the castle and the secret may get you."

"I did run into someone, but it should be fine. I doubt they would have noticed a difference."

"Please, sit." He had walked around to the other side of his desk and pulled out the other leather chair for me to sit. I did and he made his way back over to his. I waited for him to sit back down before I started.

"I do not even know where to begin." I took a long deep breath and then exhaled as I thought of where to start. "Well, Wesley and I made it to the Shadow Lands, this place where many people still have powers. There were actual Celestials there Lawrence!" I watched as complete shock washed over his face. "Before we arrived however, we found some strange temple underneath the safehouse, and it lit up with gold light once I touched the altar. Wesley and I both shared the same vision from the past."

I continued to tell Lawrence everything. About the dreams I had, to the demons we faced both in and outside of the barrier to the Shadow Lands, to Wesley and so many others being trapped there.

"But I did manage to get the prophecy," I finished.

"What? Why did you not start with that? That is amazing. Your parents would be proud."

"There was just too much to tell. I told you I did not know where to start." I laughed.

"I still cannot believe you are back, after all this time!" Lawrence tried to hide it though I swear I saw tears forming in his eyes.

"You are going soft on me. It has not been that long. Two weeks tops."

"Miss Amara." He paused.

"What is it?" I asked not knowing if I even wanted the answer.

"It has been over a month since you have left."

"What? It could not possibly have been that long! It did take us some time to get to the Shadow Lands, but I was only there for one night and then I flew back here in less than two."

"Perhaps time moves differently within the barrier. Most of those people would have been trapped for hundreds of years. The person behind this. This Shadow Lord you mentioned, may have altered time and reality within the barrier."

"That's great!" I blurted but Lawrence shot me a confused expression. "If time moves slower within the barrier, I could take more time out here fixing things and it would be as if no time has passed for Wesley!"

"True, assuming our theory is correct."

"I also should have mentioned, Calypso revealed to me the name of this evil half of her that had split. Esmeray. I believe she must be working with Shadow Lord and I don't know how many others. Why else would Calypso have shown me that unless it meant something."

"Perhaps you are right again. We do not know much about this great evil other than what Calypso has told us." Lawrence turned back to his paperwork as if there would be something in there that would be able to help us.

"She told me Avery is in trouble."

"Yes, it seems she has been having the same dreams you have had about this Shadow Lord. She has also been attacked by these things you refer to as shadow demons, on several occasions now."

"I am afraid that the other demons that were inside the barrier may somehow break free. The shadow demons are nothing compared to them. I just hope that this time difference theory is correct." I paused to stifle my tears. "It may be Wesley's only hope."

"You have to think about the positive for now. You have the prophecy, your powers seem to be getting stronger, and you are back here, safe." He smiled softly.

"About my powers getting stronger. I managed to put up a protective barrier, similar to the one I mentioned around the Shadow Lands. But this one is pure light. No demons or darkness should be able to penetrate it. Nothing and no one should be able to get in or out unless I say it so." I smiled proudly at my growing abilities.

Out of nowhere all the lights flickered and then went out completely. I looked to Lawrence but could no longer see him due to the sudden darkness, the room was pitch black.

"Do not panic," said Lawrence. Just as suddenly as the power went out, he had found a candle and lit it, placing it on the table between us. He frowned. "This does not bode well."

Trust your instincts. And nothing and no one else. Echoed in my mind. *I know I can trust Lawrence, he's the only one I know I can.*

"Oh, no," I whispered under my breath as my shoulders slumped.

"What is it? Are you hurt?" His voice was shaky with panic.

"No. It's just... I was given a warning before I came here and I did not think too much of it until now. Just as the power went out the same warning flashed in my mind and I had a thought."

"Go on." He sat back down in his leather arm chair, waiting for me to continue as he tapped a finger on his desk.

"What if I was too late?" My hands trembled as I rubbed my temples.

"What do you mean? I am sure Wesley will be fine. We will have to deal with this and then we can send the royal guard with you to save him and everyone else there." Lawrence's voice was calmer but as he fidgeted with his tie, I knew he was more concerned and frightened than he let on.

"That's not what I meant." My eyes met his again as I continued, "What if I was too late getting here. My barrier cannot let anyone in or out. What if that doesn't matter because someone here is already working with Shadow Lord or Esmeray."

Lawrence's eyes grew wider. "We need to find Avery immediately. No one can know that the both of you are here let alone exist." Lawrence ran to his coat rack and grabbed a cloak and tossed it to me. I threw it on, and we ran out the door to find Avery.

As soon as we walked out the door, a loud scream echoed from the main corridor.

Avery

That's it! I need to find Xander. I can't tell him who I am, or can I? I feel like I can tell him anything. But not this! Can I? I roamed around the corridor trying to avoid any spots that were too dark while I had a full-on debate inside my head. *What is wrong with me?*

A gust of wind swirled around me and the rest of the corridor. *What the heck? Did a window fly open from the storm?* I tried to look but had to shield my eyes with my arm from the strong wind.

Then just like that, the wind was gone and so were all the lit lanterns except for one. On the far end of the corridor was a single lit lantern. And in between me and the lantern, was one of those horrible creatures.

It hissed and loomed closer. I looked around wondering why I didn't start carrying around matches like Ben suggested.

It somehow disappeared and reappeared directly in front of me. Squeezing my eyes shut, I held out my arms and screamed in horror. It grabbed my arm and threw me against the wall.

Pain rippled through my back where I hit the wall and landed.

"It-it can touch me?" I cried as it crept towards me again. I tried to make a run for the torch on the other side of the corridor when a stinging sensation shot through my back once more. Wincing in pain, I tried again just as another demon materialized in front of me. The two of them slowly slithered towards me, backing me against the wall.

"Amara," Ben's voice sang from the far side of the corridor.

I looked over to see both Ben and Xander. Xander ripped down the lit torch while Ben grabbed another. Xander lit Ben's and they came charging.

"It actually touched me! I think they are getting stronger somehow!" I cried, still holding on to my back as the pain worsened.

Ben unsheathed his sword, attacking the demons with both steel and fire. Darkness engulfed me as the sound of shrieks echoed.

The shrieks were soon replaced with low voices whispering for me to follow them into the darkness.

A warm body held me and I reached out, opening my eyes. It was Xander. He held me tightly in his arms.

"You're going to be okay!" he muttered over and over again as he held me.

"Xander." I breathed as I leaned in closer to his hold.

"Ben, do you think I could have a minute alone with her?"

"Of course, but I will not be too far." He said as I finally opened my eyes.

Xander helped me up and waited until Ben must have been out of ear shot before he started. "I need to apologize," he said and I realized he was still holding me when I became very warm. I instantly pulled myself away and looked at my feet. I couldn't meet his gaze.

"For what? Saving my life, again." I tried to make a joke of it but I still worried.

"No, and you're welcome by the way." I glanced up to see him smile lazily and I wished I could jump right back into his arms without turning as red as a tomato. He continued, "For earlier."

"What are you talking about?" I asked, genuinely confused by what he meant.

"I didn't mean to upset you or anything. I don't know what I did but whatever it was, I'm sorry."

"I'm not mad," I blurted before he could actually give me his apology. He must have been going over this in his head. "I don't know what you're talking about, but really I'm not mad about anything." I gently brushed his hand with mine in an attempt to reassure him before quickly stopping myself and dropping my hand back to my side.

"I don't know, maybe I should have sent you a letter or something after our dinner. I know I definitely should have gone and seen you at some point before now after our date. But I wanted to give you space after what happened. I thought you'd come to me if you needed me." He took a step back as if he still believed that I needed space.

Did he just call it a date?

"I need you." *There my mouth goes again without thinking.* "Um, what I meant to say is that I needed you. I needed you, as in past tense." *Great save.* "I didn't want to be alone. I guess I just didn't know what I wanted." But I knew then, I knew what I wanted and for once I wanted to just do what I *wanted.* I took a step closer to him, closing the distance between us again.

"That's probably why she was upset earlier."

I didn't see him earlier, what is he talking about?

"There is something else I need to tell you." For once I was going to do and say what I wanted to, I wasn't going to bottle it up inside, too afraid of what might happen. I wanted him, and I wanted him to want me. *Me,* not the person I was pretending to be.

"So do I. I came to find you earlier and when I couldn't find you—"

"Xander, I'm not who you think I am." I blurted out, completely cutting him off mid sentence, I needed to get this out before I lost the nerve like I always did.

"I know."

Suddenly, I was overcome with extreme dizziness, my vision blurred, my head pounded and my legs began to weaken. Trying to steady myself, I grabbed on to Xander for balance. A ringing sounded in my ears. Xander's blurred face looked down at me as he held me, his lips moved but I couldn't make out what he was saying beyond the ringing. Over his shoulder I saw myself and Lawrence running towards me in a lazy mess. Xander's face was the last thing I saw before everything faded to black.

"Avery!" A familiar voice cried.

Acknowledgments

Years ago, I read so many stories on an app called episode interactive. One night I came up with the idea for this story while laying in bed. When I woke up, I had dreamt more about this idea and world and decided to write it on that app. At the time I was working full time and just did not have the energy to keep up with all the coding that was involved with writing on there, but I tried because I wanted to get my story out there and was excited to have a few people write to me about how they loved the idea. I would like to thank those people who may have read this story while it was not much more than an idea on there and to my friends at Spencer's that I worked with who encouraged me to start there.

I would also like to thank my amazing mom, Bev Whalen for always being my biggest supporter and so much more. Thank you for all you do.

I am eternally grateful to, Abigail Woodcock. When we reconnected, it was like we never stopped being friends. We shared so much in common, including our love for writing. You read this on the episode app and was so supportive of it. If it were not for you, I never would have turned it into a book. You not only inspired me to do so, but even helped write it with me in the beginning of this journey. Although life got crazy and busy and I continued it on my own, you were always extremely encouraging and helpful, whether it be bouncing ideas off you, editing, or just being the amazing friend that you are. I never would have dreamed I could have done this without you.

To Ashley Lavadinho, you were the first person and friend to read my book in full and probably the only one to read it as I wrote each chapter, and then rewrote those same chapters. You always gave me such great feedback and have been there from the beginning as well as throughout the entire process. Thank you so much for all you've done. You weren't just a part of my publishing team; you were the whole damn team! From beta reading to editing to marketing, you have done it all and helped me with so much more.

To Connor, thank you for the editing you have done for me. I know things got busy and the world shut down, but I appreciate all you have done. Thank you.

Thank you, Belle Manuel, my fantastic editor, for helping me get this book to where it needed to be.

To Celin, my amazing cover designer, thank you so much for the incredible cover you designed for me. I had hired several designers and even designed a few myself but nothing compares to what you made! You really captured everything I wanted and more in my cover and you really do judge a book by its cover so I really can not thank you enough.

To Stephanie for being the best beta and ARC reader I could have asked for. You helped me bring this book to where it needed to be by finding even more edits that needed to be done and took it upon yourself to mark them down as you read so I could fix those too, thank you!

I would like to thank my incredible beta readers and book besties from my book club who took the time to read and edit this so close to the release date and really helped me get it to where it needed to be with such short time. You are all so amazing and I am so grateful to you all. So, thank you Randle, Tiana, Syd, Emily, Isa, and Mandy.

To all my incredibly supportive friends and family, thank you for always being there for me throughout this long, amazing journey!

ABOUT THE AUTHOR

Danielle Hill is an Amazon Top 20 author of drama filled, swoon worthy and magical contemporary fantasy novels. Danielle first came up with the idea for A Kingdom of Sun and Shadow in late 2017 and began publishing chapters on Episode shortly after. After a warm reception on Episode, she decided to expand the story and began writing the manuscript in February 2018. She has already begun work on the sequel to A Kingdom of Sun and Shadow and can't wait to share it with the world.

Danielle resides in a small town in Ontario and spends her free time creating remarkable worlds full of magic and being a mom to her daughter and dog. She loves Marvel, binge-watching TV shows and cheesy hallmark movie marathons.

Made in the USA
Las Vegas, NV
08 February 2022

43403650R00162